DEVIL DOG DAYS

DEVIL DOG DAYS

Nick Englebrecht #3

K.H. KOEHLER

The Monster Factory

DEVIL DOG DAYS

A NICK ENGLEBRECHT MYSTERY

K.H. KOEHLER

CONTENTS

1	The Man Who Fell to Earth	1
2	Better the Devil You Know	3
3	Gun Control	12
4	Creepypasta	20
5	"Give It Back!"	28
6	Mr. Clean	39
7	The Thin Man	44
8	Number One Crush	57
9	Fun in the Sun	63

10	Queen of Babylon	70
11	Broadsided	79
12	Weird Sisters	86
13	My Hero	93
14	Synergy	102
15	Angel Breaker	107
16	Master of the Mystical Arts	121
17	Lucy-fer	129
18	Substitutes	139
19	Alternative Medicine	146
20	The Children of Endor	153
21	The Queen of Tarts	158

22	Hocus Pocus	169
23	Lord of Hell	176
24	"They Disappear."	185
25	Blackity-Black	194
26	Grunches	200
27	The Spell	208
28	Spiders from Mars	219
29	Lights Out	229
30	Wake-Up Call	234
31	A Good Catholic Boy Never Would	245
32	Bogey in the Bathroom	258
33	Into the Void	268

| 34 | Free Falling | 275 |
| 35 | Hellraiser | 283 |

ABOUT THE AUTHOR

Copyright © 2018 by K.H. Koehler

All rights reserved. No part of this publication may be reproduced, stored or transmitted in any form or by any means, electronic, mechanical, photocopying, recording, scanning, or otherwise without written permission from the publisher. It is illegal to copy this book, post it to a website, or distribute it by any other means without permission.

This novel is entirely a work of fiction. The names, characters and incidents portrayed in it are the work of the author's imagination. Any resemblance to actual persons, living or dead, events or localities is entirely coincidental.

Paperback ISBN: 979-8-8692-3939-6
Ebook ISBN: 979-8-8692-3940-2

Cover art and interior design by KH Koehler Design
https://khkoehler.net

No part of this book was created using artificial intelligence.

| 1 |

The Man Who Fell to Earth

THE CREATURE AND I were in free fall.

The atmosphere of the Angry Red Planet scorched my lungs, and it was hard to breathe as we fell through the fiery red sky. We seemed to fall for a long, long time—and every second of it was an agony.

The pain of the creature's arms tangled like barbed wire around my forearms was sending all kinds of mixed messages to my brain. Stop. Get him off. Punch him! Get away! But we were tangled together, physically and emotionally. I knew this was always meant to be—him and I. Locked in this death dance, where only one of us would survive.

It screamed, and its inhuman wails seemed to fill my brain with yet more waves of razor-sharp pain. I had never experienced so much pain as I had in the last few days. Philosophers talk about Hell on Earth, but I was experiencing it firsthand.

I roared back at it. I gave it all my pain and my rage. But in my mind, I was counting my regrets. I had a lot of those. People I had hurt. Things I had done. And not done.

"Goddamn you, angel!" it warbled in its foul language before its voice devolved into yet more primal wails.

Heh. That was pretty funny when you thought about it. How was this being going to damn me when I'd been damned long, long ago?

I supposed it didn't matter. We were both probably going to die anyway. Die like a pair of ancient warriors locked in deadly mortal combat as we fell to the Angry Red Planet below us. We would die...and no one would ever know what had happened. Certainly, no one on Planet Earth.

| 2 |

Better the Devil You Know

"YOU'RE THE WORST Satan I've ever seen," Baphomet stated on the day all hell broke loose, both literally and figuratively. "And I've seen a few, let me tell you. Your father was quite the handful, but *you*, Nicholas...*you* would try the patience of a saint..."

I did my best to block out his blathering. I was down on the floor in the back of the shop, trying to fix the fan on the industrial cooling unit. Not that I know how to do such mystical and amazing things, but that's why we have YouTube, right? I was dividing my attention between the video on the laptop beside me and the compressor on the unit.

Desperation is the mother of invention. Or something like that.

It was approximately 110 degrees in the darkened little back-room, and we were on the eleventh day of the worst heat spell that Blackwater had ever experienced. Suffice to say, I was inventing my ass off, and I wasn't open to much criticism at the moment.

"Your grandfather, on the other hand, was a natural. Why, he could wield the Morning Star in one hand and a martini glass in the other like you would not believe..."

Sitting up suddenly, I conked my head on an overhanging pipe and let out a long string of curses that would have made my illustrious grandfather blush with embarrassment. Pushing sweaty hair out of my eyes, I rubbed at my sore spot.

Baphomet was still fucking talking, so I casually heaved my wrench at my tormentor. "You know you'd be more useful, demon, if you'd stop pontificating and fetched the Philips screwdriver from the toolbox over there." I pointed at the table.

The demon tutted at that like some displaced nineteenth-century fop. Then again, that was about right for him. A high demon of the *Daemonologie*, the demon equivalent of Parliament, he had a unique position—and the attitude and attire to match. He looked like a tall, handsome black man dressed in a tuxedo and Jeevesque white gloves. A regular Mario Van Peebles in one of those oddball rolls he always seems to favor. He spoke with a posh English drawl and appeared inured to the ungodly heat pressing down like a furry blanket upon us all. As I understood it, he had once been my father's personal aide and adviser—or, as he liked to refer to himself, the *Au pair*.

He tugged on a glove. "Once again, you fail to understand my position, my liege. Or yours. I advise and council. I do not *serve*."

(Emphasis on the last word, natch.)

Lord Trash wrinkled his upper lip "And the Prince of Perdition does not do his work sitting on a filthy cement floor like some unlovely *waif.*" Baphomet accented that last with a slightly distressed grimace of perfect white teeth.

"Good to know, Baphomet," I said, rubbing an oily forearm across my sweating forehead. "But I'm not *him*..."

"Actually, yes, you are..." He stopped and sniffed—actually sniffed —while he shifted his weight on his rather disturbing-looking cloven hooves. "Oh, dear, you were attempting to be facetious, were you, my liege?"

I was about to jump up and grab him by the throat when Morgana ducked into the room. She passed right through Baphomet as if the demon was a dark, smoky veil. Her presence dissipated his essence like mist wafting away—though she did shiver slightly. "Nick? Were you talking to someone?"

"Myself." I squinted down at the YouTube video—which was no help at all, by the way.

Morgana sported a long, dark blue Celtic dress with bell sleeves and white crystal chandelier earrings, her icy pale hair carefully piled atop her head with a few spiraling tendrils hanging down to surround her slender, intense face and icy blue eyes. Normally, nothing in this world flustered Morgana—my partner, moral compass, and, lately, my significant other—but today, even she looked slightly wilted at the edges as she approached, carrying a bottle of Poland Springs in one polished hand.

"I was just talking to myself," I further explained, heaving myself upward. "Unfortunately, I had nothing of value to say to me."

In the last six months since my Ascension, I'd been visited a half dozen times by my new *Au pair*. Though I share almost every little thing with Morgana, I had yet to mention him. It wasn't that I didn't trust her. She was the best friend and steadiest lover I'd ever had. But something about cluing her in set my teeth on edge. Presidents and dictators had *aides*. Me? I didn't know what to do with him. Plus, it was like admitting that the Ascension had really happened, that I was changed into...whatever it was I was supposed to be...and I just wasn't ready to deal with that level of whatthefuckery yet.

I winced as I straightened my back. My blue jeans were stuck to parts of me in ways I'd rather not mention, and my once-white T-shirt was now sweat-and-oil-stained. I didn't look the image of the prince of hell—more like a poor man's greaser. I was dripping sweat all over the floor, and I probably smelled like a locker room. She handed me a towel and I wiped myself down, not that it did much good. I was certain I had sweated out that glass of Kool-Aid I'd drunk in fourth grade in 1986.

Despite all this, she was looking me over with a familiar commingling of pity and subdued, rawbone lust. Ever since becoming exclusive, we'd made a point of christening every room in the building with our sexual shenanigans—but I drew the line at the boiler room.

She offered me the water next. "So...what's wrong with it?"

"The thingy is broken," I said, unscrewing the bottle.

She folded her arms across her ample, yet always perky, bosom. "Can you elaborate on the 'thingy?'"

"It's the thing next to the other thing. By the way, both things are broken." Mechanical engineering has never been my forte, sue me. Growing up, Lincoln Logs and Tinker Toys had pretty much defeated me.

"In other words, I should just get a service guy over here as soon as possible."

"I think that would be prudent, yes." I drank down half the bottle in one gulp before rubbing the frosty cold bottle against my head where a cold headache was forming. "Especially if it's getting hotter. Is it getting hotter? Please tell me it's not getting hotter."

I might be the newly crowned Prince of Hell, or whatever, but I was definitely not a hot-weather guy. Give me frozen, witch's-teat-cold New England weather anytime and I'm a happy little freezy bug. Snow Miser is my spirit animal.

She gestured vaguely. "I don't know. I haven't stepped outside the shop all morning."

Not that I blamed her. Opening the front door was like being bowled over by a blast furnace. Groaning, I followed her up and into our shop, Curiosities.

The shop is small, old, and perpetually dusty, but generally comfortable, full of the rich aromas of tea and incense. Curios, jewelry, and fake pagan artifacts for the tourists line the shelves. We sell healing crystals, how-to videos, and fancy-as-fuck magicians' wands—you know, the usual crap. Normally, during the summer months, it swarms with tourists. Today, the air was cottony hot and utterly still in that way that only a late June day in the Pocono Mountains can produce. I smelled musty old books and skin-roasting summer heat under the usual odors of mint, cinnamon, and sandalwood.

Morgana had switched off most of the lights to try and preserve what little coolness remained since our cooling unit had broken down this morning, but it wasn't helping much. The shop was understandably near empty, and our feet echoed flatly against the old, scarred wooden floorboards.

An old pensioner and busybody named Mrs. Wilson was the only one here, perusing the shelves. She claimed to like our collection of wind chimes, though I suspected she visited only because we had a good view of the street and its goings-on. Rain or shine, heat or blizzard, she could be found walking the Strip and talking smack about almost everyone.

"This heat is going to kill our business," Morgana said worriedly, producing a painted Japanese folding fan from seemingly thin air and fluttering it in front of her heat-reddened face. I've never discovered if that's a magician's parlor trick or if she really can materialize items out of thin air—and she's never told me. Morgan is a very good, very learned, witch—unlike me.

"At this rate, it's going to kill me," I answered, sliding behind the glass display case and sagging down on the stool. I dug out the local phonebook from under the counter. It occurred to me then that I could probably Google a repairman on my phone, but some habits die hard—if, that is, they die at all.

Morgana moved closer to the counter to avoid Mrs. Wilson overhearing our conversation "I would have thought you'd love the heat, Scratch. Your natural environment, as it were."

"As if I go *there*."

Morgana raised an eyebrow. "You mean you haven't...gone downstairs?" She sounded surprised...but also relieved.

That was code for Dis, my father's capital city—the place that, according to Baphomet, at least, I was supposed to get my skinny ass to. He said I needed *orientation*, which just made me want to do it even less. This was like high school again. Tell me I have to do a project for credit, and I guarantee you I'll do the opposite and wind up in detention. I hate being told what to do.

"You surprise me, Scratch"

"It's not like anyone can force me. I mean, I am the guy in charge —supposedly."

I'd just picked up my cell to call the service guy when I heard the insistent *nee-naw* of our one local police cruiser dashing down the Strip. At first, I thought maybe the woods had caught on fire— which wasn't a stretch of the imagination, given the dry heat spell and the burn ban that no one in town observed. But it was followed soon after by a fleet of Staties, and then by an ambulance. In all the years I'd lived and worked in Blackwater, I had never seen a caravan quite like it.

Something was up. Something was wrong.

By the time I made it to the door of the shop, Morgana was already standing on the stoop and Mrs. Wilson was out in the street. I saw her flowered hat as she tilted far out over the curb and discreetly removed a small pair of bird-watching binoculars from her purse as she followed the caravan streaking down Main Street and turning the bend. They were heading downtown toward the newer residential area. She muttered something excitedly and not so lady-like under her breath before scrambling for her flip phone.

I came up protectively on Morgana's right side and slid a hand around her waist. She leaned into me in a show of solidarity. It reminded me of how in the months since my Ascension—and my massive breakup with Vivian Summers—Morgana and I had finally taken the next step in our relationship. We had committed—a pretty big deal for me.

It happened suddenly one night, and it was surprisingly easy for us both, like the most natural thing in the world. We worked together. We slept together. Hell, we hexed together. It seemed only natural that we should be together in a more significant way.

That night, lying in bed after some serious sexy time, I just blurted out, "We should do it. Go steady."

The brief silence that followed made me nervous.

"'Go steady?'" Morgana eventually said, pushing herself up on one elbow and looking down at me. She was naked and beautiful unashamed. You have to respect a woman like that. "Steady as in exclusive. No one else?"

Another woman might have made fun of my old, 1980s-inspired colloquiums, but Morgana didn't tease. Mostly, I think, because there was only a few years' difference between us. I mean…I *think* so. I was in my mid-40s, and she was fresh into her 50s—or so she let me believe. God knew how old she really was. She could have been old enough to be my grandmother, for all I knew. What I did know was that neither of us looked our age.

"Yeah. No one else. What do you say?"

She thought about that for a long moment. "No other men. No other women."

The *no other men* statement was for her. Both statements applied to me. "Just us. You and me. Together. Exclusive—as the kids like to say. Or whatever it is they say now. I can't keep track."

She bit her lip. "And do you think you can handle that?"

I gave it some thought. "I think I could."

In many ways, we were well-suited to each other in every way. We belonged together. I felt that intrinsically.

"The hell's going on?" I asked now.

Morgana shook her head. "Not sure." She looked over at Nathan Charles, who ran buggy rides for the tourists during the summer and fall months. His two gigantic Clydesdales were stamping their feet nervously. His beautifully polished, nineteenth-century buggy was parked in an alley across the street, and he was straining to see from his buckboard.

Slowly, bit by bit, the other shop owners were emerging like nosy little Hobbits from their Hobbit houses to see what the buzz was all about. I saw Annie, owner of Annie's Ice Cream Shop farther up the hill, stepping out onto the old-timey front porch. Mr. Fernstermacher, the antique dealer next door, was shaking his head and talking to himself. And Rooney, who owned The Dollar General across the street, looked our way as if we had the answers.

I shrugged to show we didn't have a clue.

Within seconds, all of them had their trusty cell phones in hand and were furiously calling or texting—which kind of ruined the Hobbit effect, but whatever.

At that moment, my cell went off in my back pocket. I had an app that alerted me to local emergencies, Adam and Amber Alerts mostly, as well as sudden weather warnings and fire and crime alerts. I took one look at the screen and my stomach sank. "Jesus H. Christ. It's the school."

I didn't need to say anything more than that. Morgana got it.

She swore under her breath. "John Quincy Adams or Holy Name?"

John Quincy Adams was our local high school, and Holy Name was our Catholic alternative. "Holy Name," I read.

I looked up at Morgan and she nodded.

That was code that she wanted me to go. Not that she could have stopped me.

Blackwater was finally going to make a name for itself. Another fatal shooting.

This fucking country.

**

Within seconds, I was back inside, grabbing my button-down shirt off the counter. I rushed past the back room and took the rear delivery exit to the alley behind the shop where I kept my bike leaning against the Dumpster we shared with Mr. Fernstermacher. I knew without even asking that the narrow streets of Blackwater would be a total bottleneck, and I didn't want to be responsible for blocking an incoming ambulance, so there was no point in revving up the Monaco.

Within minutes, I was pedaling like a madman toward the Catholic school sixteen blocks to the north. I prayed I wasn't too late, but by the time I'd gotten there, almost everything had already come to pass.

| 3 |

Gun Control

THE FRONT LAWN of the school—once manicured green but now a dull wheaten color due to the heat and drought—crawled with law enforcement from three different counties. I skidded to a halt on the street in front of the school and let out my breath. I had never seen so many out-of-town law enforcers in my life—not here, not in boring little Blackwater where nothing usually happened.

Sure, we got the Staties out during the parade down the Strip during the Fourth of July, then again for the Witches' Walk through Oldtown for Halloween, and sometimes they stopped by the Dunkin' Donuts on Main, but it was never like this. Unis from Buck, Pike, and Carbon County crawled like chaotic ants around the collection of black-and-whites, ambulances, and fire trucks that dotted the parking lot. Local radio vans were circling the outer edges, and a news chopper flitted by overhead, trying to get the scoop for the evening news.

As usual, Mountaintop Radio was Johnny-on-the-spot. As I biked down the paved road toward the school, I spotted the black news van with the easily recognizable MTR logo and colorful mountain illustration on the side panel. It was parked to one side, in the lot usually reserved for the school buses. Shelly Preston, their star reporter, was running hither and yon, interviewing any law enforcement officer she could pull away from the scene for a few seconds. I could hear her reciting the blow-by-blow into her Bluetooth while a host of cameramen chased her around, trying to get clean shots.

"...most shocking event that Blackwater has ever seen. It appears the last day of school has been interrupted by an active shooter who has opened fire in the middle of a class at Holy Name Catholic High School. The name of the shooter has not yet been released, suggesting to this reporter that the details of the shooting will undoubtedly be muddled in the days to come..."

I snorted. Leave it to Shelly to try and drag a colorful conspiracy out of a local tragedy. From experience, I knew she'd be the best choice for finding out all the details, but I doubted she would give me the time of day, considering the ongoing hate-on she had for me. She and I had been a thing for about two seconds because she turned on me, trying to wring whatever scandalous information she could out of me. When I refused to play ball, she tried to wreck my reputation and the shop. My reputation was questionable at the best of times, but I took exception to her trying to harm the means of my income. Her efforts failed in the end, but we were still playing the long game, she and I.

I biked past her to the edge of the barricade of vehicles. I could see Sheriff Ben Oswald stomping back and forth across the lawn, talking into his radio and shaking his head. He looked pissed to the moon. My first assumption was that someone had pulled rank and the Staties were muscling him out. That would certainly annoy me. But as I skidded to a halt, something else occurred to me, and my stomach, already bottoming out, managed to find another level somewhere near my shoes.

"What's going on, Ben?" I called.

He let out a string of curses before turning on me all wild-eyed and disheveled. Normally, he and I had a rapport—maybe not quite like what you see on TV between the cop and the private dick (he being the cop, me being the dick), but, generally speaking, we respected each other.

He motioned me to stay back. "I have no time for you, Nick. Get the hell out of here!"

That confirmed what I already suspected to be true. "Antonia? Is she inside?"

"I said get the fuck out of here!" He gestured wildly toward the road.

I was right. Ben's only daughter, Antonia, went to Catholic school. I only knew that because the few times she'd ducked into the shop, she was wearing their uniform—the vest with the Holy Crest on it.

Ignoring his orders, I said, "Is she still inside?"

He stood there and stared at me as if he wanted to shoot me. He wasn't in cop-mode right now. He was in dad-mode. In that moment, he was, beyond doubt, the palest black man I had ever seen. He was a liability and I think everyone knew it. No wonder the Staties had frozen him out.

I didn't wait for him to respond. I hit the pedals and biked down the road and around the building to the reserved parking lot where the principal and teachers parked. The lot was half-full of cars, this being the last day of school. Three ambulances were standing by, with EMTs mulling about and smoking with little to do at the moment. Unis were stationed at the back doors, checking the munitions of their firearms and listening for orders. They neither noticed nor cared when I skidded to a halt near the fence where the parking lot gave way to the soccer green.

There was a row of industrial windows leading to the basement woodworking and music classes, all of them open on this dog day afternoon—and that made me smile. Within seconds, I was inside a music room, listening to the sounds of a kerfuffle in a distant classroom. But I couldn't tell from the sounds if it was the shooter, students taking cover, or the police screwing around.

The hallway beyond was eerily quiet. And dark. Real horror movie stuff. Only about half the lights were on to cool the place off; the school had the same idea as us.

I moved down the hallway quietly and unhurriedly, trying to pinpoint noises and their direction. I didn't have my piece with me, but at some point, I had ricocheted back to my cop brain anyway. Active shooter. Go slow. Case the place. Don't do anything rash or stupid. I wish I had my firearm. Fuck it, I would do without.

The darkened hallways were lined with closed doors and religious and motivational posters. Some of them sported large, impressive crosses—three crosses atop Calvary, images of crosses fading to lions and lambs, crosses with broken chains hanging down. I eyed those warily. They were poison ivy for creatures like myself. Had anyone been there to power them up with their faith, I probably would have been crawling on my hands and knees and retching all over the nicely polished floor.

Two shots fired close together one floor up, made me start—and gave me a good idea of which direction to go in.

Seconds later, I'd found the stairs, and not long after that, I found myself coming up on the school cafeteria. Holy Name had a sizeable budget and plenty of investors, so the cafeteria was set up more like a posh food court. Instead of a closed-up cinderblock room painted prison green, like in my own dingy high school back in Brooklyn, it was set inside a vast glass atrium divided by low glass-bricked partition walls and had the type of seating arrangement similar to what you see at the mall, tables and booths. Vending and ATMs lined the walls, with a hot and cold lunch bar running the length of the room. There were even small Mickey D's and KFC kiosks to one side.

A thin, nervous-looking teenaged boy in a school uniform stood near the hot bar, clutching a handgun against the side of his cheek like it was a security blanket. He was shouting at the police stationed behind the glass wall opposite me, warning them not to come any closer. The active shooter. He wasn't more than seventeen years old, sported an emo hairdo that fell over one eye, and was weaving to the enthusiastic madness playing out in his own head.

A few kids lay face down on the floor, with a few more crumpled down in booths and under tables, but at this angle, I couldn't tell if they were down because they were shot or just scared. Mostly, they were just legs. I could hear soft sobs emerging from just behind the glass cubes I was leaning against. A girl was calling on Mother Mary for deliverance.

As I surveyed the scene, I bit my lip. I'd seen this shooter's type plenty during my time with the NYPD. He looked like one of a hundred tweakers I'd dragged in, and he'd probably make the last victim himself. The way the cops were set up, skirmish-line-style, I knew it was only a matter of time before he realized there was only one way out—and I didn't want to see happen. Whatever his problem was, I'd rather see him behind bars than in a coffin. Yeah, it was a point of contention with me, but I hated it when kids turned on their own.

So I stood there with my back to the glass wall, listening to the Chief of Police trying to talk Emo Guy down. Good luck with that. I'd seen this same situation played out countless times during my years on the force. It didn't work all neat and square like in the movies. Shooters didn't just come to their senses because they got a good, inspirational talking to.

All right. Time for an intervention. No snipers were hiding in the wings, ready to take the kid down. There were no action heroes lined up, ready to leap into the fray and save the day. And these were just local flatfoots more used to writing up tickets and citing peeps for shooting off fireworks out of season. As far as I could tell, I was the only ace in the hole, and, frankly, as heroes went, I was pretty fucking lacking.

I closed my eyes, steadied my breathing, and counted to ten. Yippee-ki-yay. My actions after that were all mechanical—all cop. I turned about-face and lit a cigarette from the pack in the breast pocket of my dress shirt and the click of the lighter alerted Emo Guy to my whereabouts almost immediately.

He swung around, aiming the shaking gun in my general direction. "Who's there? Tell me who you are!" he shouted, his voice rising in hysterical octaves.

I stepped rather casually out from behind the glass blocks, giving Emo Guy a good, unobstructed look at me. I was more than pleased to realize the wall the police were using as a barrier cut off their view of me. That made my job even easier.

"Hi, kid," I said.

"Who in hell are you?"

"And you got in one." I smiled...and something in the kid's face seemed to flinch inward.

There had been times during the past six months when I suddenly knew all about someone—usually a total stranger I had never met before in my life. I figured it probably had something to do with my responsibilities as the new Lucifer. To Serve and to Judge, if you will.

The knowledge was elemental. It wasn't a matter of visions or telepathy or any of that happy crappy, but more of instinct, a kind of *knowing*—the way you can sometimes tell the phone is going to ring seconds before it does. This felt like that.

My instincts told me a lot about Emo Guy. His name was Ken or Kenny, and he was almost eighteen years old. Antonia, Ben's daughter, knew him, and he liked her a lot, but he would never date her because he knew his mom would pitch a fit if he brought a black girl home. He had killed several of his classmates and friends a few minutes ago—kids he had liked and loved. People he still liked and loved. And he was willing to kill more. He was on a mission. A holy jihad of the mind. This was something he had to do.

That's all the information I got from him, and it was making my brain hurt. The rest was a lot of white mind static, and I was finding it hard to cut through it.

"Who are you?" Kenny bellowed. He was shaking more than ever, and when he raised the handgun—a 9MM pistol, the cop in me noted, which was a pretty standard gun used in home protection—the weapon wavered before centering on my chest. His eyes were wild and unfocused, and he kept gulping nervously as if he were choking on air.

"You know," I said, still working on autopilot as I moved a few inches out from behind the low wall, trying to make a target of myself so he'd forget about the crying girls lying on the floor at his feet. "I think maybe we've met?"

Kenny weaved on his feet and touched the gun to his forehead as if he had a massive headache and the coolness of the weapon was a relief. He squelched his eyes shut and gritted his teeth so hard, I could hear his molars grinding in his jaw. "Don't know you, man. Don't wanna know you....!"

"Kenny," I said as reasonably as possible. "Kenny, put the gun d—"

"Fuck you, Tempter!" Kenny aimed the gun. It dipped downward slightly, and he took a bead on my chest.

It all went down pretty fast, then.

My wings exploded outward, all four pairs of them, the way they were wont to do at certain times in my life. Kenny screamed in response and jerked the trigger on the pistol. The whole affair lasted no more than a fraction of a second, but the sonic blast from my wings disintegrated the bullet and blew Kenny back into the hot bar. Suddenly, the whole atrium was awash in glass and chaos as the police, seeing their opening, surged forward, pouring from around the glass walls. I heard radios squealing and the Chief of Police telling his men to *move, move, move!*

Kenny had rolled to the floor, moaning. The first officer on the scene moved to disarm him, kicking away his gun and holding his automatic on him while his brothers wasted no time cuffing him and reading him his rights. Kenny screamed throughout it all—which was good because it prevented the officers from even noticing me standing there. Within seconds, the officers were bustling Kenny away and checking on the students lying wounded or dead on the floor.

Antonia, huddled under one of the booths, emerged, spotted me, and sprang to her feet. "Nick!" She started running toward me across the apocalypse of glass. By then, my wings had disappeared...or she would have gotten a very bad surprise on top of her very bad day.

"Antonia," I said. She threw her arms around my neck so hard that she almost unbalanced me. Within seconds, she was sobbing uncontrollably into my hair.

"It's okay, baby. I've got you," I said as I lifted her and carried her down the hallways of the school and out the front door. Before I even knew it, Ben was racing toward us, wearing the expression of every horrified parent everywhere who'd expected the very worst.

The irony of it all was that Antonia kept saying things like *Thank you, Jesus* the whole time—and Jesus...well, he had nothing to do with any of this.

| 4 |

Creepypasta

THE POLICE BLAMED the heat. The school blamed society. The internet blamed the lax gun control laws of Pennsylvania. Whatever the cause, whatever the reason, the shooting had put Blackwater on the front pages of every newspaper and Internet news site in the country, and in the days that followed, the town filled up with such a media circus that even the heat couldn't keep people from swarming the streets.

I stayed out of the whole mess. The police hadn't noticed me, and Antonia didn't say a word, which suited me just fine. I had other business to worry about in a place where no human had any business going.

***

The frozen white landscape stretched on forever.

It looked like the landscape of one of those survivalist TV shows set in the Arctic Circle—an endless plain of painfully white nothing with no visuals to break it up. Just horizons of hard-packed snow that rose up and up toward a looming, cobalt-grey sky. Ice was falling, and the wind was gusting against me, but I didn't feel any of it. The wet, heavy flakes blew against my exposed skin and eyes but then vanished like ash.

I took one step, then another, crunching down into the ever-deepening snow. I thought again of those survivalist shows on TV. I'd always wondered why the poor fool out in such crummy weather didn't make better time than he did. Now I knew. Just moving through this shit was tiring as all hell.

The saying *hell freezing over* came to me and made me laugh, though the storm carried my voice far away. Okay, I admit it. The first time I'd visited Hell, I'd expected something a little more flamboyant...more of an Ecclesiastical lake-of-fire and burning brimstone type of situation. But I guess Hell was a matter of perspective. Or maybe there were different sections of hell, like in Dante's Divine Comedy. It's not as if I had a Google map of the place.

For all I knew, Hell was a series of continents on another planet—places as alien and diverse as anything that existed on earth. Or the moon. At one point, Baphomet had mentioned several cities. He'd also taken me to my father's keep a few times, the place he called The Watchtower, but he hadn't bothered to mention *this* business. I supposed he figured I'd find out sooner or later on my own.

Despite being dressed in just jeans, a T-shirt, and a long grey raincoat, I wasn't cold. Quite the opposite. It was hot and snowy, and that made it hard for my brain to wrap itself around the concept. Despite sweating, I couldn't bring myself to remove the coat.

I walked with my head down, hands in the pockets of the coat. I was being violently buffeted by the storm and had to stop periodically and pull the collar of the coat up around my mouth. As I had on my previous visits, I hiked a few hundred feet before stopping to cup my hands around my mouth and call Peter's name. I howled it into the wind. But, with the gale-force winds blowing around me, the name was sucked away.

"Peter!"

Nothing but howling whiteness and nothing as far as the eye could see.

"Peeeeeteeeeer!"

Baphomet suddenly appeared beside him, dressed in his proper British suit and cravat, walking on top of the snow as if he had snowshoes on—which, by the way, he did not. "My liege, I don't see what any of this accomplishes..."

"No," I mumbled down into my collar. "You wouldn't, demon."

I walked on, repeating the cycle every hundred feet or so though the landscape didn't change at all. I called and no one answered. No one but Baphomet.

"You come here often, but you've never explained who this Peter is whom you seek."

If it's one thing about demons, they're incessant gossipers. It really is ridiculous what they get hung up on. They love to get the goods on damned near everything that wasn't any of their business. I secretly imagined a demon kaffeeklatsch somewhere dark and desolate, with Baphomet and his coworkers whispering gleefully over the ridiculous goings-on back on Earth.

"Isn't there somewhere you need to be?" I said, sloshing knee-deep through the pseudo-snow toward the next ridge. Baphomet trailed stubbornly behind, hands clasped in the small of his back, head cocked slightly as if welcoming me to explain.

I stopped so suddenly, and he was so close on my heels that he nearly plowed into me. I swung around. "Leave. Now. Back to Dis!" I commanded. "And don't come back!"

Baphomet continued to sniff even as he faded from view.

Years ago, I had asked my father if Peter, my partner of seven years on the NYPD, had wound up in Hell after the Arcana had ritualistically murdered him, but the bastard never answered me. Never even gave me a fucking clue. Well, I was determined to find out on my own one way or another, and if he was—which I dearly hoped he wasn't—I would liberate him.

I was the theoretical ruler of Planet Hell, right? I could do those things.

Ahead, something stirred on the horizon, dark against the very white snow. I hurried to see what it was, but running in knee-deep snow was harder and less graceful than you think, and I was nearly winded by the time I reached the top of the next ridge. I had wings in this world that I could not hide. I could probably have flown, but I'd never done that, and, frankly, the idea freaked me the hell out.

Down below, I spotted a foraging demon. As demons went, it was pretty damned weird. It looked like a skeletal horse on wagon wheels with a long trunk and the faces of old men on either side of its misshapen head. It made nervous warbling sounds and rolled its many eyes at me as I approached it. "Please, my liege," The Bosh-inspired, nightmare-fueled creature said to me. "Do not hurt."

I sighed. Since this wasn't the first time I was getting this reaction to my presence, I could only conclude that my dad was a total asshat. In addition to running into no humans on Planet Hell, the few demons I did encounter were scared shitless of me.

I decided to call it a day and summoned a portal back to earth.

I was alone and dripping wet when I stepped into the loft. I immediately shed my clothes, which smelled like burned sugar, and took a long, hot shower, trying to forget how the little demon had freaked out at the sight of me. Well, this wasn't the first time I had garnered such a reaction, and it probably wouldn't be the last.

Ruminating on it made a kind of frustrating, impotent rage boil up inside me. I hadn't asked for any of this and there were no obvious benefits. It wasn't fair, and if I could have handed this thing off to someone else, I would have, but there was no one I could turn to. I was the sole heir to Planet Hell. Not my father's only child, but...still...the one who had gotten the rotten inheritance.

I quickly toweled myself down and took myself off to bed.

"Humhn," Morgana said sleepily as I slithered under the cotton sheets beside her. "You smell funny."

I always did for a few hours after I returned to Earth. I turned the fan so it would rotate towards Morgana, then tried to get a few hours of shuteye, though sleep (as always, for me) was hours away, and when it finally did arrive, brief and sporadic and full of shadowy things I'd just as soon not describe.

With the influx of press and gawkers in town, the rest of the week was unsurprisingly hectic in the shop. On Saturday night, sometime after midnight, I turned off all the lights of the shop, turned the sign to Closed, and clomped up the stairs to the loft while contemplating the many secrets of Hell.

I thought about taking another look around for Peter, but Morgana had waited up for me and set the kitchen table with a white linen tablecloth, candles, and boxes of Thai from the new place down the Strip. She was standing at the kitchen counter, pouring white Chablis into two glasses. I plopped down into one of the kitchen chairs and undid the laces on my boots.

"Set the alarm?" she asked, referring to the overcomplicated burglar system we'd installed in the shop last year after someone broke a window to try and get in. Protip: Breaking a window is harder than it looks, makes a lot of noise, and is not optimal for an entry point. The tweaker found that out the hard way when we found him moaning and writhing on the floor of the shop with shards of glass sticking out of him.

"Yes, dear," I answered and took a moment to appreciate the care that had gone into the table setting. "You cooked!"

"I'm a regular June Cleaver," Morgana said cheerily as she carried the wine over. She leaned down for a kiss. We both laughed because neither of us can cook and Morgana was most definitely *not* June Cleaver. More like Samantha Stephens.

After we had decimated the Thai and wine, we took a fresh bottle and went to cuddle on the sofa like an old married couple. Netflix and chill. Yeah, that was pretty much us these days. Only a year before, I had spent many an evening on Vivian's sofa, doing the same thing. (I like adventure that way.) But I had done an excellent job of decimating *that* relationship—not the first time for me.

In the soft blue light of the TV, I looked at the scratches on my left wrist, the ones that wouldn't go away. The last time I had seen Vivian, we had passed each other in the dairy aisle at Sam's Club and Viv had taken pains to pretend I wasn't there. Only a short time before, we had been screaming like a pair of juvenile delinquents at each other in the parking lot of her duplex. Frankly, I'd been too scared to get too close to her. I thought she might set me on fire or something—not that I didn't kind of/sort of deserve it, I guess.

She'd discovered I'd lied to her about my father—our father. The lying part was pretty bad, granted, but I think a lot of her frustration had to do with the fact that she'd been banging her half-brother for almost a year. That had really sent her over the edge, even though neither of us had known about that until rather recently. It hadn't bothered me the way it bothered her, which probably meant I wasn't a very good person.

Morgana, lying with her legs in my lap, channeled surfed while I played Hokey Pokey under the hem of her robe. Soon enough, she muttered a curse when the local news came on and an anchorman started jabbering on about the details of the school shooting as if everyone and their dog didn't already know most of them. Sighing, she prepared to hit the button once more when I stopped her.

"Don't."

"Aren't you tired of this stuff?"

I took the remote from her and turned up the sound. "The police finally got a statement out of Kenny Johnson."

"Is he as disturbed in real life as he looks on TV?"

"I don't think he's disturbed at all," I said, remembering some of the stuff that I'd seen in his head. There had been violence and blood, yes, but no madness that I'd detected. "Just the opposite. I think he knew exactly what he was doing."

Morgana looked at me as if I was insane.

The screen showcased a pan shot of Pocono Medical Center. The reporter stood outside the hospital and announced that Kenny was under observation in the psychiatric ward. He started rambling off the details of the kid's statement, including Kenny's confession that he'd shot four of his fellow students in an attempt to free them from the influence of the Thin Man, an Internet creepypasta legend he believed had taken control of them. Things got pretty weird after that.

We watched until it all became too depressing. Eventually, Morgana changed the channel to an old, safe wartime Bogart movie. We watched for a little while, not watching at all, lost in our private thoughts. Mine were going to bad places, as usual.

Suddenly sitting up, Morgana decided to play some Hokey Pokey of her own. I bit back a moan as she slid her hand under my open shirt and down to my naval and started playing with the belt of my jeans. "Why do old romantic movies make you so horny?" I laughed.

"It's not the movie, it's you," she laughed back.

"Do tell."

"Can I help it if I like scruffy, burned-out P.I.'s with daddy issues? I used to have a crush on James Garner in *The Rockford Files* when I was in high school."

"I don't look like Jim Rockford."

"That's right. You're a pretty boy."

"Demon," I corrected her.

"Half-demon."

"You have some weird fetishes, lady, do you know that?"

"Oh, you're one to talk about *fetishes*," she said, arching an eyebrow.

I didn't answer that. I liked a little tie-me-up sex sometimes. And, hey, crops and whips are a thing. I didn't exactly see Morgana complaining.

We moved things to the bedroom. But Kenny's story was so strange and unusual that later, after Morgana had dropped off to a sound sleep beside me, I lay there wide awake, staring up at the darkness, running the whole scenario through my head over and over and replaying what the reporter had said about the Thin Man —whatever the hell *that* was.

Near four in the morning, I slid silently out of bed and took Morgana's laptop with me into the kitchen to look up this Thin Man Internet story.

Two hours of googling later, I wish I hadn't.

| 5 |

"Give It Back!"

THEY HELD THE memorial for Kenny's four victims the following Sunday at St. Joseph's Cathedral. Since it was also my one day off work and I wasn't minding the shop, I figured it was a sign from Heaven that I should be there. Well, maybe not *Heaven*, exactly, but you get the idea.

The church wasn't more than a couple of miles from the Strip, but the temperature was clambering with all the persistence of a crazed, crime-fighting Spiderman into the high nineties, with humidity to match, and it was too damned hot to bike that far out. So instead, I took the Monaco down the road and parked it in the visitor's lot beside a hundred other vehicles ticking in the heat. I noticed that at least half of Blackwater had turned out for the service.

I carefully leaned against the too-hot hood of the car, chewed on a piece of Red Vine, and considered my options.

1. I could go up to the church and take my chances or…
2. I could use my head and not go anywhere near the modest cathedral for fear I would burst into flames like someone had doused me in diesel and lit a match.

This wasn't my first rodeo, in case you haven't noticed.

Luckily, the decision was made for me when the people moved en masse through the doors of the church and out to the shady green behind the building, most waving programs in front of their faces to drive the heat and mosquitoes away. Evidently, the cooling system had gone down inside the church and no one wanted to risk melting in the middle of services.

I hovered on the edge of the crowd, dressed in dark jeans, a black dress shirt, and sunglasses. I was nearly indistinguishable from the other men who had gathered, except, of course, for my height—both the blessing and bane of my existence. At six-four, I stand out like a sore thumb even among the tallest of men. But the advantage of it was that I could easily survey the crowd.

Mrs. Wilson had turned out, as I suspected she would, as well as most of the shopkeepers on the Strip. Sheriff Ben was there with his wife, Brenda, and their daughter, Antonia. The other students and their parents had gathered. It was quite a turnout—though I jarred slightly when I recognized a red-haired woman dressed in a black lace mini standing under a stately old maple.

Jesus. Vivian was here, hanging onto her new boyfriend's arm. I was rather confused by that until it occurred to me that she, like her brother, Josh, had graduated from Holy Name. It made sense that she should be here to pay her respects.

Vivian had lost a lot of weight since I'd seen her last. That depressed me. I had loved her curves, loved losing myself in them—and her. She'd always thought she was fat, but I'd thought she was perfect. Now, she looked tall and as slender as a dark crane in her four-inch black leather Mary Jane platforms. They put her at almost the same height as the guy whose arm she was hanging onto. The lace of the dress clung to her in ways that made it just this side of scandalous for a funeral, and her hair was fixed in a chignon, with little scarlet spirals falling down around her ears. I saw she sported huge silver hoop earrings with little skulls attached to them. I'd given her those earrings for Christmas.

I must have been staring too hard. She turned her head to glare at me, and I saw she was wearing a dab of mascara and her lips painted the color of heart's blood. Otherwise, her face was untouched and virgin—as always, milky white with high cheekbones and eyes like aquamarines on fire.

She was my father's daughter. She was beautiful and surreal and otherworldly. Men and women alike turned to look her way as she passed. She could bespell an entire room simply by walking into it.

I mean, I was no different. Certainly not immune. Just the sight of her put a catch in my throat. She was beautiful in a way that made your heart ache, that made you wonder why she wasn't a model or an actress. Some kind of TV star. And then you wondered if she was even real at all or if you weren't just making this stuff up in your head. But you weren't. She was that beautiful, that perfect. A daemon, a witch. The devil's only begotten daughter.

I knew the truth about her: She could never be a model or movie star. She loved the kitchen. It was her whole world. She'd graduated from Lincoln Culinary only the year before and was well on her way to being the greatest local pastry chef that Blackwater had ever produced. I imagined her running her own catering business, writing bestselling cookbooks, and getting her own Food Network TV show. Vivian had been created for greatness.

And, yet...something had happened along the way, something I still didn't understand. She'd given up on cooking and catering in the last few months and seemed more interested in partying, even though she had never been what one would call a "party girl." She spent her weekends in New York and New Jersey. There was a biker gang she had attached herself to, and a coven she frequented in Philadelphia. Along the way, she'd hooked up with this Goth dude named Oberon, and they'd been an item for the past few months.

Oberon was a typical Nugoth guy—six foot even, wore Hot Topic from head to toe even on the hottest day of the year, had a David Bowie haircut from 1985, and not a tat in sight. He did have pierced nipples and a Prince Albert.

Yes, I'd done a background check on the new boyfriend. He was a pretty rich boy transplant from New Jersey. His real name was Mike Bartholdi, which had mafia written all over it—though, supposedly, he and his uber-rich *Soprano*-style family weren't on speaking terms.

Yes, I hated the new boyfriend with every fiber of my being. That goes without saying. Somewhere in my heart, I felt he was corrupting Vivian. Several times in the last few months, I'd thought of picking up the phone and calling her, but Vivian had pretty much warned me if I went anywhere near her, she'd roast me like a side of beef on a barbecue. As the devil's daughter, she had the means to make good on her threat.

And, yeah, I understand the concept of boundaries. I know no means no. But it still fucking hurt to watch them together. Vivian had given me hope as well as love. In the short time we'd been together, I had learned to distrust the world a little less.

Her mark on my wrist throbbed. I knew it was the same for her. Anytime we were near, the witches' marks acted up. She patted Oberon/Mike's arm and whispered in his ear before stalking toward me in her tall, inky high heels. A few honeybees swarmed her as she made her way across the green toward me, but she absently waved them away. No fear. But then, bees—and all manner of stinging insects—were hers to command.

"I figured it was you."

"What gave it away?" I grinned from behind the shades.

She ignored my baiting.

"What are you doing here?" she said, and not in some friendly way.

"'Here' as in the church, or 'here' as in this town?" I sounded like such a wise guy. Vivian had stated in no uncertain terms that one of us had to leave Blackwater. And soon. I just felt sad and disappointed that things had come to this.

Her bright, otherworldly witch's eyes narrowed. "I can feel you a mile away, Nick." She held up her arm to show me her mark, then looked me up and down as if she was appraising me. "Same coat. Same hair. And, as usual, you look like you slept in a doorway."

I ignored her criticism. When I hadn't immediately told her we shared a father and a bloodline, she had assumed the worst about me, that I was trying to entrap her, use her, as others had in the past. As if I'd deliberately lied to her when I had only wanted to protect her from the truth.

"I'm here for the memorial," I explained, sticking my hands in my coat pockets and trying to sound casual about it. "The same as everyone else."

She gave me a dangerous side-eye. "You're not here to collect...you know...are you?"

It took me a moment to catch on. "Souls? From the kids who died?" I virtually guffawed. "You must be joking. For one thing, I haven't figured out how to do that. For another, why would I want the souls of some murdered kids?" Did she think I was that horrible?

"I never know with you, Nick." She pressed her lips together bitterly. "You're always up to something."

Oberon/Mike stood under an old magnolia tree, lighting a clove cigarette. He looked like what he was—a bored, rich fuck.

The sight of him made me mean. No, it made me *territorial*.

There, I said it. Vivian had been mine, and now she wasn't, and I didn't know how to deal with that yet. Sue me. "What about you?"

I pointed at her boyfriend. "Have you told the King of the Fairies about us yet?"

Her eyes seemed to flare to life. "What *we* are is no concern to him. You just leave Oberon alone!"

I lit a real cigarette and sucked in some cancer-causing fumes, trying to hide my anger behind the smoke. "So you haven't told him anything about our dear father. Or what you are. Or what I am. How very like me you are," I quipped and then regretted it because my sarcasm was making me sound like a total asshole, and I didn't like that look on me.

She stepped closer, but cautiously as if she were walking on invisible shards of glass with me. Her eyes, formerly bright, flashed dark, the way my dad's eyes were wont to do when he was upset. "I want it back, Nick. I want you to give it back to me. And then I want you out of my life for good."

"What?"

She shook her head and bared her teeth. "You *know*."

We'd lived together; we'd borrowed a lot of each other's stuff. But that wasn't what she was referring to. I knew that. And she knew that I knew. I just wanted her to say it. But when she didn't, I blew out more smoke. "*That* I can't give you, Viv."

"You took it. You can give it back!" She raised her wrist to me, where my mark looked red and sore. Blood seeped from the wound —not a lot, but enough to ruin the sleeve of her gothy little club dress. Around her, several honey bees reappeared as they tended to do whenever she was agitated. I watched them carefully, afraid they might swarm me. I'd seen what Vivian's familiars could do, and, let me tell you, it ain't pretty. Also, I don't like bees.

She shoved her arm in my face. "I want it back and I want this to go away!"

I clutched my wrist where her mark had started to fucking hurt like hell. Some years ago, when the angel Malach had pursued her, she had given me her soul for safekeeping. But when I'd marked her, I'd found her mark on me, which made sense *now*. She was a Lucifer like me; she, too, could mark souls. Essentially, we had marked each other.

"I don't know how to do that," I said, raising my voice in indignation. I threw my cigarette, half-done, away in the dry grass. I hoped it made me look tough, but probably I just looked like a giant asshole. "I don't know everything about this...whatever I am. I'm still *learning*, Viv."

Vivian started sputtering in anger, then stepped back, her eyes suddenly wide as she turned them down toward the ground. I followed her gaze and saw that my big, elongated Nick shadow was all wrong. Even though I had not manifested my wings, I could see the shadow of them fluttering in agitation, and everything that had fallen under those shadows was wilting and turning brown. The grass, the dandelions. Even the insects caught under it were curling up and dying.

I hadn't meant to frighten her. I started taking a step toward her to take her by the hand, to tell her I was sorry, but the wilted grass was spreading like some kind of vegetative cancer—and it was slowly creeping toward Mike/Oberon. She noticed, too, and it kept her from coming any closer. She always was a sensible girl.

Anger and confusion warred across her face. I knew how much she hated me. And desired me. It was the same for me. A terrible, endless ache.

For a few seconds, she worked to get herself under control and then said in a softer and more reasonable voice, "Well, when you figure it out, give it back. All right?"

"Yes," I said, lowering my voice. We needed to act like adults instead of petty, rage children. My shadows stopped crawling toward the Fairy King and started to dissipate. Vivian still took a step back. I did, too. Space between us was good. "When I know how, I'll give it back."

* * *

I didn't stay for the memorial. Vivian and I had nothing else to say to one another, and no one here liked or trusted me anyway. I'd been here for almost ten years, and half of my family came from these hills. But I was still the outsider. Why had I come?

Feeling a little like a kicked puppy, I headed back to my car. On the drive back to the shop, I put the radio on as loud as I could bear it. Some horrible, sugarcoated hip-hop tune bounced around the old Monaco, because, apparently, rock no longer exists on any of the local stations, and my only other choice was country, and—well, fuck that noise. But I didn't care. I just wanted it loud. I wanted not to think.

Peter, I thought. I had to concentrate on that. I still needed to find him. I needed to know where he was, and if he was in hell—if he was all right.

But today I didn't go hunting Peter the way I usually did on my day off. I was too scatterbrained, too angry. Too apt to make bad life decisions. Instead, once I got home and I was alone, I opened a portal to Hell and into my father's personal quarters in the Watchtower in the City of Dis, the Capital City of Hell.

I suppose I had to stop thinking about things that way. My father's this and my father's that. They were my quarters now.

He had a luxury mansion out in the middle of nowhere. And I mean nowhere—nada, nothing. Oblivion. There were no doors in or out, and when you looked out the tall, arched windows, there was absolutely nothing to see, just swirling, chaotic colors. The mansion itself looked like something out of old Hollywood. Honestly, I'd expected something more Bela Lugosi, if you know what I mean, but if there was one thing my father has going for him, it's good taste.

Wainscoted walls and pillared porticoes. Italian marble floors and spiral staircases that went absolutely fucking nowhere. The rooms went on forever. Literally. For every room I'd discovered, there were at least a half dozen doors leading elsewhere, most of which I had yet to explore. It was like living in some kind of freaky, never-ending TARDIS. The rooms also seemed to move around a lot, which made it that much more confusing.

"My liege, it's good to see you back," Baphomet announced when I stepped through the portal and into the foyer with its rearing Greek columns and long, hanging red glass lamps.

I didn't answer him, because...why? He was dressed in a white apron and standing on a ladder, changing a light bulb in one of the pendant lamps. From what I understood, one of Baphomet's functions was to keep my father's house when I wasn't around. A part of me wanted to fuck with him. If I asked him to wear a cute little French maid's outfit, would he feel compelled to do so?

I surveyed the foyer, searching for what had changed this time. Stone angels stood in lighted alcoves, wielding swords and spears, most in poses so defensive, I had a feeling they had probably been real at one point but had somehow fallen victim to my dad's spells. I knew he was a notorious hoarder. It sort of reminded me of being in the White Witch's castle in Narnia.

I ignored Baphomet's greeting and took the long, winding stairs down to what I had come to think of as my dad's throne room. Baphomet followed me, of course. I seemed unable to shake the bastard, no matter how rude I was to him or how much I ignored him. That's another thing about Baphomet: He's perpetually perky and always has a smile for me. I hate perky people.

The throne room was something else. It was dim and cavernous like some Grecian temple, and, yes, it was much too large to fit inside the mansion, but the normal rules of time and space did not seem to apply here. Physics had been fucked over well and good, and if someone bothered to take the time to go over the whole joint, I was certain they would go insane from their analysis of it. As it was, I'd failed physics in high school, so I figured I was inured to such madness.

I stood there, taking in the breathtaking size of the place. My breathing echoed, it was so vast. It was lined on both sides by more of those stone angels, most cowering away from whatever had taken their lives and changed them into...whatever they were now. Torches lined the walls, casting muted, flickering light along the huge, black and white parquet tiles that made up the chessboard floor and the walls adorned with strange, floor-to-ceiling runes.

My father's throne lay just ahead on a raised dais, a gigantic seat made of angel bones and covered in what I feared might be angel skin and dry, broken feathers. I had yet to sit there because...yanno...skin...creepy much? Besides, I wasn't that kind of dude.

Here, in this gigantic place, I'd learned that my father had several tools at his disposal—a scrying pool I had yet to master, a stone chess set composed of game pieces I could not identify, and the weapons barracks where he kept the bident, the symbol of the House of Lucifer.

I did know how to use the bident—sort of. I mean, basically, you just pushed the pointy end into someone you didn't like. If they were human, they were judged for their sins—usually with dismal results. If it was an angel, it turned them to stone and you had yourself a nice new statue like something from Pier One Imports.

Then there was the curio cabinet. It was huge—at least a story high—and looked like something from an ancient alchemist's lair. It took a long iron hook to release the catch on the front of it so the doors could swing open, revealing hundreds of narrow shelves containing thousands upon thousands of tiny, empty glass vials no larger than your thumb. They stood dusty and dark on their shelves—empty except for one.

The one on the far right, near the bottom, glowed faintly blue. I climbed the rolling ladder and reached for it, taking it down off the shelf. It felt warm in my hand and pulsed like the heartbeat of some living animal. Uncorking it, I let the small glowing creature—it resembled a tiny, pretty starfish—slip into the palm of my hand. It lay there, squirming and beating with a life all its own.

Holding it made me feel warm and comforted.

"It's very special to you, isn't it?" Baphomet said from behind me.

"More than you know," I answered. If I could, I would have taken it with me back to Earth. I would take it with me everywhere like a sacred talisman—my own personal crucifix. But I knew if I did that, I would lose it forever.

"You can have more, my liege," Baphomet suggested with a grinning leer. "As many as you want. Your father had millions. There are always desperate men and women willing to give you *more*."

But I didn't want more. I only wanted this one small, precious creature. I kissed it gently before putting it back into its jar and setting it back inside that giant, magical curio cabinet.

| 6 |

Mr. Clean

A FEW DAYS later, Morgana sent me down to Sam's Club to pick up cleaning supplies for the shop. The cashier—a seventeen-year-old girl with a nose piercing—had to run our corporate card twice because it wouldn't work. Suddenly, she looked down at the name on it. "Hey, you guys aren't too far from that school that got shot up. Wild or what?"

"I wouldn't call it that," I said. "Four students died because of a mentally ill boy."

"Four more souls for the Thin Man," she said as I grabbed up my plastic packages. She glanced up, eyes dancing, obviously taken with the whole sordid affair. The most excitement the town had seen since Cassandra Berger disappeared a few years back.

Then she said, "Maybe they'll come back."

"Excuse me?" I thought I hadn't heard her right.

"The dead kids. They're supposed to come back," she explained, obviously well-schooled in her creepypasta legends. "But they won't be right if they do. They'll be zombies or whatever."

Ooookay.

Crossing the gigantic parking lot cooking under the oppressive 90-plus degree heat while bearing the weight of fifty pounds of Mr. Clean and Clorox left me feeling like Lawrence of Arabia crossing the Nefud Desert. The soundtrack of twittering heat bugs didn't help much. My shirt was stuck to my back and my sunglasses kept sliding down my sweaty nose. Ahead, I spotted Antonia standing near the old Monaco.

She was a pretty young thing. I could see why Kenny liked her. She was tall, slender, and leggy. She had Ben's coloring and no-nonsense expression, but I could see the Shawnee in her face, as well. She wore a light blue halter dress and her afro hair was carefully crimped. As I approached, I encountered a quick surge of primal energy like a heat wave blowing off her. Ben was slightly clairvoyant; I suspected his daughter had inherited the same ability —or one similar to it—though whether it was due to their Shawnee or African roots, I had no idea.

"Hi, Mr. Englebrecht!" She raised a hand in greeting.

"Is everything all right?" I immediately asked, a true testimony to my outcast status in this town. No one approached me unless they needed something from me, whether it was a spell, a potion, or the kind of help only a witch and daemon could give.

She looked momentarily confused. "No…everything is fine. I saw you inside, so I waited. I wanted to come over to thank you." She gave me a hopeful smile. "You know…for being there at the school the other day."

"As long as everything's all right,"

"Yeah…well, as all right as it can be, under the circumstances."

I could see the age in her young face. This whole experience had changed her.

"Let me walk you to your car," I said. "There are a lot of out-of-towners around of late."

She didn't resist my offer, which was good. As teens went, Antonia was smart and sensible—not that I expected anything less from Ben's loins. But at least she didn't give me teenage lip for wanting to look out for her. I locked my packages inside the Monaco, picked up her shopping bags, and together we walked toward the blue Kia runaround that belonged to Ben's wife.

"Sure is hot."

"Like hell," I admitted without really thinking about it.

"I wonder why they say that—that hell is hot," she said, surprising me.

"Maybe it's a Catholic thing?"

She laughed.

I thought about this opportunity I had been given. "Can I ask you something about Kenny?"

"Sure," she said, sounding guarded suddenly. "I guess."

I thought about the statements that Kenny had given the police at the psychiatric hospital. It was all very odd. "The police are saying he was the victim of bullying..."

As we reached the Kia, she cut me off with a shake of her head. "*Some* of the kids gave him a hard time, but it wasn't like that. Everyone liked Kenny. We looked out for him." When she saw I didn't understand, she turned and tilted her head up at me. "I know you think all teenagers are awful, but we're not. Not most of us."

"I never said that," I stated even though that was exactly what I was thinking.

"Kenny was...special. Autistic. But he was sweet. He wouldn't have done this."

"Kenny was autistic. I did not know that."

She looked at me uncertainly. "Now you'll just think the worst of him."

"I will think no such thing," I assured her.

"Not many knew. And Kenny..." She shook her head. "That wasn't the real Kenny. That wasn't even autism."

I went over to the car and opened the back door, wincing a little. The whole car was as hot as the bottom of a frying pan. "What's your take on things?"

She gave me an incredulous look. "You're asking me?"

"I'm asking you," I said, slamming the door with her packages inside. "You knew him better than the police."

She brightened at the prospect that I wanted her honest opinion. "Kenny was strange sometimes...had meltdowns...but he *never* would have done something like this if he felt he had no other choice."

"How do you mean?" On a hunch, I added, "Does the Thin Man story have something to do with this?"

Her eyes widened; her nostrils flared. Jesus, she was scared half to death. "You know about...that?"

"I looked it up on the Internet. It's some shadowy creature who steals children, right? Something like Slenderman—"

"Not Slenderman. Slenderman is a *joke*. Slenderman was never real." She took a deep breath as though she might start hyperventilating. "This is real."

Her reaction surprised me. She really believed in the Thin Man. According to the stories I'd read online, the Thin Man stole (usually naughty) children...and then bought them back. That part had thrown me. If this was real...if *he* was real...why would he bring them back? That seemed counterproductive. But the one caveat? They weren't *right* when they returned. Zombies, as the cashier had said. Or something like it.

Antonia's voice was low and whispery, and she glanced around the parking lot as if she was afraid of summoning something. "Slenderman just steals children and they're gone. *Him*...he's something else. He...takes them somewhere else. He does something to them, and then he brings them back, but they aren't the same. Kenny called them Subs. Substitutes—the kids who come back."

I started leaning against the hood of her car to hear the rest of this but then thought better of it. The Kia felt like a pressure cooker. All this was suddenly getting very interesting to me.

She stared at her feet. "It's...a story."

"Tell me."

She licked her lips before she began. "The Subs...they look the same...they even act the same...but when you really look at them, they aren't in there, you know?" She looked up at me. "They're...empty. Substitute people."

"Is that what he was trying to destroy? The Substitutes?"

"I think that's what he believed."

I crossed my arms across my chest and quirked an eyebrow. "And what do you believe?"

"Does it matter?" she said, getting defensive suddenly. "No one will believe Kenny. No one would believe me. Hell, no one believes anything teenagers say." She let out her breath in exasperation. "Sorry, Mr. Englebrecht. I gotta go." She got in the car and started it, then rolled down the window even though she had the A/C on full blast. "Forget I said anything, all right?"

I nodded but thought, *Oh, hell no.*

| 7 |

The Thin Man

I CHECKED THE time on my watch—a cheap plastic Pokémon watch I'd found one day in a parking lot of a Wawa and made mine forever. After four years, it was still going strong.

I had only been gone half an hour. I figured I could squeeze in a quick field trip before I headed back to the shop. All I had to do was tell Morgana that they didn't have some of the stuff we wanted and I'd needed to go down to the Walmart in Lehighton for the rest.

It was a small lie...and not one that sat well with me, honestly. But I needed to do something. I needed to know more about what Kenny was going through.

The school was still on lockdown, but I knew that after a week, the forensics team would have scrubbed the place clean and security would be lighter. I pulled into the parking lot and cut the motor. The A/C in the Monaco had never worked right in all the time I had owned her, so the blast of heat when I got out wasn't nearly as bad as it could have been. I was already drenched in sweat, so no biggie.

The fence that lined the soccer field to the east was covered in cards, photos, straw crosses, and stuffed animals. I went over and looked the memorials over. Pictures of the victims dotted the fence. A brown bear with button eyes and a picture of the victims from a class photo pinned to it glared back at me. On the tarmac at the foot of the fence, someone had chalked the words LET THEM GO THIN MAN in angry green chalk.

Suppressing a light shiver, I turned back to the building.

A side door had been propped open by a chair to let in some air and, I presumed, to prevent any summer staff from spontaneously erupting into flames. I ducked into the darkened hallway but found no one around.

I sniffed the scents of books, chalk, and industrial-strength cleaner as I made my way down the empty hallway to the cafeteria where everything had gone down. It was a nice school, nicer than the one I'd gone to. Mine had been made of all green cinderblocks and teenage angst and underpaid teacher frustration. We hadn't yet reached the point of kids mass shooting each other, but it was definitely going that way, and in my last year of high school, they had started putting in metal detectors to keep kids from knifing each other.

Yellow police tape had been tacked up around the open doors of the cafeteria in an "X" pattern. I ducked through it and took a walk around, looking at the broken glass and investigative flags and markers. I was alone. Contrary to what you see on television, chalk and tape outlines are no longer de rigueur. Too much contamination of the crime scene. But I didn't need the markers to remember clearly where most of the bodies had lain.

I crouched down near a dark stain on the floor and just looked at it. The walls had bullet holes in them. What in hell could mess a kid up so badly he'd shoot his fellow students? Kenny was autistic— not violent. Okay. But the investigators were just going to see the autism. That, I was certain of. But, according to Antonia, they were wrong. How had some stupid internet meme made him do this terrible thing?

I heard the squeak of sandals behind me. "Oh, I'm sorry," came a deep, resonating voice. "I didn't see you there, officer."

I stood up and turned around. A man in a priest's black cassock and white collar stood in the hallway, carrying some ledgers. He was a tall, chunky sort, with steely grey hair and a creased but otherwise pleasant face. He was wearing Birkenstocks. I couldn't peg his age correctly. He looked thirty and sixty at the same time—wise and warm. Someone's jocular uncle, I thought. His grey eyes squinted at me myopically from behind his square, rimless glasses.

"I'm not an officer," I said, then regretted it. He'd probably throw me out now.

"Oh?" He lifted his head slightly and looked directly at me, but not in an accusing way. Instead, there was something open and full of understanding about his expression. He looked like someone you could really talk to. Someone who would never judge. I bet he was very good at being a priest. "Not one of those reporters here to gawk, I hope? It's all such a tragedy."

"No, not that, either. I'm a friend of Ben's."

"Sheriff Ben?"

"That's right."

"Are you sure you aren't an officer?"

"Why do you say that?"

"You have the bearing." He made a vague up-and-down gesture with his free hand. "You look like a TV cop."

I laughed at that as I ducked under some more police tape so I could approach him more easily. The warmth and humor in his eyes was strangely infectious. "No…well, I was, but that was a long time ago. I'm Nick." I didn't give him my last name. No one ever remembered it anyway.

"Dr. Theodore Lamb." The man extended his hand. Despite the graying hair, I realized he was much younger than I had first thought, closer to my own age. "Doctorate of Sacred Theology."

I was so surprised he was offering me his hand, I almost didn't know what to do with it. Aside from Morgana and a small handful of others, most people are physically intolerant of my touch. It's not that they make a show of it, but they do subtle little things to keep their distance from me—change lines in the supermarket, or suddenly find something very interesting to look at when they have to shake my hand. I'd learned long ago to avoid casual physical contact where possible. Dr. Lamb seemed unperturbed, however. He held out his hand for a few heartbeats longer than was strictly necessary before withdrawing it. His face showed no insult.

"Sorry," I said anyway. I felt bad to have shunned him.

"No, you're quite wise. Do you know how many bacteria you can pick up from a handshake?" He wrinkled his nose. "I should quit the habit myself."

I laughed at that—and then I smiled. Suddenly, I couldn't seem to stop smiling. I found I liked this beautiful man even if he was a man of the cloth. He was the type of old soul I knew I could talk to for hours and never grow tired of.

We started heading down the hallway together almost as if the whole encounter had been choreographed. You would have thought I was friends with him forever. Along the way, I said, "Should I call you 'Doctor' or 'Father?'"

"Why not be casual? Call me Theo. You're looking into the shooting, correct?"

"Yeah," I agreed. "But only unofficially. Ben would kill me if he knew I was stomping all over his crime scene."

Dr. Theo Lamb nodded. "Then I shan't tell him."

"Thanks."

"No thanks necessary. You seemed concerned, and heaven knows we need more of your kind of person in the world, Officer Nick."

Along with his Birkenstocks, he also wore socks. Socks and sandals. For some reason, that made me smile, as well.

"It's a terrible thing. Worse that it happened here." I waited for him to pontificate on the mysterious ways of God and the universe the way men of the cloth usually do, but he just nodded to himself and sort of hummed in sympathy as he stepped into an office with his name stenciled on the door.

A boy of fifteen or sixteen, dressed in the school uniform, was standing on a step stool, furtively straightening a shelf of crooked books.

"Carl, my assistant," Lamb said, indicating the boy. "He helps me in all kinds of ways—mostly with the computer." He indicated the source of his frustration—an open Mac laptop on his desk. "Can't get the hang of it. Can you?"

I shrugged. "Computers don't like me either."

Carl laughed at us Luddites.

Nodding toward a rather elaborate, stainless steel coffee machine sitting on a sideboard, he said, "Carl, can you get a couple of cups out of that infernal machine?"

"Of course, Father." Abandoning the books, Carl quickly climbed down the ladder.

"Can I tempt you?" Lamb asked me.

"If you're having it."

Carl set about getting frothy cups of latte from the machine and into two large mugs with scripture printed on them while Lamb moved around his desk, which was groaning under the weight of un-filed paperwork. "I've been counseling the survivors of the shooting and their parents. It hasn't been easy."

With his back to us, I noticed Carl's shoulders stiffening while Lamb explained.

"How does one instill a sense of God when He's such an esoteric concept?"

I sat down in the big, comfy leather chair opposite his desk. "You don't believe in God?"

"If you mean God as in our Holy Father? Not exactly. I see Him as more of a lofty concept born of our ancestral lizard brains than anything else. Thank you, Carl." He took the cups from Carl, who was smiling and seemingly unperturbed by Lamb's heretical beliefs.

"Sugar?" Lamb asked me.

"Please. And how can you be a priest and not believe in God?"

Carl, balancing a tall stack of books, quietly exited the room, humming to himself. Meanwhile, Lamb, having doctored my cup, carried the two mugs over from the coffee station, setting one down in front of me. "I don't have much of a choice, I'm afraid," he said, taking a sip of his own. "I was born clairvoyant. Specifically, with the gift—perhaps curse—of charisma."

When he saw I didn't fully understand, he explained, "It's defined as personal influence over other people, either individually or as a group. For instance, you followed me to my office without fear or invitation. As a cop, how often have you done such a thing, I wonder?"

And, just like that, I felt like some spell had been broken—or that I had woken up suddenly. I stopped gulping coffee and set my cup down, bristling. I hated coffee. I didn't follow anyone anywhere. I didn't go walking around, grinning like some fucking idiot.

"This isn't me," I bit out, annoyed, angry, repulsed by my own behavior. I glanced around the office as if it were a trap. "You mean you *control* people."

Lamb pursed his lips. "Not deliberately. I mean, not in some psychic 'Professor X' kind of way. It happens whether I will it or not. Wherever I go, people follow, and they listen to me, even if

I'm sprouting gibberish." He sat down in his chair, which groaned a little under his weight, and put his hands in his lap. He looked at me—I wanted to say shrewdly, but his face was plain and open and almost breathtaking in its sincerity. It was the face of your father, mentor, someone you trust and love implicitly. A sensei. A caregiver. Someone you know will always be there for you.

Someone you loved.

Christ...I *loved* him. I didn't *know* him, but I knew even without consulting my deep inner feel-feels that I loved the man. And it was revolting. Unnatural.

I started standing up but found I didn't want to. I didn't have it in me to leave just yet. I searched Lamb's face for evil. For darkness. For manipulation. I could find no deceit in it at all.

Lamb sighed tiresomely. "It's happened since I was a child. For instance, if I suggested you go home, find your state-issued firearm, and shoot yourself in the leg, you would do it. If you're a strong man —and I suspect you probably are, Officer Nick—you might spend a few days rationalizing it, but eventually you'll do it just the same."

I was still drinking his damned coffee. I put the cup down and pushed it away, sloshing coffee over the edge. I finally did stand up —too quickly. I didn't want to be here anymore, but now I couldn't trust myself. I couldn't decide if that was *my* decision or his, so I just hovered in place, undecided, like some kind of moron.

"I don't want you to hurt yourself, Officer Nick. I was only trying to make a point," Lamb said, sounding sad and rather lonely about it all. He pressed his hands together hard as if he was trying to hold something back, something in.

I studied him, waiting for the kicker...the shadow that said he was evil. That he was Otherkin like me. It never happened. "If what you're saying is true"—And I had no doubt it was, by the way.—"do you really think you ought to be working around children?"

Lamb didn't look surprised by my question. Perhaps he had been expecting it. "I have no choice but to be here. To do this."

I was getting angrier by the moment. "What do you mean?"

"If I hadn't become a priest, I would probably have been a dictator—or, at the very least, not a very nice person." Lamb looked sad about that.

I shook my head. I couldn't fucking believe this!

"I suppose you use your...power...in counseling," I said, eyeing him uncertainly.

"I try not to, but it slips out sometimes. All for the good," Lamb hastily added. "Or, that's what I tell myself." He seemed to shrink a little in his seat as if he was ashamed of himself. "I expect you think I'm perfectly mad."

"No, I believe you." I thought it might even be possible he was a daemon like me. Like Vivian. I wondered about his parentage. His power seemed too strong and elemental to be anything learned or conjured up. Even a natural-born witch couldn't do the things he was doing.

I should have left right then and there, but I saw another opportunity knocking and decided to readily answer it. I sat down again. "The counseling sessions...do the kids talk about this Thin Man I've been hearing about?"

He looked up quickly, his glasses flashing, his mouth slightly open. "That old legend? Sometimes." Lamb frowned at that and nervously pushed some papers around his desk. "Do you know the story?"

"From the Internet..."

"I mean the *original* story."

I didn't, but I wasn't sure if I wanted Theodore Lamb telling me it. I couldn't be certain if he would tell me the truth. Daemons aren't to be trusted. Still, I was a little too curious to simply flee his office. Curiosity and the cat and all that.

I sat back. "Tell me."

He brightened up when he realized I wasn't going to flee his presence or take him to task. With a happy grunt, he pushed himself up and out of his seat. Maybe, like me, people instinctively shrank from him. Maybe he was just as lonely and isolated as I was. Or maybe that was just what he wanted me to feel at the moment.

"I'll do you one better, Officer Nick. I'll show you."

He walked around me and moved to the back of the office. The wall was completely covered in shelves of books and ledgers with papers sticking out of them haphazardly. Theo Lamb the daemon wasn't much of a housekeeper, I noted. But then, neither was I.

It took a little bit of digging and rearranging, but he finally found the book he was looking for. An old tome with a torn and ragged cover entitled *History and Folklore of the Lehigh Valley Railroad*.

"This is one of my favorites. I'm a bit of a local history buff, you see. I bought this one from the curator of the Lehigh Valley Heritage Museum," Lamb explained, opening the book to one of many plastic bookmarks. The spine was weak and the pages flopped, a testament to how many times it had been used. "It's mostly about the railroads, of course, but there's a section about the No. 8 Mine, the one that's supposedly haunted."

"Lucky 8 Mine?"

I wasn't deeply into local folklore—at least, no more than I had to be when the situation warranted it—but even I had heard about Lucky 8. It had been one of the deepest and richest veins in the country for Anthracite coal. You know, the black stuff high in carbon that gets used in...well, almost everything. But like almost all the mines in Eastern Pennsylvania, it was dangerous as hell, with plenty of accumulated stories, legends, and local folklore.

Lucky 8 was supposedly haunted by dead coal miners. Nothing too original there, sure. They said that about *every* coal mine in the Lehigh Valley region. The only thing setting it apart was that it really did host a few "knockers"—that is, low-level demons that lived down there. Despite all your assumptions about demons, they don't all fall into the "bad" category. There's a lot of grey areas to be found. Knockers are demons that were willing to either help or hinder miners, depending on their mood that day—and if they liked you. But I didn't mention that little tidbit. I seriously doubted Lamb would believe in demons if he didn't even believe in God.

He showed me a page that featured some pretty freaky woodcuts. In one of them, several miners were fleeing the tunnels while a shadowy figure with extremely long arms seemed to reach for them out of the darkness.

"In 1857, an Irish immigrant miner by the name of Seamus Wogan kidnapped a number of children from Central, a mining village located in the Susquehanna Valley..." Lamb read from the book, then looked up briefly overtop his glasses. "That's only a few miles from here. Anyway...to summarize, he took the children into an abandoned mine shaft and gave them figurines to play with that he'd carved from the coal. Then he systematically butchered them and boiled them into a soup."

I winced as I looked over some of the other woodcuts he was showing me. Pretty graphic stuff. "Reason being?"

"They say he came over during the Great Potato Famine and that, even though there was ample game in the woods, he'd grown accustomed to eating human flesh for survival. They say he was addicted to it." Lamb paused for dramatics.

I could tell he enjoyed having an audience for his grisly tale.

"Do you believe that?" I asked.

"I think he was one of the first examples of a human touched by the Thin Man. I think being down in the mine led to him being...influenced by him somehow."

I thought of Antonia. She had called them *Substitutes*.

"In any event," Lamb continued, "eventually the disappeared children increased and the town grew wise to what was happening. They sent a search party out into the woods, and the men eventually found his cabin. By then, he had used the dead children's skin to bind his books and make furnishings. They captured Wogan, tried him, and hanged him for his crimes. They burned the body and scattered the ashes all along the Blackwater River, but"—Again, he paused for dramatics, even raised a finger to make his point.—"it didn't do much good, because the abductions continued for another seven years."

"Seven years?" Now that's tenacity for you.

Lamb nodded. "Sometimes, a child got away and talked about what he or she had seen—a ghostly figure reaching for them while they were asleep. Long arms and fingers. They said the specter moved spider-like along the ceiling or made long shadows on the wall. That's why they called him the Thin Man. He was known to make a strange rattle before he took the children."

"Creepy," I agreed.

"The townsfolk initially attributed it to Wogan because he used to abduct children after they'd fallen asleep in bed." Lamb pointed to the first woodcut. "Several miners even went down into the abandoned tunnels to investigate, but they were frightened off by what they thought was Wogan's spirit."

I took the book from him and looked it over, turning a page. "But the abductions did stop?"

"Eventually. But only after the mine was finally closed down and abandoned in 1864."

I thought about that a long moment. "But that mine was still in operation all the way up until…the 1970s, wasn't it?"

"1972, to be exact. Yes, but it's always been haunted, or so it seems. It goes in cycles, you see. A powerful investor sweeps in and tries to mine the deepest veins, then something goes wrong—a cave-in or a disappearance—and they wind up boarding up the mine again. They say there's still a billion dollars in untapped veins down there."

I chewed my bottom lip over that. "So you think this Wogan fellow worked in unison with the Thin Man?"

"I'm not sure, to be honest, but he may have been an agent of the creature."

I gave him a smirk. "According to the stories I read online, the Thin Man's victims come back—they just aren't the same. Could Wogan have been one of his victims-turned-agents?"

Lamb took the book from me and offered a smirk of his own. "I don't know…do you believe any of this?"

"It's a local legend. There's a hundred of those around here." I shrugged. "I mean, probably there's some small truth to it. There always is. Can I keep this book for a little while?"

He shoved it at me as I stood up. "By all means. In fact, wait one moment."

Lamb returned to the wall of books, got on the step stool, and took down what looked like one of those giant photo albums every family seems to have. In this case, though, it was full of newspaper clippings. "I have a fairly large cache of these. As I said, I'm a bit of a history buff."

He blushed at his admission, which made him seem far more boyish than was probably healthy but offered me the scrapbook anyway. "This journal traces a lot of local legends going back to the turn of the last century, but you'll find some things relevant to these types of crimes." He nodded over the clippings. "Recent things, too—things leading up to the mine closing in '72. I even took the liberty of adding a few clippings about the recent reopening. Those are at the back."

That surprised the hell out of me. "They reopened the mine after all that?"

"I told you—it goes in cycles, Officer Nick." Lamb rubbed his fingers together to indicate money. He offered me a pleasant, if noncommittal, smile. "It's all in the journal."

Thus armed with Dr. Lamb's research literature, I turned toward the door...then had a thought and turned back. "Why give this to me? I'm not actually an investigator, you know. You could have given all this information to Sheriff Ben."

But Lamb's benign smile never slipped. "Young man, I have a feeling you'll know exactly what to do with it. Besides, you can give it back to me when you're done with it. I have a feeling we'll be seeing each other again very, very soon."

| 8 |

Number One Crush

WELL, THAT REGISTERED pretty high on my creepy-o-meter, I thought on the ride home, Dr. Lamb's research material sitting in a stack on the passenger seat beside me. I mean, in the greater scheme of things, not uber-creepy. I'd seen uber-creepy. Angel-eaters. Ancient gods birthed from out of alternative dimensional voids. Angels that could turn men to stone. Real hair-raising shit. But Lamb was pretty much up there.

I kept rolling my encounter with the man around in my head, trying to determine if he was friend or foe, but I couldn't make heads or tails of him. On top of it, I had this weird feeling of déjà vu that wouldn't let me be. I felt that I had met Dr. Lamb somewhere before—or, maybe, I had always been predetermined to meet him, and this was just psychic backwash. I wasn't sure.

Normally, I encounter three different kinds of people in my life—those I immediately like and respect, like Morgana and Sheriff Ben, those I immediately dislike, like those monstrosities I've previously mentioned, and what I called Blanks. Blanks are people who gave me no reading at all, and no sense of either good or evil. They're just...blank slates.

Vivian had always been blank to me. The more I thought about it, the more I realized Kenny Johnson was the same. And the same was now true of Dr. Lamb.

Blanks.

In a clear moment of utter non sequitur, I suddenly remembered I'd picked up a bag of Raisinets at Sam's Club. I dug them out of a shopping bag as I rode over the railroad tracks and back into Blackwater proper, but I'd left them too long in the car while I was messing around with Dr. Lamb and they'd turned into one big melty pile. That didn't put Lamb too far up on my likable list—through no fault of his own.

With a little whispered curse, I drove around the back of the store and down the narrow service alley where I normally parked the Monaco. In the process, I nearly ran down Josh Summers, Vivian's brother, and his dog Tiger, sitting on the back steps. I hit the brake and my thirty-five-year-old heap shuddered to a halt inches away.

The last time I'd seen Josh, he was on the run from some angels who had a bone to pick with his sister—which was pretty crappy on the part of the angels, in my own humble opinion, considering Josh was an ex-veteran who'd gotten an honorable discharge after a bomb in Afghanistan had blinded him one bright, sunny day. I didn't feel he deserved that level of shit thrown at him.

These days, Josh spent his time playing gigs down in Philly dives for a pittance. When Vivian and I had been together, she had offered to put Josh up in her apartment multiple times, but Josh insisted he liked the circuit and liked spending his nights playing blues tunes to drunks and insomniacs. It gave him a sense of purpose, and I could dig that. I was independent that way, too, as well as good at making bad life decisions. In many ways, Josh and I were flip sides of the same grimy, nearly homeless, coin.

I grabbed my packages and walked around the car.

Josh stood up. He was carrying a brown, military-surplus duffel bag and a guitar case. He was a tall, rangy guy in his early thirties, sexy in that disheveled Kurt Cobain kind of way that never really goes out of style. He had a scruffy, dirty blond mop-top and goatee, and his plaid and denim clothes looked like they hadn't seen the inside of a washing machine for a few weeks.

Didn't matter. As soon as I saw him, I remembered I'd had a bit of a crush on him in the not-too-distant past—not that I was likely to act on it. For one thing, he was my ex's brother. For another—and, most importantly—Josh was a sweet guy, and sweet guys had a bad habit of coming to bad ends around me.

His shades turned my way and he flashed me a familiar grin. Tiger, his service Rottweiler, stood up as well and gave me a big doggy smile and a stumpy tail wag.

"Hey, Nick, sorry to drop in so unexpectedly," he said, adjusting his pack on his back.

"What are you doing out here?" I asked, giving Tiger a scratch behind the ears. "Didn't Morgana let you in?"

"Yeah, she did, but your shop smells...no offense. All that incense." He wrinkled his nose. "It's making my hay fever worse."

Now that I thought about it, he did sound nasally—well, *more* nasally than he usually did, which was his signature singing voice.

He looked at me uncomfortably. "I have a favor to ask and you're probably not going to like it."

"Shoot."

He hesitated as he gathered himself. "Is there any way I can leave Tiger with you for a few days?" He again pauses, thoroughly embarrassed to be asking for this favor, then hurried to add, "I'd asked Viv, but she's at the club all the time with Odin, and..."

"Oberon."

"Yeah, *him*. And there's no one to look after my buddy properly, and I don't really have any friends anymore in this town. None that I trust with him, you know?"

I was more flattered than anything else. First, a man like Dr. Lamb wants to shake my hand, and, next, a sweet, sensible guy like Josh wants to trust me with his dog. It was a real Red Letter day for Nick Englebrecht. Maybe, I thought, the universe was starting to hate me just a little bit less.

"You going out of town?" As far as I was aware, Josh never went anywhere without Tiger.

"California. Well, L.A., to be exact. There's a surgeon out there who's had some success at repairing corneas and..." He turned his head down as if this mortified him to no end and mumbled some other excuses I didn't care about because this was Josh, and I'd do almost anything for him, with or without an explanation.

"Ahh. Sure. Why the hell not?" Morgana probably won't dig it, but I'll burn that bridge when I got to it.

Josh's smile grew, beaming at me. Shit, what a heartbreaker. It was a good thing he was blind because a smile like that was capable of giving me a decent bit of wood.

He started digging into his pack. "I have money for Tiger's food..."

"Don't worry about it. The shop is doing great this summer." Not *exactly* true. The heat had killed our customer base, but the shooting was bringing in a few curiosity-seekers, just nothing serious. But what Josh didn't know couldn't hurt him.

I grabbed up Tiger's leash. "Tiger and I will have a good time. We'll do doggie things," I said, not exactly sure what those things were, but I'd figure it out as I went along. Growing up, I'd never had pets, though I'd always wanted a dog.

Josh tilted his head uncertainly. "Are you sure you're cool with this?"

"Sure. Don't worry about Tiger. Just worry about getting better."

"I owe you one, man." He checked his Braille watch. "I gotta get down to the airport for my flight."

"You need a ride?"

"I have an Uber coming, but thanks." He unfolded a white cane from his jacket pocket, then crouched down to rub the sides of Tiger's broad head. "You be a good boy for your Uncle Nick, got it?"

Tiger made a nervous whining noise. I tried not to take that as an insult.

After he was gone, I led Tiger inside. Tiger sneezed from the incense, so I figured maybe he had hay fever, too.

"What's that dog doing in here?" Morgana asked, breaking the curtain of beads that separated the back room from the front of the store.

"Josh asked me to watch him for a few days while he's in California. He's seeing a top surgeon who's had great success with corneas. He thinks Josh might be able to see again." I was stretching the truth a bit, admittedly, but I didn't want Morgan kicking Tiger out.

Tiger, for his own part, sat down, clomped his jaws, and drooled onto the floor.

Morgana considered it for about two seconds before sighing. "All right, fine. But keep him upstairs. I don't want him rampaging through the shop and scaring the customers."

I touched my heart dramatically. "I'll have you know Tiger is a well-trained service dog and does not 'rampage.'"

Morgana rolled her eyes.

I started up the stairs with Tiger at my side. Almost got to the top, too, before Morgana said, "Nick?"

"Yes, dear."

"You might want to put a cap on some of the fibs. It's becoming something of a habit with you."

Oops. Sometimes I forget what a powerful witch she is.

"Yes, dear." I tipped an invisible hat to her and then hurried up the stairs like some reprimanded teenager.

| 9 |

Fun in the Sun

"NICK, ARE YOU happy with us?" Morgana asked me that night while we were fooling around.

Since I was down under, I almost didn't hear her. "What?" I said, my voice coming muffled from between her legs.

"Are you happy? With me. With us?"

"Morgana, I'm working here."

"Answer the question, Scratch."

I looked up at the cool, wintry blue eyes set in her sensual, ageless face. Her body, like her face, was flawless. I only hoped I looked as good as she did at her age. Then again, who knew what I would look like in ten years? Maybe I'd have horns and a tail by then.

"What's all this about?" I sighed, moving up alongside her in bed and leaning on my elbow.

She pulled the sheet up to her breasts, which was a good sign I'd pissed her off in some arcane Morgana way I was about to learn about. "You saw Vivian."

I didn't ask how she knew that. Being a witch, and a woman, beauty has her way. "I ran into Vivian at the memorial service on

Sunday, if that's what you mean." I kept my voice carefully neutral. No quarter given.

"She showed off her new pet—some Goth boi with a bad haircut. Then she got pissy with me for no reason at all." I made sure to add the last, lest Morgana tried to steer this convo into waters I wasn't ready to weather. "Her pet's name is Oberon."

Morgana gave me her poker face, which is always infuriating. "And is this 'Oberon' still standing?"

"Walking, talking, and smoking pansy-ass cigarettes." I held up two fingers, scout's honor. "Why the hell is everyone treating me like Tony Soprano? What in my past history makes you think I'd bump someone off for dating my ex?"

She gave me a droll look.

"I promise I won't kill the Fairy King," I said, a little annoyed by the fact that I'd had to promise that twice in two days.

Finally, her angry face broke and I could read her concern as she snuggled against my chest. "I worry about you, Nick. I worry that you put yourself...at risk."

"Of what?"

She ran her fingertips up and down my chest. She didn't say it, but I didn't need her to. She was afraid I would act irresponsibly. Recklessly. That I would hurt myself. Or her. Or someone else. Or everyone around me.

"I don't want things to change," she confessed. "I like us where we are. Hell, I love us. But if something does change...if you feel something changing in you...I want you to feel you can come to me. Talk to me."

Oh, so that's what she was worried about.

"I won't change, I promise," I told her, kissing her hair. She had sacrificed so much for me. For us. She and Anton McGinley, her main squeeze for just over a year, had been well on their way to a handfasting when things fell apart between me and Vivian. I went to a very dark place for a time, but Morgana had been there to shore me up. Her mothering quickly turned into something else, and, along the way, we'd decided to give us a try. Not friends. Not friends with benefits. A real *us.* A real try. A real relationship with all the messy strings attached. I wasn't about to screw that up. Not with Morgana.

She was too precious. She was worth too much to me.

To make up for all my lies and general asshole-ish behavior of late, I even promised to watch the shop all day tomorrow so she could get out a bit and visit the Wiccan Fair in Cherry Hill.

"Do you promise to stay put?" she asked me the next morning just to confirm I meant what I had said in bed. "No shenanigans?"

I yawned, all sleepy-eyed, as I stood at the stove. "When do I ever engage in 'shenanigans?'"

"Nick."

I kissed her hand in passing. "No shenanigans, dear."

I had even gotten up at the ass crack of dawn to dress and put the kettle on. I fed a bowl of kibble to Tiger, who proceeded to sloppily spill it all over the kitchen floor.

"Now I *know* you did something wrong," Morgana quipped as she made her way to the island. She was dressed in one of her flowing, painted Japanese silk robes. Her long, white-blonde hair braided away from her face. She gave me a cynical look as she slipped on her reading glasses and started perusing the morning paper spread out over the countertop.

"Is it wrong for a man to want to be a better boyfriend?" I said, pouring us both some organic rose and lavender tea. I carried two cups over.

"You're not a bad boyfriend, Nick."

My spirits sank. Just a bad man, she was thinking. Someone she didn't fully trust. Hell, most of the time, *I* didn't trust me. Not entirely. But I didn't say that. I've never been one to bare my insecurities, even to Morgana.

"Enjoy your day," I said and kissed her on the cheek. I almost winced; I sounded so artificial, some ridiculous and demonic Ken doll playing house with an angelic Barbie who was too damned good for me. "I want to get downstairs and work on that stock before I open up."

After I got the new stock open and had the displays up, I flipped the sign in the door to Open and started taking customers. It was still ridiculously hot, and our newly repaired air conditioner unit seemed barely able to keep up, but there was an endless stream of people today. I should have been ecstatic about that. For once, we wouldn't need to worry about covering the lease, but the extra traffic was a reminder that several teenagers were still dead, a seriously messed up teenage boy was still in custody, and I still hadn't figured out what was going on, or how it was connected to some scary Internet meme.

After Morgana left for the fair, some boys started roughhousing back near the incense burners while the parents stood around, idly examining healing crystals, texting, and generally not parenting. Before the little family left, I slapped the father with a bill for the merchandise that one of his boys had stolen.

"My son is not a thief! Who do you think you are, anyway?" he barked in my face.

"Check his pockets," I said. "Back left jeans pocket. He has a rose pendant."

"My son doesn't steal! My son—"

The boy in question started screaming and clawing at his back pocket even as the red teardrop pendant burned its way through his denim-clad ass and dropped to the floor with a clink.

"You did something to him! What did you do to my boy?" the father screamed hysterically. "I'm going to sue your ass for everything you're worth, mister!"

I was about to raise my hand and completely wipe his fat mouth away when the wife intervened. "He's okay. Shane's okay, Bill. Just look at him!"

The two started arguing viciously in the middle of the shop, and they were still doing so when they both left.

And this, I thought obliquely, is the definition of Retail Hell. I leaned against the glass of the display case and worked on getting my temper back under control. I wasn't proud of myself, not by a long shot. I'd wanted to hurt that man, and I didn't normally lose it like that. Maybe I needed more sleep, or to eat or something. Yeah...when was the last time I'd eaten something other than Twizzlers or Gummy Bears?

I shut the shop down for lunch and went out to buy a hoagie from the Turkey Hill at the end of Main Street. While I was checking out, I saw someone waving from the parking lot. I stepped out into the blistering heat with my sandwich and iced tea and saw David Breyer with a couple of his college friends hanging out near the Bike Tour shop. Back when Vivian and I were an item, David had rounded out our little polyamorous clique. He was a Penn State graduate like Vivian, specializing in medicine. Reconstructive surgery, to be exact.

The sight of him immediately lifted my spirits. I'd thought he'd left for Florida at the end of last year. When I walked over to ask him what the hell had happened, he said he was only back temporarily to see his parents since his aunt had died a few weeks ago. He quickly detached himself from his college buddies and walked with me back to the shop. He walked close but not touching.

"Sorry to hear about your aunt," I said.

"Thanks, man. She was sick for a long time. Lung cancer, you know? The radiation treatment did her in. She had a weak heart."

"I'm sorry, David," I said. My own aunt had died of a bad heart.

He bowed his head a little. He was still the lithe, foxy guy I remembered. Lots of beautiful Jewish hair and good teeth. Glasses. I'd always enjoyed his company. I let him into the back room where we kept the stock and said, "Can I make you some tea?"

"Nick and tea." He shook his head. "I could never figure that. You never seemed like the 'tea' type."

I shrugged.

He leaned back against one of the tall racks we keep for stock and said, "How's Vivian?"

I knew what he meant. "We aren't together anymore," I confessed, breaking the seal on my iced tea, which wasn't so iced anymore since the walk back to the shop in the 90-plus, heat-bug-twittery humidity.

He looked shocked. "I never would have guessed that. You two seemed like forever, you know?"

"Looks can be pretty deceiving."

I didn't feel sad, just nostalgic. Yearning for something long gone. Maybe something I'd never really had, only imagined.

I knew he felt it, too. A few minutes of polite chitchat later, we were fumbling with each other's buttons and belt buckles, running hands over ridges of muscle, rib bones, and tacky summer flesh. I kissed him the way I used to kiss Vivian, all sweet, melting honey and sharp, hungry teeth. I bit his lip and we clinked our teeth together as we sought entry into each other's bodies any way we could.

"Fuck, Nick!" David said when I turned him around and pinned his upper body against the metal racks, which at least were a little cooler than the rest of the room. He bucked his ass and made low groaning noises while I set my teeth in his shoulder and shuttled my way deep inside of him. Vivian liked it rough; David, too. The sounds he made quickly turned to mewls of pleasure and things clanked on the shelves high above us as we reached our end.

It was over pretty quickly, and when he turned back, I touched the marks of my teeth in his flesh, which looked a little too ragged and fierce to be made by human teeth. It made me want to touch what was in my mouth, to discover if I had those horrible hooked angel teeth my dad had.

"Sorry," I said because I was.

"Are you fucking kidding me? At least something good came of this rotten trip. I got a kickass souvenir." He rubbed the mark before hooking a forearm around my neck. He ducked his head to kiss me, then reached for his T-shirt, sliding it sweaty wet over his head.

He drank some of my iced tea and gave me a sticky summer kiss goodbye. Too soon, he headed back down the street to join his college buddies. I tried to go back to my lunch, but, by then, I'd lost my appetite.

Around two, I closed the shop down for the last time and took the old Monaco out into the country, all the windows rolled down and the hot arid wind raking over my sweaty skin. I had no idea where I was headed until I finally got there.

| 10 |

Queen of Babylon

BACK IN NEW York, when I was eleven years old, this kid Vinnie and I used to play a game behind the projects called Break the Bottles. Spin the Bottle was still about four years off for me. We'd collect glass bottles and use a stickball bat to knock them into the wall. We made a hell of a mess and got into loads of trouble for it. My foster father at the time didn't give a shit what I was up to, but Vinnie wasn't a foster like me, and his dad ragged on him for it. The homeless guys and the Puerto Rican gangs got pretty pissed with us, too. This one time, a gang caught us in the act and kicked the shit out of both of us. Vinnie got two black eyes and I got a busted nose and a kicked-in rib.

The next day, looking like two prizefighters who had done a couple of rounds with Mike Tyson, we were back at it again, breaking bottles and getting knocked around. Fun times.

I thought about that time in my life as I drove out to Serenity Falls, the retirement home ten miles east of Blackwater. Why the hell did Vinnie and I do something that brought us so much pain? Or, rather, why did we *keep* on doing it?

Beats me. Because it was fun? Because we were bored? Because we thought we were tough guys, when, in reality, we were both just hurting and angry? Why does a kid do anything he's not supposed to do?

Why does a man?

As soon as the endorphins from screwing David started wearing off, I started feeling like dog shit. I kept asking myself why I had let it happen.

To hurt Morgana? To hurt myself?

I didn't have any answers. I told myself I would tell Morgana as soon as possible, be upfront and honest about it, but I knew I wouldn't. I was only fooling myself. The only way she would ever find out was if she used her woo-woo or David told her. I was lying to myself again. Big surprise there.

I pulled into the parking lot of a large, rambling, butt-ugly building. It was obvious it had once been a large residential home once upon a time, but wings had been added to it over the years. It sprawled in three different directions, but none of the dirty vinyl siding matched. I parked at the end of a long line of vehicles and got out and went inside.

I'd never been here, but Serenity Falls had a reputation for being a good place to dump your loved ones when you no longer had the time or patience to take care of them. I found myself in a front parlor of sorts, with a TV snugged away in the corner ceiling and about two dozen old-timers sitting around in wheelchairs. *The Price is Right* was on, and one of the contestants was guessing on a fancy billiards table. No one in the room seemed to be paying much attention, though everyone was watching.

Something about the antiseptic smell of the place, combined with the natural odor of the relics sitting, or slumping, in wheelchairs, just weirded me out. Evil, I know, but there it was. I didn't like the place and I didn't like being here.

I started toward some swinging door that led to a short hallway I could see through the windows dead ahead, but halfway there, an old woman with her hair in curlers grabbed my arm. Hard. Her grip was frighteningly powerful and her hand felt dry and almost claw-like. It felt like a mummy had me.

"Mammon," she said quite clearly.

I stopped and looked down at her. Yeah...this wasn't my first rodeo.

"Mammon." She had a doll lying in her lap. When she said it a third time, it sounded more like "Mamma," though I knew that wasn't what she meant.

I yanked myself loose from her grip. From another part of the room, a man called in a soft, hoarse voice (the voice you use after midnight), "Son of Aurora."

"Mammon," said the old woman again.

"King of Babylon."

"Jesus Christ," I whispered and moved quickly out of the room and into the hallway, feeling like I'd run some kind of damned gauntlet. I was sweating worse than ever, and my heart was ticking in my throat. It took me a moment to realize I was standing in front of the nurse's station. I wiped the burning sweat out of my eyes.

The pretty young black nurse behind the glass partition looked up and said, "Are you all right, sir?"

"I'd like to see Everett McCarty."

"One moment." She started tapping on her computer.

According to the news clippings that Lamb had given me, the abduction of four young people had occurred in 1970, just two years before Lucky 8 Mine was closed down once more. Some simple Google-fu had told me the rest. All four had turned up—or been returned, depending on how you wanted to look at things. Two had died in State Penn some years back—one on death row—but two were still alive. One lived out of state, a woman who had been rendered catatonic since her abduction and never spoke a word again. The last lived here at Serenity Falls.

I had chosen to visit McCarty for two reasons.

1. He had given the police the most detailed description of his abduction, even if no one had ever believed his outlandish story. And:
2. He was the same teacher who'd seduced Vivian when she was nine years old, basically ruining her whole fucking life.

The two of them had carried on a yearlong affair before he got tired of her and threw her away, leaving her to deal with the emotional fallout all alone. He'd wanted Vivian scared and at his mercy because that's what it took for him to get off, but Vivian didn't scare easy, not even then. She'd told me once that she'd liked it, that, at the time, she had considered him her boyfriend.

I knew that in her heart, she had never forgiven him. Or herself. I knew what stuff was in her soul, good and bad. Particularly these days.

"What relation are you to Mr. McCarty?" asked the nurse.

"I'm his nephew. Nick Englebrecht."

She looked me over with more interest than was probably appropriate. I figured that since I was sweaty and still disheveled from having sex with a man only an hour earlier, my devil charm was working overtime. With a wide, friendly smile, she buzzed me into the private wing after—didn't even ask to see my ID.

I was a little surprised that security was so lax. Then again, looking at the withered souls sitting slack-jawed in their jammies in wheelchairs in the hallways, I couldn't see Serenity Falls as being the kind of place where truly violent confrontations were apt to break out.

I found his room—113. Another pretty nurse in scrubs with Scooby-Doo on them was just stepping out, pushing a medicine cart. "Are you here to see Mr. McCarty?" she asked in a perky Southern accent.

"Yeah, I'm his grandson," I said, forgetting I'd said nephew at the nurse's station. Oh well. But she never blinked.

"Such a nice man," she said, grinning at me in that naïve, untouched way that so many young people have about them before the real world gets its claws into them. "It's a shame no one ever visits."

"Really? No one?"

"Not a one. But that's not unusual here." She looked sad about that. "I didn't even know he had a family."

"Yeah. I'm here to fix all that."

"God bless you, sugar." She waltzed off, none the wiser.

McCarty's room was dim and small and far too warm, even with the A/C on. It sported a narrow bed and a tiny seating arrangement in the corner. The drapes were pulled closed and he was sitting in a wheelchair, breathing into an oxygen machine, and watching the same *The Price is Right* episode as the people out in the parlor.

He wasn't what I'd expected.

I'm not sure what that was.

What does a child predator look like? Monstrous and twisted, frightening to look upon?

The man looked half my size, with a balding pate and grey, paper-thin skin. His face was drawn and skull-like in that way of people facing terminal diseases, a permanent, painful sneer on his lips that said he would die as miserably as he had lived and that, soon after, it would be like he had never existed at all. To me, he looked like he would crumble at the slightest touch.

He turned just his head to look at me. He cut right to the chase. "Who the hell are you?"

"My name is Nick Englebrecht," I said, not expecting him to react to that, and I was right.

He just looked annoyed. "So? If you're one of my sister's kids, I ain't got no money. But you can have my shit when I'm dead."

There was nowhere to sit down, so I just moved to stand beside the tiny, old-fashioned box TV on its aluminum stand. There were cheap, soulless prints on the walls, the kind you buy from Target, and a couple of family portrait collages, but, otherwise, the room looked destitute and sad.

I decided to cut to the chase, as well. "I'm not here for your money. I'm here to talk to you about your time at the No 8 Mine, and your abduction when you were twenty-seven years old."

According to the clipping in Lamb's book, McCarty had taken a job feeding the miners as a line cook. He and the three others disappeared not long after—two miners and a prostitute. They vanished one night from the bunkers, stolen away by what witnesses claimed was a shadowy figure with long arms. But, three days later, all four returned, stumbling drunkenly through the woods. They had no injuries on their person and were mumbling nonsense. Most people thought they had gone off into the woods to drink and carouse and had just lost time.

No one believed the eyewitnesses' statements. Two of the disappeared miners ended up in trouble with the law, doing life in State Penn for second-degree murder. The prostitute, from what I understood, was the one who'd gone catatonic. McCarty had turned into a child predator—though he had never been convicted of his crimes. Viv told me she was only one of many he had corrupted over the years.

I expected him to take some small interest in his past. I was wrong. He took a deep breath from his oxygen machine and said,

"Don't know what the hell you're talkin' 'bout, asshole, but get the hell outta here."

"The Thin Man," I insisted, closing my eyes and swallowing hard to try and rein back my temper. I did not need to be losing it. "Witnesses said they saw the Thin Man take you and the others, but no one believed them."

"That's a lie! Nothin' happened that night!"

"But they said..."

"They didn't say *nothin'!* Get the fuck outta here, you cunt!"

I hovered a moment uncertainly, trying to decide what to do.

And then, just like that, I lost it. I lunged at the old bastard and pinned him against the back of his wheelchair. "Vivian Summers," I growled in his face, inhaling the sweet decay off his fetid breath. I bared my teeth, which were anything but human at the moment. "Does that name mean anything to you, *you cunt?*"

I expected fear. Most folks lose their shit around me big time, especially when I was in devil mode. Instead, he smiled as if it was the sweetest memory he had. He nodded to himself and said, "That sweet lil' piece of ass. Goddamnit, but she was a freaky bitch. Liked me to paddle her ass before I fucked it." He laughed and, again, he nodded as if to himself. "Thank you for reminding me of her, young man—"

I didn't think. I grabbed him by the throat and pulled him right up out of his chair, the oxygen mask falling to the floor. Light as a fucking feather, "She was nine years old! Nine fucking years old!" I rasped, breathing the words out hoarsely.

Cold smoke actually poured out of my mouth and nostrils as I spoke as if I was a goddamned dragon. I was shaking with rage and completely unable to control my actions. At some point, my wings emerged. They were now spread wide across the length of the tiny room, brushing against the walls. They beat wildly at the air while my body hummed with unspent rage and electricity. God knows what Everett McCarty saw in my face. In the ensuing silence, I heard and smelled his bowels loosen into his colostomy bag.

And still, he grinned at me. Grinned and licked his lips! Break his neck, I thought obliquely, even practically. *Break his goddamn neck.* I'd been a cop. I knew forensics. I could make it look like a bad fall, an accident...

He didn't deserve to live, to breathe the same air as Vivian. Those children who died at the school? Innocent children just starting out in life? They didn't deserve what had happened to them. But this piece of shit...it lived on and on, laughing and grinning and spreading its shit around. Where was the justice? Where was the fucking justice in *that?*

I tried to throw him down. I had every intention of breaking every goddamn bone in his body. Instead, my body acted of its own accord and I released him gently into the chair cushions. I wasn't being merciful. It wasn't some change of heart. I simply had no control over my body at the moment.

It mystified me until I realized I had never actually seen my father murder anyone. He'd harmed them, sure, and he'd collected their souls—deliciously speared upon the family bident like wriggling fish. He was an expert at interrogation and torture. But he'd never actually taken any living person's life. Maybe, I thought, the crowned Lucifer couldn't do that. Maybe he could collect their souls after their natural time of death, but he couldn't actually kill anyone.

It made a certain kind of insane sense.

"Vivian Summers," McCarty croaked. "Vivian-Fucking-Summers. The Whore Queen of Fucking Babylon..."

"Shut up!" I told him.

I turned away, still shaking with rage and wanting to tear the walls down around me. That meant I was staring at one of his collages on the wall, this one full of newspaper clippings of the Lucky 8 Mine. Some were old and similar to what Lamb had, but a few were more recent, dated to within the last year. Like Lamb, he'd been collecting them.

Without thinking much about it, I used my elbow to crack the glass dust shield and ripped the most recent ones off the corkboard they were stuck on. When I turned back, I saw McCarty grinning and playing with his dick while he continued to chant Vivian's name over and over again like some sick mantra.

"One day soon you'll be mine, you piece of shit," I told him before ducking out of that place of the sick and the damned.

| 11 |

Broadsided

YEAH, SO...I was busted for leaving the shop unattended for more than two hours. By the time I made it back, Morgana was already behind the counter, having left the Wiccan Fair early because of a rainstorm that wasn't showing any signs of letting up.

"It's a Saturday, Nick. A Saturday!" she roared even before I was in the door. "And where the hell were you?"

I was truly and completely shocked by her outburst. It wasn't very Morgana-like. Morgana is one of the coolest, most collected people I have ever known. Nothing shakes Morgana. This display of emotion was like the Dalai Lama getting drunk and winding up in a bar fight.

I told myself to stay calm. To rise above it.

But of course I didn't.

Shit, I couldn't change my stripes even if I wanted to. She knew something was up—probably not, exactly, what that thing was, but close—and it was setting her off.

I dropped my car keys on the counter and roared back, "Well, fucking excuse me for stepping out to get a meal. I'm so fucking sorry that offends you."

"A meal. For two hours. Sure." She was sorting Wiccan medallions out on a black felt jewelry board, another job I was supposed to have done today. I'd dropped the ball on that, too, and something about that just made me madder than ever. Not mad at her. Mad at me. I was letting her down. I was letting everyone down. Again.

She was pressing her lips together to keep from screaming, which showed me just how pissed she really was. It wasn't her fault. She was in the right. But I was still angry and wound up from my confrontation with McCarty.

I marched up to her like a soldier but shouted like a two-year-old in her face, "What exactly do you want from me, Morgana?"

She stood up, the stool behind the counter squealing as she pushed it away. "I want you to be honest! I want you to stop disappearing and lying about where you go!" She paused to take a deep breath. Her eyes were the color of summer lightning. "It's the school shooting, isn't it? You're investigating it!"

"Are you kidding me?"

"Tell me it's not."

"Fine." I took a deep breath. "I'm not investigating the school shooting."

"Oh my god!" she exclaimed, tears in her eyes. "You think I'm stupid, don't you?"

"Of course not!"

"You're still lying! Do you ever stop lying for one second, Nick?" Her tears just set me off. "Don't talk to me like I'm four years old!"

"Then stop acting like a fucking four-year-old!"

We both stopped when we realized people were browsing through the shop—and most of them had stopped what they were doing to watch the two of us scream at each other. Shit.

Morgana at least had the sense to grab me by the shirt and drag me into the back room for more privacy. Once we were there, she let go and took a deep breath before she really laid into me. "It's Saturday. Our busiest day. And you're gone!"

"I told you—!"

"Tell me the goddamn truth for once, Nick. Where the hell were you?"

The heat, the pressure. It was all too much. It was wearing me down. "You want the truth?" I roared back. The back room was narrow and we were practically pressed up against one another. Even with a small rotating fan on, the closed-up room felt like a pressure cooker. It was the kind of suffocating heat that made you want to either pass out or commit homicide.

I grinned nastily. "I'll tell you the truth. I went for a ride to clear my head."

Morgana studied me, but I could see she wasn't convinced. She probably sensed I was lying by omission. "You just got in that piece of shit car of yours and went for a ride for no apparent reason."

"I had to try and make sense of it all."

"Sense of *what*, Nick?"

I threw my hands up. "I don't know. All of it. You. Me. What the fuck we're doing here…"

Morgana bit her lip and looked away. "I should have seen this coming."

"What?"

"This." She pointed at the floor, but I knew what she meant. "You. Me. Is it because I'm not Vivian? It's all about Vivian again, isn't it?"

I don't know, something about the hideous way she said Vivian's name just set me off like a grenade. I simply exploded—not one of my better moves, not that I had any *good* moves to brag about anymore.

"No. It's not about you and it's not about me. It's about me and David. He dropped by. We talked. Then I fucked his brains out in this very room—right up against this fucking rack where you're standing." I kicked the rack I was referring to as if she couldn't figure that out.

"David?" she said slowly. She blinked in confusion. "David Breyer?"

Honestly? It felt so good to confess everything, to watch Morgana pale further than I've ever seen her before. I pushed up against her. I was enjoying this way too much. Her pain. It washed over me. It made me feel so damned good.

"Yeah. *That* David. He was a good lay. He didn't bitch me out afterward."

I felt her pain like warm, yummy chocolate going down my throat. I wanted it. I craved it. And I wanted more of it.

"That's what you want to know, right, Morgana? How good it is to fuck someone who isn't trying to tie you down like some slobbering dog or trying to make a fucking Stepford boyfriend out of you..."

I stopped. I was weaving on my feet. Felt sick.

Jesus. Jesus-fucking-Christ.

What the hell was wrong with me?

I staggered back a step and slammed into a rack. It took all my power not to manifest my wings in that moment. God...the pain...the power. I felt both hot and cold at the same time. It was as if my blood was both ice and fire and was surging through every part of my body. I felt like I could do anything. Burn this place to the ground. Burn Morgana. And it would feel so fucking good...

It took some moments to get my labored breathing under control. When I finally dared to look up, I expected Morgana to explode into tears and rage, as well she should. Instead, I got her pity face. Pity of all things! I couldn't believe that. I fuck a guy right in our shop, right under her nose, and shred the memory of the good relationship she'd had with a decent man she might even have married someday...and she was giving me *pity?*

It enraged me.

I started to scream. I kicked. I knocked some boxes down off the rack in front of me. One of them fell with a heavy thump and stuff spilled out and all over the floor. It crackled with a peculiar kind of energy, as did the racks, which seemed to be conducting that same power all over this narrow space, making it hum with unspent electricity. I smelled ozone.

"Nick..." she said with concern and started to reach for me.

I jerked away. Something in my face must have been pretty off because she didn't pursue me. She didn't even try to reach for me a second time.

"Don't touch me!" I felt the nasally annoyance of tears in my nose and throat. I felt the electricity dancing all over my skin like bug bites, and I knew—just knew—if she touched me now, it would kill her.

I moved past her, toward the service exit. She turned with me, boldly grabbing my arm.

She didn't die, and her touch was warm, soft, strangely comforting...but I didn't want comfort. I didn't want her to try to heal me. I wanted her to hate me. I wanted her to damn me. Damn me down to Hell.

"I know you're struggling," she told me softly. "I know this is hard for you...what you've become. All this insanity. But you don't have to go through this alone."

But I *was* alone. I could be standing in the presence of a million people who wanted me, who wanted to be with me, who wanted my magic or my sex or whatever it is I could give, and I would be forever alone.

I wondered if this was what my father felt, and the reason he'd coveted my mother the way he had.

"No," I told her without looking up. "Let me *go*, Morgana."

She did.

I jerked my arm loose. I hurried out of there faster than a speeding bullet and jumped in the car. Then I saw that Tiger had been leashed outside in the alley, probably so he wouldn't explode from the heat upstairs. I got out of the Monaco and walked around it to untie his leash. Tiger jumped up and wagged his stumpy tail like crazy. He looked happy to see me.

He wasn't afraid. Somehow, that made me feel better.

"Come on, boy. Want to go for a ride?"

Slobbering, he jumped into the backseat, and I closed the door and went back around to the driver's side. At least Tiger didn't hate me, I thought as we rocketed out of the delivery alley and onto Main Street.

I had no plan. I just drove to the edge of town, and then past the limit and out into the countryside full of dirt roads, trees, and deer that could kill your car if you went too fast. The roads were bumpier here, potholed from winter, and less often maintained. I'm pretty sure there are fewer bears in northeast Pennsylvania because they all fell into the goddamn potholes.

While Tiger and I bounced along, I noticed the bag of Raisinets on the floor of the passenger side. I'd forgotten all about them. I took my eyes off the road for maybe three seconds while I was fishing them out of the footwell.

When I turned back, I saw a dump truck up close and personal, bearing down on me in the wrong lane. It just came out of nowhere.

I didn't even have time to swerve and try to avoid it. It filled the whole windshield.

I heard the crunch—though, strangely, I felt no pain, just a sense of weightlessness as the truck plowed into the front of the Monaco and spun it 360 before momentum rolled us off the side of the shoulder. There were no guardrails here. Funding had run short. So Tiger and I easily and efficiently rolled down the side of the mountain toward the Pontiac River far, far below.

| 12 |

Weird Sisters

I RECALLED SOMETHING Vivian told me while we were still seeing each other: *"You're not a true Pennsylvanian until you've rolled your car at least once."*

We'd been in her bed, in her apartment, and we'd been fooling around. She'd produced her stash of cheap, all-natural, PA-grown ganja, and we'd both lit up because we were adults like that. Somehow, we had segued into car rolling, and Vivian, sitting up naked in bed, held up two fingers as she giggled.

"You're fucking joking," I said and started to laugh, too. "Twice. In little Daisy?"

Daisy was her secondhand jeep. Not a nice modern jeep. One of those boxy little things from the late 1980s that the Duke Cousins might have driven around in.

"Daisy's my *second* jeep, dumbass!" she said, still laughing. Because it was *that* funny. "One day you'll roll that junker of yours and it'll be like a rite of passage for you, Nick. Then you'll be one of us. One of us! One of us…!"

* * *

I woke up with my face on a nest of prickly brown pine needles—ow. Grunting and sweating, I managed to push myself up from my prone position and roll over so I was lying on my back and looking up at the grey summer sky. I saw a large collection of frothy evergreens hovering over me, their branches so low they were practically in my face. The branches were shaking as if a squirrel was up there, flash dancing for cash, and fresh green needles were falling down onto my exposed face.

I groaned. I was somewhere in the woods, under a tree—though how I didn't know. It seemed too remote and isolated, and my last memory was rolling the car along the shoulder of the road leading out of Blackwater.

My first clue came when I heard a soft, crystalline voice say, "He's awake!" Someone answered, a whisper on my left side. The voice was so soft that, at first, I thought I had imagined it. "Sister, he is awake!"

Then I heard the response.

The voice was similar, just a few octaves lower. "You should not have brought him here, Sister! He is one of them! One of the humans!"

"Silly, he is not human. He only looks human!"

"We should get Husband," said a third voice, this time from my right. "He will know what to do with the daemon."

"No!" answered the first voice with alarm. "He is Otherkin, but he is not like us! If Husband knows, he will make us set him free."

"The daemon is dangerous, Sister."

"We are dangerous, too!"

By now, I was concerned. Some strange people are living in these woods. Real *The Hills Have Eyes* type of folk. I wondered if I had fallen into a colony of them. I'll be honest—I was having some dark thoughts here. Some people have disappeared into these woods, never to be found again. And some were, but just their remains...

It hurt to heave myself up, but I managed it. I felt dizzy from the impact, but I managed to get myself turned around on the damp ground and clunked my shoulders back against the trunk of the pine. My three companions had temporarily retreated, I noted, though the tree was shaking again as if they had gone straight up into the boughs.

Awesome, I'm being besieged by squirrel girls, I thought. My head hurt and my thoughts were pretty scrambled. Still, I thought that was pretty funny, like the name of an 80s-style pop band, though the sounds I made that were supposed to be laughter sounded like I was choking to death. There was blood in my eyes, and my scalp felt like it had been sheared straight off. My arm hurt, too, and hung limply at my left side. That concerned me. I thought it might be broken.

Whether I liked it or not, I was going to need help to get out of here. "Who...who are you?" I said, hoping the Squirrel Girls would return. Maybe they could get me some help, or get me to the nearest road, at least.

The trees rustled above and pine needles fell into my hair.

"You can come out. I won't hurt you," I said.

While I watched, three lithe girls slowly descended the tree. And they did as if they really were squirrels, with their heads down. Their bodies moved oddly, though, slinky and snake-like like they had all soft bones. Definitely not human. I felt a cold shock at the sight of them until I figured out what they were: dryads. Wood nymphs. These forests are full of them, though almost no one ever notices them—unless the nymphs wanted them to, that is.

The first nymph descended the trunk of the tree until we were face to face—or, rather, my face to her upside down one. She was magnificent, though not what you probably remember from Greek mythological studies in school or RPG campaigns with your local D&D club. Not some hot, naked chick with big boobs—though she was, in fact, quite naked.

The wood nymph was much taller than a human and sinewy like her whole body was a set of living vines tangled together. She twisted her body around the branches of the tree in unnatural ways. Her eyes were white and pupil-less, and dark green and black moss grew in patterns on her face and surrounded her eyes. Her hair, like her body, was comprised of something that looked closer to moss, branches, and vines bound together than actual human hair. It moved, too, in unnatural ways that crackled and writhed and made me want to freak out just a little.

All three were naked but covered in that mossy substance. However, I noted it covered no part of their private anatomy. Rather, it grew in random patches and strange patterns over their lengthy, muscular arms and around their small, pert breasts. The second one who had spoken had recently given birth and her baby-thing—it didn't look like a real baby—clung to her woody, mossy skin, its tiny mouth fasted hungrily around one of her sturdy, upward-curling nipples.

While I watched this fascinating, slightly grotesque thing play out, the second one touched my hair with her fingertips. I jerked my head around to face her.

She was hanging upside down from the tree like her sister and smiling at me, her mouth full of shark-like teeth. When she reached out again to touch my face, I jerked away. "He is so pretty. I want to keep him, Sister."

"We may not," advised the second Sister. She slid farther down the tree, her body doing all kinds of weird things, though the baby thing managed to hang on despite them all. "He will make Husband jealous."

"But I want him for a pet!" said the third with a simpering expression on her beautiful, terrifying face.

"Look at him, Sister!" the first advised. "He will make me such pretty young ones for us..."

"Sister is jealous," said the third, looking at the first. "She has a babe and we do not!"

Well, shit. Objectified by wood nymphs. I forcibly pushed myself up but lost my balance in the wet needles and collapsed back against the tree.

The two Sisters without a young one slunk closer, surrounding me on two sides. They smelled musty and moldy, like a basement after a hard rain. Not the most pleasant smell. But under that odor, I could smell their desire. Their sex. They smelled female and extremely fertile. I tried to shift away, but Mamma Nymph suddenly whipped around the tree, cutting off my escape

She put her fingers on my shoulder and I could feel her immense strength. "He is hurt!" she said. I wasn't sure if this pleased her or concerned her. "Summon Husband!"

"No! I will care for him," said the first nymph, her mouth contorting into what they used to call a moue back in the 1800s as she stretched a hand out to touch my face.

"That's...not necessary," I said, shrinking against the tree.

These were Brownswick's wives, I suddenly remembered. And Brownswick was the King of this forest. He was also my animal familiar—a particularly pushy, hypersexual Faun I had no desire to run into while staggering around all wounded in the woods. Not to mention, if he thought I was making time with his wives, he'd probably crack my spine like kindling over his knee.

Trying again, I managed to get myself to my feet, though I weaved like a drunk and the forest wouldn't stop careening around me. The first one didn't like that much, so she slid down to the forest litter and snagged hold of me by the front of my jeans.

I made distressed noises, you bet I did. I was about to be gang-raped by wood nymphs in the woods outside Blackwater. But they didn't hear or care about my distress. Almost bristling with desire, the one attached to my jeans started squirming up my body, her mouth open, and her slinky fingers gripping my shoulders for purchase. Her long, multi-forked tongue unfurled like a wet tangle of vines to taste my cheek, and I could feel things going on lower down on her body—like she had hands or something...down there.

My panic edged all the way up. If wasn't wounded, I might have been able to fight them off, but I could barely stand up, never mind fight off two oversexed tree nymphs. I had no choice. I opened a random portal behind me and just sort of fell backward through it and into Hell.

* * *

I was never any good with the portal thing. Probably would help if I practiced, but I've never had the patience.

I landed pretty damned hard on my dad's creepy-ass throne in the room in the Watchtower, which scared me so badly that I compulsively opened another portal beneath me. This time I smashed down on my back next to the Monaco, which was officially upside down and lying in a creek. I was walking wounded already; the double impact, so close together, didn't help at all and knocked the ever-living breath out of me.

I said some sweary stuff I need not go into here and then suddenly remembered Tiger in the backseat. And then I said some more sweary stuff while I scrambled up onto my hands and knees and did an impromptu military crawl along the creek bed and back to the car those naughty, oversexed wood nymphs had dragged me from earlier.

The back door had been ripped away by the impact it was still lying on the shoulder of the road—and as I neared the poor, busted-up Monaco, I could see Tiger's head lying limp on the ground, with the rest of him angled up and lying on his side on the roof of the car, which was now the floor. I swore some more as I scrambled around on my one working arm to his side. Every motion was an agony.

I needn't have hurried. I knew even before I reached him that it was too late. That he was gone.

I'd killed him. I'd killed Tiger, Josh's service dog. I was officially a dog murderer—and I was crying about that because I had done some pretty shitty things in my life, but this topped my Shittiest Things I've Ever Done in My Life List, and if I could fix it in any way, I would.

I would fix him. I would undo this whole shitty mess I had made.

Reaching out to the deceased dog lying half in and half out of my equally deceased car, I put my hand on his stony black head. He felt so very cold—and that made me cry even more. I felt that crackling surge again like electricity was pouring from my fingers and into his body.

Tiger's body jerked once, twice, like someone was sending short jolts of raw power through it as if he was Frankendog. I stopped crying after that because, seconds later, Tiger opened his eyes, sat up, and whined at me.

| 13 |

My Hero

TWO HOURS LATER, I was sitting on a gurney in Emergency at Blue Ridge Medical while a pretty young, chatty nurse named Sandy put stitches into my scalp. She had also needed to pop my arm back in—which was dislocated, not broken as I had feared. It was a good thing she was cute because her endless chatter was grinding into my brain, which was tender from the stitches she was currently stapling into my scalp.

They said I was damned lucky, considering what I had done to my car. Or, rather, what had been done to it. A few gashes, plenty of bruises, and a dislocated shoulder. I was glad about the arm. They'd wanted me to get X-rays to be on the safe side, but I had refused. I didn't want to have to explain to the staff of Blue Ridge why I had four pairs of wings in the X-ray scans. That would have been awkward.

"...I loved this sweet potato pie I found at Hellman's Market, but they're only open from June to October, and I told them, I said, 'Why do you close just before Thanksgiving? Where's the logic in *that*?' And you know what they said? You wouldn't believe what they said to me..." Nurse Sandy hesitated as she finished up with the last staple. "You like sweet potato pie, honey?"

"I...I don't remember," I said in truth. My head was spinning.

I think she was about to go fetch the doctor for her concussed patience when I spotted David coming around the privacy curtain separating my gurney from the one next door. He stopped and gawked at me all wild-eyed and said, "Holy fuck, Nick. What the hell happened?"

I rolled that around my head and could come up with nothing that sounded even vaguely sane. Instead of explaining, I said, "You seen Tiger? I tied him outside..."

"I've got Tiger," David explained. "He's in my car."

Nurse Sandy looked over with concern, so David hastily added, "I left it running with the air conditioner on. Don't want anyone breaking my windows." Pushing past Nurse Sandy, who was starting to look disappointed by David's sudden appearance, he grabbed my hand. "Dude, you look like you got dragged by wild elephants."

"Feels that way," I said, wincing with the pain in my skull from the too-tight stitches.

I got a script for Tylenol 3 and then the hospital discharged me. Honestly, I was a little disappointed that David had come to pick me up instead of Morgana—but not overly surprised. I deserved that. I deserved worse. I deserved to have no one pick me up, but I was grateful nonetheless that David was here.

I'd left a message on Morgana's voicemail about the accident. I'd hoped she would come, or at least send an Uber to get me, seeing how I didn't have wheels and Blue Ridge was miles from the shop. Well, she'd sent David. I wasn't sure if that was her taking pity on me or sticking it to me and good. Maybe both.

When we got to David's car—a kickass Jeep Wrangler that had honest-to-god A/C—Tiger popped his head over the side of the seat and gave me subdued doggie kisses.

"It's good to see you, too, boy," I said, cradling his big head. He made a moaning noise that I interpreted as a response. While David drove us toward town, Tiger wouldn't remove his head.

"That dog really likes you," David said.

"He's warming up to me, I think."

"You want I drop you off at the shop?"

I didn't answer that. I was pretty sure Morgana did *not* want to see me right now or she would have picked me up herself. But that left me with what? I didn't have any friends or family I could stay with, and all the local B&Bs were too expensive to crash in for a few nights. Then I remembered the old Motel 8 way up in Mount Pocono. It was a real fleabag, notorious for its hookers and drug deals, but it was also cheap. I asked David to turn the car around and head up that way.

"You can stay at my place until you're better. It's over in Birch Hollow."

That was the newer, swankier part of town.

"The development?"

"It was my aunt's place. Turns out she willed it to me."

"She left you her place?"

David shrugged in a kind of humble brag way. "I was the only one in my family who gave half a damn about her. So, yeah."

Thus, we wound up in Birch Hollow, a place I had honestly never been to before. I mean, Morgana and I had clients who lived there and who wanted séances done—mostly rich old ladies trying to contact their dead husbands—but we did the séances in a space we rented in a local B&B in Blackwater that didn't have special spiritual attachments. Those tended to interfere with Morgana's natural ability to channel dead people, and neutral was always best. We didn't go to the clients' homes.

The development looked pretty snazzy from the onset. There was a security booth—wow—and then a long drive through some carefully cultivated woodsy hills before you found yourself in the most manicured neighborhood you have ever seen. It was a far cry from most of Blackwater, which was made up of a lot of clapboard houses of different shapes and architectures from the old coal mining days. Those houses, mostly saggy, hundred-year-old side-by-sides, had been thrown together almost overnight for the miners and their families.

These were new, deluxe, two- and three-story homes, all airbrushed-looking and squared away on perfect tracts of green lawn. New-looking, black-paved driveways swirled in front of each perfect gingerbread house, and there were garbage and recycling bins on the curbs, in-ground swimming pools in the back, and swing sets and trampolines with kid-safe guards everywhere. The houses themselves sported different architectural designs, but you could see the same developer had planted them all. The colors and materials were the same—lots of white, sunny yellow, and organic green siding and modern metal roofs. Strangely, despite the different-looking houses, there was a certain cookie-cutter sameness about them that was almost Stepford-eerie to behold.

We wound through a maze of streets before David parked in the driveway of a huge, yellow, pseudo-Victorian. It was almost brand new, built in the last decade, but it sported all the proper gingerbreading, the ornate gables, and a vast wrap porch. It even had a porch swing.

"Is it okay to bring Tiger inside?" I said because this place didn't look like it could handle a giant, rampaging dog.

"Of course. We can't leave him outside!"

He led us up the paved driveway, which smelled strongly of tar in the relentless heat, and ushered us inside. It was cool and dim. Nice, middle-grade Shaker furniture made amorphous shapes in the dark.

"You can put a light on, if you like," David explained as he headed down a long hallway toward the kitchen at the back of the house. I spotted French doors that led to a vast pavilion and what looked like a tennis court beyond. "It's just been so hot..."

"That's okay," I said as I followed him.

He gave me a Dasani from the fridge and filled one of his aunt's bowls with water for Tiger. While Tiger slopped water all over the nice parquet floor, I looked around. "It's nice, David. Real nice. But I can't just stay here, surfing your couch."

David guffawed. "Dude, who said anything about the couch? Come on, I'll show you the bedroom." He grabbed me by the front of the shirt and dragged me away with a wicked, wide grin.

* * *

Things went the way you'd expect. We ended up doing some heavy petting in David's bed—nothing too serious, though. David said he needed to see someone about his contract with Doctors Without Borders and didn't want to have to take a shower after he sweated himself up too much.

The central A/C, as good as it was, was barely able to keep the huge place cool. I stayed in bed after David left and dozed through the rest of the day, high on pain meds and general exhaustion. That surprised me. I usually healed like a superhero. But then it occurred to me that I might have used up all my manna points after putting the spunk back in Tiger, so maybe I was going to heal human-slow for a while until I was able to recharge.

My phone went off in the early evening hours. It was Morgana.

"Are you all right, Nick?" she asked. She still sounded pissed, but there was an undercurrent of concern there, too.

I tried pushing myself up on one arm, but that hurt too much, so I resigned myself to just lying in David's bed, staring up at the ceiling fan whirling gently above me. "Well, they haven't killed me yet."

"Don't joke. That was a bad accident." There was a pause. "They?"

I thought about coming clean, then decided to just go for it. Call it the new, better Nick. "You're right. I lied to you. I was investigating the school shooting. And I think someone found out. I think something out there has it out for me now."

I paused and winced as I moved my bad arm "You know, the usual kind of clusterfuck I attract."

She didn't reprimand me now. "Where are you?"

"Do you really care?"

"Yeah, Nick. I do."

"I'm safe. I'm alive."

"But where are you? With Vivian?"

"Don't ask me where I am if you don't want me at home."

She didn't answer that. I knew she didn't want me home. I could feel that, even at a distance. If I went home, we'd fight. I didn't want to fight anymore. I couldn't handle it.

"I'll be fine," I told her finally. "I took care of myself just fine before you, Morgana. Hell, I've been homeless on the streets of New York. This is a walk in the park for me."

She took a deep breath. "Nick, we need to talk about us."

"I know. But not tonight."

"You can always come home." A lie.

"Not tonight. I'll be fine. Promise. I'll call you." And then I hung up on her, looked at the phone, and tried not to cry.

***

David got back after dark.

I pulled myself out of bed and staggered into the massive living room as he came in the front door. He was sporting a pizza and a six-pack of Yuengling. My hero.

"You hungry?" he asked.

"Starving."

"I couldn't remember what you liked on your pizza, so I just got plain."

Between the two of us, we decimated the pizza and beer.

"We celebrating?" I asked, biting hungrily into a big, greasy slice.

"Yeah," David said as we settled on the floor around the coffee table. He went on to explain that his tour with Doctors Without Borders was ending and he was thinking of taking a position at Pocono Medical. They wanted him, and he was thinking of settling here on a semi-permanent basis. He asked my opinion of that.

"I think you should do what you want."

He laughed. "Typical Nick. I'm asking *you*, stupid. You know...after the other day."

I finally caught on. He was wondering if we had a future together. When I didn't immediately answer him, he shrugged. "Eh. Forget it." And he grabbed the big screen TV remote.

The beer must have been reacting with the pain meds I'd taken because David put on *Inspector Gadget* on Netflix and we just laughed our asses off as if we'd smoked a bowl or something. When he, Vivian, and I were an item, we didn't always go out and make a production of it. Sometimes, we'd just crash at each other's places with lots of takeout and junk food and chilled in front of the TV until sexy time.

One thing led to another, and eventually, David's head wound up in my lap, making me moan and writhe against the back of his aunt's ugly flower print sofa. When my phone went off, I ignored it. The second time it happened, David dug it out of my pocket and handed it to me. "It's Morgana."

I groaned. "She can go fuck herself."

I tried to grab the back of David's head, to pull him in for a beery kiss, but he jerked back. "What happened between the two of you? You used to be best friends."

I didn't say anything to that, but David was no dummy and figured it all out in a matter of seconds. He put my phone down on the coffee table and climbed back up onto the cushions of the sofa. "Seriously, Nick?"

"What?" I growled, not looking at him.

"You and Morgana?"

"What about it?" I was getting annoyed now. I didn't want to talk about this. I just wanted to stuff David's cute mouth with my big hard—

"You're with her while you're with me?" he said, sounding appalled. "*Real* classy, Nick."

"So? It used to be me, you, and Vivian—"

"That's not the same thing and you damn well know it. We had an open relationship. No one went sneaking around behind anyone's back—"

"I'm not sneaking!" I shouted, because, technically, I was, and I hated being caught in a lie. "Morgana's being bitchy and we're not together right now."

"Bullshit." He got up and started cleaning up our mess, bagging things with exaggerated drama. "You're sneaking. Worse, you're putting *me* in the middle of your mess with her. With Morgana, Nick!"

"So what?"

"It's *Morgana*," he explained as if I was an idiot while he shoveled empty beer bottles and the crusts of our pizza into his garbage bag. "Just *the* most powerful witch in all of Blackwater—maybe the northeast. Christ, she's gonna make my hair fall out like that chick that screwed you over—"

"Don't get dramatic."

He moved toward the kitchen but then stopped in the doorway to glare at me. I kept my back to him. "You like rolling around in your emotional messes, don't you, Nick? You get off on it."

"Fuck you, David."

He shook his head as he ducked into the kitchen.

Tiger immediately crawled up to me and laid his big head in my lap as a sign of solidarity. "I'm back on the couch, Tiger," I said as I petted him.

Tiger whined in sympathy.

| 14 |

Synergy

I COULDN'T SLEEP. No surprise there.

Around three in the morning, I kicked the blankets off David's sofa, took another pain pill, and got dressed. I got Tiger into David's jeep and drove us down to the impound yard where my car had been towed.

Bunny Killborn worked the impound yard at night. I knew she was sweet on me, so when I got to the guardhouse, I saw her eyes light up. She put down the magazine she was reading and stepped out to greet me. I tried to roll down the window of the jeep, then realized this wasn't a 1970's model and it had electric slide windows. After I got it down, I said, "Hi, Bunny. How's tricks?"

"Tricks are for kids," she said, our private joke. Her smile grew, then fell off her face. "You know I can't let you in, Nick."

"I want to see the Monaco."

"You *totaled* the Monaco, Nick. I mean, that was some hardcore shit right there."

"Yeah, and my stuff is still inside, including my wallet. Can I just see her for a sec? Get my stuff? Please?" I gave her sad puppy dog eyes.

She was a cop. I was an ex-cop. We had a camaraderie. She let me in. ("But only for a few minutes.").

I found the Monaco at the back of the lot where they keep the wrecks for imminent crushing. The wrecker had dropped it under one of the sodium parking lot lights, and up until I laid eyes on her, I'd had a sliver of hope. I'd fantasized about taking her to a body shop somewhere, getting the dents knocked out, her insides fixed up and replaced, and maybe driving her again one day. But when I finally saw her, haloed by the sallow, angry light of the lamp, I knew it was over.

Her roof was caved in all the way to the backseat, and her doors were little better than crumpled bits of twisted steel—those they had found. The windshield was not just shattered, just mostly missing, and there was nothing left of her front end, just twisted steel like an inside-out accordion. It didn't even resemble a car any longer.

She was my first. The only thing I could afford when I was eighteen. She was old and secondhand in '91 when I bought her with the money I'd saved up working at a Laundromat over one long, incredibly hot summer.

I crept closer to her corpse and felt like mourning. I had no idea how Tiger and I had escaped this deathtrap alive. It seemed a miracle.

I went to the passenger side, which had no door. My side of the car had the door crumpled inward in a way that suggested it would never move again. I found McCarty's clippings all over the seat and floor. Some of it had flown into the backseat. That stuff I couldn't reach.

Gathering what I could of the clippings, I went and stood under the lamp, trying not to look at the shell of my deceased Monaco. One clipping was just over a year old. It announced the reopening of the Lucky 8 mine and showed a picture of the investor standing at the mouth of the mine, holding an oversized pair of scissors.

He had just cut the ribbon over the entrance of the mine. I had to squint to read the caption under the picture: Justin Alexander, CEO of Synergy, a Fortune 500 company that specializes in alternative energy and wind farms.

"Justin Alexander," I said. "You and I have one hot date."

But first...

Lifting my head, I looked over at the Monaco. My one constant. There was even a time I'd slept in her for a while when I was between places. I wasn't just saying goodbye to a car. I was saying goodbye to my home, my past. A relic of my lost years.

I felt like I should say something. Eulogize her. Tell her she would be avenged.

Revenge. I think that was the moment the thought started permeating my admittedly rattled brain. The idea of revenge. The wreck was no accident, even though I was listing it as such in the police accident report. No. What happened yesterday was a message, and it was coming in loud and clear:

Leave well enough alone.

"Yeah, well, fuck that," I said and started toward the jeep.

* * *

I needed wheels bad so my next stop would have to be the only car rental place in town. Unfortunately, they wouldn't be open until seven in the morning, and it was barely five now. To kill some time, and to get a change of clothes—which, admittedly, I badly needed—I drove to the shop and let myself in with my key.

Upstairs, in the flat, I took a quick shower and dug a change of clothes out of my bureau. Morgana wasn't home, and for that, I was grateful. I didn't want to get into it with her right now. Well, ever. But that was another fish I needed to fry.

I had this feeling I wouldn't be back here in a while—if ever. While I packed an overnight bag with some personal items, David's accusation went round and round my head.

You like rolling around in your emotional messes, don't you, Nick? You get off on it.

I don't know. Maybe? Maybe I liked making drama because it validated my existence. Except that was probably too deep for me. I couldn't help but think that the reason I screwed everything up was simply that I was a world-class screw-up. I'd screwed up school. I'd screwed up being a cop. I was a rotten witch and an even worse Satan. I was a pretty terrible boyfriend and had messed up every single relationship I had ever had. Basically, I couldn't do one damned thing right.

No, that wasn't exactly true. I had one thing going for me—I was good at getting to the bottom of things. I was a damned good detective. And my detective's instincts were screaming that it was all connected. Kenny's breakdown. The Thin Man. Dr. Lamb. My accident. It was all *one thing*. And that *one thing* was somehow linked to the mine—the one Justin Alexander had just reopened. I just needed to discover *how*.

Everyone was pissed at me, and I had no allies at present, but that was okay. I would get by on my own. I always had.

"And you like me, right, Tiger?" I said to the dog as I threw my overnight pack over one shoulder.

He grunted in response.

"Thanks, buddy," I said and patted him on the head.

Morgana blew into the flat just as I was leaving. "Nick," she said, turning to follow me. "Nick, wait..."

But I slid past her. "I'm just here for some of my things."

She reached out and touched my arm. The moment she did, I felt her pain—sharp and fresh and deep like a newly re-opened stab wound. And under that...an older pain that had been dredged up in the wake of my betrayal. Something to do with family. It hit me so hard, it nearly buckled my knees and forced me to stagger back. I was no longer angry with her for being angry with me. I was just deeply ashamed of the pain I had caused her.

"We'll talk. I promise," I said, meaning it. "Just not now."

She let me go.

| 15 |

Angel Breaker

I GAVE THE rental place my credit card and they gave me a late-model Jeep Grand Cherokee. I'd already decided I didn't like driving jeeps—or modern cars, in general—but they said that was the only one available. So I took the jeep with its modern electric windows and GPS and everything annoying and not the Monaco and decided to put up with it.

I threw my stuff in the back, loaded Tiger in, and together we took off toward Philadelphia. Some more Google-fu had rendered Alexander's home address in the pish-posh section of Chestnut Hill. Since it was the weekend, I hoped he was home and not jet-setting around. Sure, I could have waited till Monday, but I didn't want to have to hunt him down at his high-rise in downtown Philly. That would entail going through security measures and secretaries and such, and I was determined to suss this out *now*.

It was a three-hour drive that, given the weekend traffic, was so not going to happen in anything less than four hours. Four hours. In Nick Englebrecht GPS, that's the equivalent of two packs of cigarettes, one small bag of Jolly Ranchers, a medium Gummy Worm, and one large Icee from 7-Eleven—in case you ever wondered.

Tiger and I were officially on a road trip. To where, I wasn't sure. I just hoped it wasn't hell. I was getting a little sick of that place.

* * *

I spun some Journey tunes on the fancy CD player (because who doesn't want to stop believin'?), worked through the candy stash, and almost hit a deer coming into Philly. I lost count of the roadkill total, but it was something like eleven. We stopped twice for bathroom breaks and once for grub. I got an Italian sub from a Turkey Hill, a carton of iced tea, and a glazed Tastykake pie. Tiger got a sub, too, a water, and a packet of Beggin' Strips. Probably, Josh wouldn't have liked the sub, but what he didn't know wouldn't hurt him.

I walked Tiger back to the jeep and put his sub on the open paper on the floor—shh, don't tell the rental place—and then went back into the Turkey Hill to pee. When I got back to the jeep, I saw that half of the sub—which the deli girl had been good enough to cut in half for me—was gone, with the second half still sitting there, wrapped in paper. Tiger was snoozing on the floor. I thought that was odd but then thought maybe I'd only given him half. With the head injury, I couldn't be sure I was remembering things right.

I got in and started the engine.

We were almost to Philly when I heard the paper wrapper crunch in the back. I looked in the rearview mirror, but the angle was bad, with the backseat obstructing my view. A few seconds later, a crumpled-up ball of deli paper came flying between the seats and landed on the dashboard.

I stopped the jeep on the shoulder of the road, put the emergency lights on, and got out. When I went around to the back and opened the hatch, I saw that Tiger was sound asleep again. Okay, then. There are some mysteries never meant to be solved, even by me.

Getting back into the jeep, I followed the turnoff into Philly, then used the GPS to find Chestnut Hill, another place I'd never been. It was manicured and full of important-looking estates tucked behind wrought iron fences. It occurred to me that, for supposedly being the King of Hell, I never got to live in any of the nice places. That was kind of a bummer.

Eventually, after checking the address again, I found the Alexander estate. There was a guardhouse in front of the iron gates with the Alexander name scrawled across the top. I could feel the opulence emulating from a hundred feet away. I figured this wouldn't go well and they'd throw my bum ass out in minutes, if that. But when I gave the guard my name, he looked at me funny.

"C-can you...spell that out, please?"

Again, not my first rodeo. When I went to Starbucks, I got all kinds of variations on my name. "Nick Englebrecht. E-N-G-L..." I started spelling for him, then got frustrated. "*Englebrecht*. It's German..."

"I know," interrupted the young guard, staring at me with deer-in-the-headlights eyes. He seemed awed and couldn't seem to decide what to do for a moment. Finally, he picked up a phone on the wall. "It means 'angel-breaker.'"

That surprised the hell out of me.

After mumbling some words into the phone, he quickly raised the barrier and then rushed out of the guardhouse so he could step up to the jeep. "G-go right in, Mr. Englebrecht. And...can I say what an honor it is?"

Okay. I wasn't sure how to take that. Normally, I had to hustle my way into places like this. All this seemed...too easy. I drove cautiously up the paved driveway to the gigantic colonial mansion perched atop a hill, half-expecting an ambush from between the tall, painstakingly maintained shrubs that lined the road.

The mansion was regal and rambly and looked like something out of a British period drama. What do they call those? American castles? Yeah, this was about as close to an American castle as you were going to get in this country. There were maybe two dozen vehicles of different makes and models parked under the portico, and not far from that, a huge, ornate fountain depicting Lilith, Adam's first wife, with horns and hooves, lying on a throne with snakes writhing around her stone feet. It was a beautiful sculpture, but what really got my attention were the naked young people frolicking in the water and splashing each other.

In front of the house, several tables and benches were set up under awnings and umbrellas, with more young people, naked or otherwise scantily dressed, lounging around, playing board games, eating, drinking, or listening to portable iPod stereos, and sunbathing. Several strapping young men were cutting the lawn or trimming hedges. They didn't look unhappy to be doing so while their comrades relaxed alongside them. It reminded me of some kind of modern and better-organized mini-Woodstock. Or maybe I was thinking of Jonestown. Whatever it was, it gave me a bit of a chill.

I parked in a spot at the edge of the portico and got out with Tiger. Everyone had stopped what he or she was doing and seemed to be waiting for me. That was *really* creepy. I had stumbled across some kind of weird cult, I thought, but before I could start worrying, a feeling of great warmth and power washed over me like a wave of cool ocean water. I'd never felt anything like it before. Like ice and fire—but not unpleasant. I felt almost drunk on it—the goodness, the wellness. Yes, that was what I felt. Incredibly well. Incredibly healthy and good. My injuries no longer ached, and I felt as if I'd slept well for a good long while for a change and been refreshed. As if I could do almost anything.

They would never hurt me. The thought came to me as I moved toward the two dozen or more young people standing on the front lawn of Justin Alexander's house, many holding hands in a sign of solidarity. I wasn't certain of much in my life. But I was certain of that fact. They won't hurt me.

The young people watched me approach. They started to smile—big welcoming smiles that made me happy to see. That made me feel...

They love me.

I was certain of that, though I'd never met any of these people in my life.

I moved closer and closer to the house, and, as I did so, that feeling of goodness and power expanded inside of me. I felt their love...their peace...and a lot of other things that I'd thought were lost long ago in me. I no longer felt the guilt of what I had done to Morgana and David. I no longer felt the terrible, carved-out loss of Vivian in my life. I no longer felt that simmering, always-present anger toward my father.

All that felt insignificant now.

I felt...loved. Cherished.

I'd never felt that way before. Not ever.

And it scared the ever-living hell out of me.

* * *

The young people started to chant as I reached the house. I had no idea what they were saying. Something in Latin, maybe—but I didn't know Latin. I didn't care, I decided, because whatever it was they were saying, it sounded like love.

One young woman, very dark-skinned, hair in a carefully crimped afro, and dressed in what looked like a long, strappy white nightgown, stepped forward and met me halfway to the stairs of the mansion. The nightgown was diaphanous and I could see her soft sable skin beneath it. Even her perk purple nipples. I loved the contrast. Looking on her made me ache with a longing I didn't know I was still capable of. It was embarrassing.

"You came, my Lord," she said with a dazzling white smile. "We knew you would, one day. The prophecy has been fulfilled."

I shook my head. "I have no idea what you're talking about. What prophecy?"

She reached out and took my hand. "I'm so glad you came."

I looked at her hand. There were runes painted on her fingers, but it was difficult to see them because her skin was so dark. Or maybe they were supposed to be invisible and only I could see them?

"My name is Sada. I am the magus's second."

I looked up at her heartbreakingly beautiful face. No idea what she was talking about. But, then, I was finding it hard to concentrate, I wanted her that badly. "I'm...N-Nick—"

"I know," she answered. "We know who you are, my sweet Lord Lucifer."

I loved her voice. It was husky but musical. I wanted her to speak again, and she did! "Come, Lord," she said, stepping backward toward the house. "The magus is eager to meet you."

The other young people had fallen to their knees, still chanting, though it was more of a hymn now. It rose up and up and seemed to fill the whole world with passion. I felt that incredible power swell inside me once more. It made me dizzy with pleasure.

I let Sada take me. She led me past the worshipers and up the wide, Corinthian stairs toward the castle. I felt too loved to let go of her hand. I don't think I could have resisted her if I tried.

Up close, the castle looked more like a temple than anyone's home. The architecture was old and gothic, full of arcane engravings and sculptures of maidens and monsters built right into its stone fabric. There were runes in the lintels of the door and around the arched windows, and the glass of those windows was painted with different scenes like you might see in a grand cathedral—but all the stories looked pagan, full of swords and crones and ancient symbols of power.

I started when I saw the symbol engraved above the great oaken double doors—an upright bident, the sign of the House of Lucifer. Things were slowly coming together. I went with Sada and together we stepped into the castle to meet the magus.

"Take me to your leader," I said.

So, yeah, put that on the top of my list of Weird Shit That's Happened to Nick.

* * *

To say it was opulent was an understatement. Wainscoting and chandeliers and a lot of Queen Anne furniture—that dainty, delicate stuff that makes you nervous to sit on it. There were gigantic, nine-foot portraits on the walls under the looming cathedral ceilings. I recognized what looked like original oils of Peter Gilmore, Kenneth Anger, Marc Almond, Jayne Mansfield, and Anton LaVey—all known Satanists. I'm not really a stupid guy; I just play one on TV.

Sada led me through the labyrinth of the house, taking more turns than I could follow, and finally bringing me to a pair of grand double doors. She pushed them open on a huge conservatory with a glass cupola. Sunlight flooded the place, and it was full of flowering vines and statues from out uof Greek and Roman mythology. In some respects, it reminded me of my father's throne room in Dis, just sunnier.

Books lined the walls, and there were tables and banker's lamps for study. A huge brass telescope was tilted toward the glass ceiling, and world globes and glass cases full of curious artifacts were scattered around. A full-scale Tyrannosaurus skeleton dominated one whole corner. Finally, an aisle paved in colorful stone cut a swath down the middle of the huge, cathedral-like space and ended at a truly gigantic, one-story statue of Baphomet on his throne, two fingers pointed toward heaven.

"Welcome to the Order of Endor, my Lord," came a voice to my left.

I turned to face "the magus," surprised by what I found.

I'd expected Justin Alexander, but an older woman in grand red and black robes stood there. Tall, with dark, close-cropped hair and large, dark eyes. Like Justin in the newspaper, she looked rather serious. Another Blank. But she had an energy about her that I tend to associate with those who've followed the craft for most of their lives.

"You're not Justin," I said.

"Indeed." She looked me up and down before extending her hand. "Juliette Alexander. I'm Justin's sister. His twin, actually."

Still riding the high this place was giving me, I took her hand without hesitation. As with Sada, I felt no malice from here. Quite the opposite. She immediately went to one knee and bowed her head. "We are so very honored to have your presence with us at long last, Lord Lucifer."

* * *

I walked with Juliette Alexander along the pavilion in the back of the house while she explained the history of the castle and the Order. Her followers—the Children of Endor, she called them—had gathered around us and were laying out a gigantic feast for me.

I watched them decorate and fill the tables while she explained how the Order had had its start as a humble offshoot of the Church of Satan created by Anton LaVey. While LaVey's church slowly descended into self-serving Bohemian chaos, the Order of Endor attempted to retain its focus on the "importance of discipline." That's exactly how she put it, by the way.

Juliette's grandfather, Martin Alexander, had been one of LaVey's stoutest followers. But one day, he had a vision that the great Lucifer they worshiped would walk the Earth like a man—just not in Los Angeles, where LaVey's coven was currently located. He tried to convince LaVey to move the coven east, but the man was too caught up in the glamour of his movement and his decadent Hollywood lifestyle. Feeling disparaged, Martin and a small group of dedicated followers relocated to eastern Pennsylvania and built this house, and founded the Order to wait for the great Dragon's arrival. Martin never saw it happen, but he had instructed his children and grandchildren to keep a faithful vigil—which they had.

Juliette looked up at me as she finished her story. "I always knew you would arrive. Not what day or hour, of course. But I knew it would happen. I only wish my brother was here."

"Where is your brother?" I asked.

"He stays in Philadelphia, running our company, Synergy. Without it, we wouldn't be able to maintain all this." She spread her arms to encompass the grounds. There were endless stretches of manicured green, a glass atrium, a garden with more elaborate fountains, what looked like a hedge maze, and a giant, Olympic-sized swimming pool.

"And you all stay here?"

She nodded sagely at her followers. "The faithful do. We were waiting for your arrival, my Lord."

"So...Justin isn't the magus, then?"

"*I* run the coven," Juliette announced proudly. I could tell she'd had to explain this many times. "*I* am the magus. But Justin runs the business end and he's the face of the company, allowing the rest of us to operate more...privately."

The coven had finished setting up and had turned their attention to me. Slowly, one by one, they approached me. As they grew closer, I once again felt that strange, happy-drunk feeling surging through my body. I'd never really been big on drugs or alcohol, to be honest, but the few times I'd been pretty high, it had felt like this. When they knelt and started to chant in Latin once more, I felt that unique euphoria kick it up a notch. Frankly, I didn't like it one bit. Like most people, I much preferred to be miserable and in control. I had to grab the back of a lounger to steady myself.

"You feel it," Juliette announced. She, too, knelt. "Do you feel our worship?" Spreading her arms out, she hummed a few words before extending her hands toward me. It made the drunkenness grow. "We are yours, Lord. We are yours to command. Yours to use. I hope you will accept this, our most precious gift—our obedience and our love."

I knew what she was doing. Sort of. My dad once explained it to me—one of the few things he'd bother to tell me about myself. If I wanted to "level up," I needed followers. Worship. Their love and devotion would work to bolster my power. It worked the same with all deities everywhere. But I'd never sought out followers or a coven because who the hell wants a bunch of weird groupies following you around all day?

Their chanting increased, becoming one voice, and despite my every desire not to do so, I lost all control and my wings burst forth. Their chanting—their power—actually lifted me up off the ground a few inches.

It was like being bathed in love and sunlight. Power. Delicious, never-ending power...

And despite my misgivings and all my rebellious inclination, which I had always held close, I realized that if I wasn't careful, I could get used to this.

* * *

They wanted me to stay the night. They planned on doing a formal ceremony.

Even though I was feeling an urgent need to segue into my reasons for being here—the Lucky 8 Mine the Alexanders owned and its possible connection to the Thin Man—the witch in me was too curious to pass up the opportunity to see a real Satanic ritual in the flesh, so to speak. I'd been to dozens of pagan sabbats and esbats, sure, but I usually went as an observer rather than a participant. Magic was a complicated process, and I didn't trust my powers to behave themselves out among the masses. In this case, however, I would be the thing they were summoning and beseeching. I thought that might be interesting—I mean, being summoned had always sort of been on my bucket list. I blame all the Hammer horror movies I'd seen growing up.

Juliette led everyone to what she called the Study Hall—that gigantic observatory I'd seen earlier. There, all the followers disrobed so they were unashamedly naked and joined hands to form a circle—no different from any other pagan ritual I'd witnessed. Morgana did this frequently, sometimes alone and sometimes with a coven, so none of this was surprising to me.

Juliette, the magus, produced a black athame that looked like it might be made of the horn of an oryx or springbok and moved around the circle, carefully blessing each member and touching the horn to each member's lips. Sada, her second, stepped forward. Naked now, I noted her entire body was covered in those strange glyphs that seemed to glow slightly. With great care and obvious experience, she called the corners and secured the circle for ritual making. Soon, all the Children of Endor began to chant.

During this time, I stood, still fully clothed, outside the circle of their joined hands. I knew better than to enter a magic circle. Once closed, it was like being inside a *Star Trek* force field. No way out.

The coven's chanting increased, and I suddenly found I didn't like it anymore. The pressure was building around me in uncomfortable ways, even though I was standing there alone. It occurred to me—finally, after all this time—that what they were chanting wasn't Latin. They were talking in Divine, Angel-speak, and they were telling the story of the Fall of Lucifer. As far as I knew, no human being on Earth knew the language of the angels. Hell, *I* didn't even know it, technically speaking, though Morgana had informed me that I was wont to speak it in my sleep.

Too late, I realized these dudes were the real deal. Not a bunch of kids play-acting at being Satanists. They really did believe in and worship me.

I tried to take a step away from the circle, but it was too late. I was stuck in place, held down by their ritual. Well, I thought, this sucks balls. I looked down at my feet, trying to lift them, but I saw the stones beneath me were loosening and seemed to be...drifting apart? Creating a kind of Tetris void beneath me? I started to struggle to stay on top of them, but the more I did, the more the stones shifted.

Then I was falling through a long void into...who the hell knew where?

***

I had no sense of time. I drifted in darkness for what might have been minutes or centuries. I knew I spent a lot of time thinking about my life decisions and, essentially, how shitty most of them had been. I had just begun to despair of ever getting out of here when I felt a gust of force lift me upward so quickly and forcefully that I was afraid I was going to lose my lunch.

Above, a pinprick of light appeared, as if I were at the bottom of a well, looking up at the sky. Seconds later, I burst through into the light and sort of just *glided up* through the stone floor of the Study Room and hung there in mid-air. The circle of Satan worshipers came back into sharp focus, and it was then I realized that, very likely, little time had passed. Seconds—if that. They had drawn me into their circle, they were that powerful. Worse, they had summoned me in wings and robes—and I *hated* the wings and the robes.

Juliette had her arms raised, the athame gleaming in her left hand, but when she opened her eyes and stopped chanting, I saw her expression had changed. She didn't look beatific in worship. She just looked...surprised as hell.

I wasn't the gorgeous, otherworldly, white-winged angel she had expected. I mostly looked like my father, sure, but there were subtle differences. My mother had been an extremely powerful witch. I had her eyes—and plenty of people told me her attitude, too. And she'd been a Black woman. No, really. I just didn't look like her because my dad had basically cloned himself in me. But something had happened when I'd earned my wings. They weren't *his*. Mine were black wings, tipped in white, and they glowed faintly as if with a black light—the total reversal of my father's. Some weird genetic fuck-up, I don't know. Humans and demons are *not* supposed to do the horizontal hustle.

"My liege!" she cried, and I almost cowered away from her criticism before she added, "You *are* a pretty devil, aren't you?" Then she smiled, almost more to herself than anything else. "And so very...human."

The power drained out of the circle and I found myself crashing to the floor on my hands and knees, my wings and robes dissolving as the circle broke up around me. I was back to looking like the bum I was. I touched my head because my ears were faintly ringing and I was getting a headache from all the magic swirling around me. "Yeah, not what you expected," I said as she approached me and offered her hand.

"But perhaps exactly what we *need*," she answered sagely.

| 16 |

Master of the Mystical Arts

"YOUR FATHER LAY with a human," Juliette said after dismissing her followers and guiding me upstairs to the suite they had prepared for me. It was a real Downton Abbey affair, as big as the entire flat above the shop, with huge, arching windows overlooking the grounds, and a four-poster bed that was larger than king size. A portrait hung over the unlit mantel of a man who looked just like me—just with crueler, more arrogant features. I'd have to pull that fucker off the wall and dump it in one of the many closets before I'd get any sleep tonight.

"I've always found that interesting," Juliette went on as she pulled the heavy velvet drapes back over the windows. "I would not have expected it of him. He always seemed a bit of a...a..."

"Snob," I offered, slumping down on a nearby crushed velvet divan, my bag at my feet. I looked up at the ornately painted ceiling and the huge glass chandelier hanging down and ran my hand over my spiky, cowlick-y hair. In this setting, I felt a bit scruffy, to be honest. As much as I'd rather not admit to it, a no-tell motel was more my style.

"Did you know him?" I asked.

"We had an accord," Juliette said.

"You slept with him."

She didn't deny it. But then, he slept with everyone.

"Who was the woman?" she asked, turning around. "Your mother?"

I hesitated to say her name—not sure why. "Wilhelmina Wodehouse."

"Willa?" She looked shaken for the first time since I had met her.

I sat forward. "You knew my mother?"

Juliette went to fetch me some tea off the service one of her coven had brought up with us. Nothing magical or herbal. It was just plain ol' Earl Grey, my favorite. "We belonged to the same coven, back in the day. We were sisters in the craft. I would never have expected...well..." She sat down beside me on the divan and drank her tea.

"Go on."

She shook her head. "Willful Willa. That's what we used to call her. Stubborn, wild..." She looked me up and down. "Bit of a hot mess."

I found this fascinating. My memories of my mother from so long ago were much different. Even though they were only vague shadows in the back of my child's brain, I associated Willa with all things soft and safe. I knew she never raised her voice to me. She never, ever struck me—though I'm sure I'd probably deserved it. She was like this sweet, sacred Madonna hovering at the outer edges of my waking dreams. "Willful Willa" was a whole new side of my mother I was learning about.

I had never really gotten a proper picture of who she was until now. My father had taken her from me when I was four years old. I'd spent most of my formative years in foster care. In my ego and self-delusion, I'd told myself it was his way of protecting me by hiding my identity from his many enemies. Then I learned the truth from him. He took my mother because he'd wanted her all to himself.

I was his heir, but I was also his *inconvenience*. I existed for no other reason than because my father had lusted after my mother and their coupling had been unnaturally fertile. I was the Chosen One due entirely to good timing and circumstance.

Juliette looked at me with such a sad expression, I got the feeling she was picking up on these little things—maybe not in the sense of telepathy, but just intense empathy.

"Tell me about Willa," I said. "What was she like?"

Juliette bit her lip. "The thing I remember most about Willa is her strength—and her selflessness. She was obsessed with helping others. I expect you probably take after her."

"Well, I don't take after *him*."

"You don't speak to him."

"No, we don't speak." I drank my tea.

She got up and moved around the room. I think because she was feeling agitated. Or maybe she was feeling the past. I certainly was. Turning, she pressed her hands together. "I'm sorry he hurt you, my Lord."

"Nick," I said. "Don't call me 'my Lord.' It's creepy as hell."

She nodded. It took her a moment to speak. "Like my grandfather, I always knew you would come. And now that you're here..."

I grinned at that. "Yeah. You didn't expect a weak, sloppy, unlearned, hot mess Satan."

She squared her shoulders at that, seemingly offended by my self-critique. "Not at all. I was going to say...I never expected someone so willful and powerful..."

I laughed at that. "Lady, you are delusional."

Juliette didn't take offense. She did examine me closely as if she were puzzling together all of my pieces. "You think you are weak and...less than the sum of your parts. You aren't, Nick. You are quite unique—a rather extraordinary creature."

"If you say so."

"You aren't learned. I agree with that. You've never really applied yourself to the craft—or anything, really. I suspect you wield it while looking down your nose at it—which is dangerous. For you, it's a parlor trick. A convenient tool to get you out of scrapes. But you do not love the craft the way the craft loves you, Nick. In that way, you are an extremely lazy witch."

I set the mug of tea on a side table and grinned at that.

"There it is. You hide behind your incompetence because you're afraid if you really applied yourself, if you truly embraced the craft, you might be rather good at it."

Juliette held her hand up to keep me from protesting. "Nick, you've spent your whole life being told you aren't good enough. That you are stupid and weak and useless. As a consequence, you have become...what do the young ones call it? A slacker?"

"Whatever," I said, getting defensive now. "What are you, a psychiatrist?"

"A therapist." She spread her hands. "When I'm not attending to the coven."

That explained so much. I got up, but she got in my way. "Don't go. Please." She looked up at me with the kind of motherly concern I had only ever seen in Morgana's face. She put her hands out as if to stop me, but she didn't touch me. "You can learn things here. You can be so much *more*, Nick."

"More? More what? More of a fuck up?"

"Don't do that to yourself," she said, sounding angry now. "You do realize you undermine your own power when you have those thoughts? You undermine the craft..."

I leaned down until our faces were inches apart and I could see the deep, dark cognac of her eyes. "I'm not weak."

But even as I said it, I knew she had a point. Ever since I had ascended to my father's position, I'd had issues. I mean, you'd think as the new Lucifer, I'd have been bursting with wisdom and magical powers, right? A regular Doctor Strange, Master of the Mystical Arts, and all that jazz. Instead, I felt overwhelmed by all the craft represented. As a result, I'd just stopped doing it.

Juliette nodded as if she understood all this mental floss I was struggling with. "No, you're not a weak *man*. But you are a poor witch. Why do you think it was so easy to draw you into our Circle? Your father would not have been summoned so easily."

I clenched my fists together at my sides. I was getting just a little bit sick of Juliette's sage wisdom and advice.

But the magus stood there, continuing to nod to herself. "As the new Lucifer, you need your worshipers, Nick. Believers, at the very least. Without them...you may not survive this."

"I need your coven."

"Yes."

"There are covens back in Blackwater—"

"*Wiccan* covens—who do not believe in the devil," she explained to me with infuriating patience. "*They* are of no use to you. No source of power, at any rate." She took a step toward me and pointed at some random spot in the wall behind me. "It's like plugging yourself into an electrical socket when there is no power in the whole house. Nick, as the new Lucifer, you need *your* believers. Your power. You need your Luciferians. Understand?"

I stumbled on a response. She was making perfect sense, of course. And only now was it starting to penetrate my thick head. Still, I didn't want to admit I was that stupid. Instead, I decided to steer things in a new direction.

"I didn't come here for you, Juliette, or for your worshipers. I came here to talk to Justin about the mine."

She was good. I'd give her that. She never even blinked, even though I had broadsided her. "The mine. Number 8? What do you want to know about it?"

"Well, for one thing, if Synergy is into renewable power...wind farms and such...why buy an old, dilapidated mine? Or are you guys after the Anthracite that's supposed to be down there, after all?"

For the first time, she looked truly surprised, as if I should have been able to figure this out on my own. "We bought it for the same reason we've bought every other mine over the past few decades—so it *can't* be mined."

"You're not mining it?"

Juliette virtually threw up her hands. "Heavens no! My brother and I want to push consumers into renewables—green energy. The only way to do that is to cut off the supply of coal and natural gas. We've been doing this for years to stop fracking."

I stared at her a long moment before returning to the divan. She fetched me more tea, and as she did so, she explained that she and Justin had already begun the long, complex process of getting the permits they needed to collapse the mine. Once they did, the whole system of tunnels would be closed off forever from any living thing —including humans.

I watched her. I could detect no duplicity in what she was saying. Okay, I would confirm all that later when I had time to look deeper into Synergy's activities. For now, I briefly explained about the school shooting and the possible connection to the Thin Man legend, which was also (somehow) connected to her mine.

Juliette's eyebrows went up as if this was the first she had heard of this. "And you learned about the Thin Man, how...?"

"The Internet. And also from Dr. Theodore Lamb, the priest at the school where the shooting took place…"

"Oh," she said, voice low and eyes narrowing. "Him."

"You know Lamb?"

"Not in the way you imagine," she admitted. "He was never part of our coven."

"Explain."

She gave me a shrewd look. "You know about his…ability?"

"Charisma? Yes."

"So you know how he uses it."

"In counseling, he says," I said, suddenly feeling foolish and rather ill-informed.

Juliette threw her head back with a bark. "Is that what he calls it?"

"What do you call it?"

"Abuse."

I swallowed. "He abuses his patients?" It took me a moment to find the rest of my voice. "Sexually abuses them?"

"Not sexually. But still…" She thought about that for a moment, then added, "We call him the Beast."

I blinked at that. "The Beast?"

"That's right."

"Rising out of the sea. Seven heads and ten horns. *That* Beast?"

I admit I was having a hard time resolving the image of the paunchy guy in glasses as being the frightening, mystical monster from the Book of Revelation.

"Therion—that's his real name, Nick. Therion the Beast." Her voice was soft but sour. "But he doesn't come from the sea. He comes from out of the earth, and his job is to create chaos and make all people worship the Dragon."

That would be me.

I just stared at her for a long moment. This was some seriously fucked up shit. "If you believe that, then why aren't you allied with him? Aren't you both big on 'the Dragon?'"

She leaned sideways against the seat as she explained. "I don't think you understand, Nick. Luciferism aims to maintain free will. You, Nick, are the sentry of free will for all humankind. It's a part of your very fabric. But him...that *creature*..." Her lip lifted at the corner in disgust. "...he would have all people enslaved and down on their knees, worshiping you blindly. That is not the way. It is not *our* way. And it should never be your way." Her fist clenched in her lap. "It flies in the face of everything we are trying to do here."

"Which is?"

She straightened up, suddenly peaceful again. It was kind of eerie to watch her transform so quickly from angry Luciferian to the picture-perfect therapist. "To prepare you, of course. To prepare you for the Coming."

"The Coming," I said, an eyebrow raised. This was getting better and better. "The Coming of what? The Antichrist? My stuff from Amazon?"

She never flinched, but her eyes grew sad at the flippant way I was handling this. "War, Nick. A great and terrible war between Heaven and Hell."

| 17 |

Lucy-fer

YEAH, SO, I still didn't have a clear connection between the mine and the school shooting—and that concerned me far more than some fancy, fictitious war between Heaven and Hell. By then, it was getting late and I didn't relish driving back to Blackwater in the dark. The drive up to Philly had taken it out of me.

I decided to crash in the suite that the nice Satanists had provided me. Juliette offered me all the "companions" I might want. I turned her down on the companion part. The monster in my pants had gotten me into enough trouble of late, thank you very much. I didn't need more failed relationships dogging me. Achievement unlocked.

My sleep was rough and choppy. My arm was hurting again, so I took another of those pill bombs the hospital had given me, which knocked me straight out for a few hours. Unfortunately, I was wide awake by three in the morning, so I spent the rest of the night surfing the Internet, checking out that info on Synergy—Juliette's story did check out—and looking at funny cat videos.

Early the following morning, I stepped out onto the pavilion where I'd last seen Tiger being pampered by Juliette's followers.

Everyone was off doing whatever it was Satanists did when they weren't worshiping me. Only Sada was here, sunbathing with my dog on the lounger beside her. Tiger looked like he was on vacation and having a damned good time.

I wasn't halfway to her when Sada pushed her oversized sunglasses down her nose and sat up. She was again naked, dark, and stunning on the white lounger. I was learning that the coven's house was very much clothing optional.

Her African skin made the runes stand out almost as if her entire body was painted with gold leaf. It reminded me of black leopards with those markings you can still see, sort of. The glyphs—too old and arcane for my limited witchy education to properly interpret—sparkled under the bright sunshiny morning light. She had gold charms piercing her ears, her belly, and…her labia. Those were visible when she uncrossed her long legs and sat up to address me.

It took me a moment to tell myself to calm the fuck down. Then I looked at her face. That didn't help. God, she was gorgeous. All that beautiful wooly black hair. Those dark cat eyes with their strange, almost golden, hearts. Those soft lips gently parted in a sweet smile. The sun glinted off the gold rings in her full bottom lip. A thought jumped to my mind so suddenly that I just knew she was planting it there: *The Sun Witch.*

It fit her.

I cleared my throat. "I'm going to need my dog back now."

"Your…what…?" She looked confused, then seemed to realize. "Oh, you mean this dear creature." She reached over to touch Tiger with her long, gold-painted nails.

"Um, yeah." I looked at her eyes, trying not to be a perv and stare at the rest of her. It wasn't easy. "Come on, boy," I said to Tiger. "We gotta hit the road."

Tiger got his ponderous body up but gave me a reluctant slide of the eyes. I think he wanted to stay with Sada.

"Now," I said. "We gotta go now."

Sada got up as well and threw on a thin white wrap that concealed absolutely no private part of her delicious body. "I'll need a few minutes to dress, my Lord."

Maybe I hadn't heard right. "Excuse me?"

She looked surprised. "The magus wishes for me to accompany you back to Blackwater."

"I don't understand."

Sada smiled serenely. "She said you need a worshiper if you wish to overcome your current enemy."

"No. Absolutely not."

Sada stood there, looking crestfallen. "But she said I must. To help you. And to help protect you."

Jesus Christ. "I don't need protecting. I certainly don't need worshipping." I started walking away.

"Your demon won't be enough," she said.

I stopped and turned to face her. *Come on, Nick...stop ogling the gorgeous naked chick!* "Demon?"

She extended her hand, and Tiger raced to her and eagerly licked her fingers. She smiled at me. "He is a lovely creature, your demon dog. But I fear he won't be enough."

She danced off to get dressed.

* * *

So, that's how I wound up back in the rental with Sada in the passenger seat and Tiger, the devil dog, in the backseat.

Sada, now dressed in a long, strappy, yellow sundress and sandals, put on her oversized sunglasses and said, "This is going to be fun. I've never been on a road trip before."

"I'm glad you're enjoying yourself," I said drolly.

"It pleases me to please you, Lord."

"Nick."

"It pleases me to please you, Nick."

I shook my head. Before I turned the motor over, I said, "What did you mean about 'my demon?'"

She looked confused before pushing her glasses up her forehead. "Tiger."

"My dog."

"Tiger is not a dog." When she realized I didn't follow, she reached over the seat toward the subject of our conversation. Tiger lifted his paw and met her halfway, a doggie high-five. Now, I *knew* something was wrong.

"Perhaps he was a dog once, but..." She turned her head as if she suddenly realized something. "You didn't make him on purpose, did you?"

I chewed my tongue and looked over at Tiger, who rolled his eyes as if he couldn't believe it had taken me this long to figure everything out. Okay, so I have my blond moments. Sue me. "There's a demon in there?"

"That answers my question. You didn't make him on purpose." Sada pursed her lips and gave me a stern look, and I suddenly gained the impression that this beautiful creature made of sunlight and magic was taking me to task. She lifted a finger and tapped my nose. "This is what happens when you wield the craft without the proper knowledge of it. And that's why *I* am here."

Smiling, self-satisfied, she turned back to the windshield and settled her sunglasses into place. "Just wait, Nick. You'll soon be very happy I'm with you."

I looked her over, the way she filled out that too-thin dress. Yeah, I thought as I started the car. That was what I was afraid of.

* * *

We were halfway to Blackwater when it occurred to me that Sada might be hungry. Neither of us had eaten anything before we left Philly. I was in too much of a hurry to get the hell out of there. As we were passing a Perkins on the highway, I asked her if she wanted a late breakfast.

"Thank you, yes," she said, all very prim and proper. She had sat there, quiet and uncomplaining, for the last two hours. Sometimes she closed her eyes and hummed a little tune, or she played with the radio, but other than that, she hadn't done much of anything.

It was as if she was doing everything in her power to not be a distraction. In that way, she was the biggest distraction of all.

Frankly, I found Sada puzzling. She had seemed rather…voluptuous back at the mansion. I could imagine her seducing unsuspecting men by the dozens. But now she was acting like a church mouse.

"How does a nice girl like you become a Satanist?" I suddenly asked as I took the off-ramp.

She looked over—shyly. I expected her to say something along the lines of, "I'm not a very nice girl," but instead she said, "I don't understand."

I parked the jeep in the little bit of shade cast by a Dumpster, for all the good that would do. "I can't leave Tiger in the car—whatever he might be. And he can't come in with us." I pointed to the "No pets" sign. Truthfully, I had his service dog apron, so I could fake it, if I wanted to. I was just afraid of what he might do.

"I'll go in, get some grub. Can you take him down the hill?" I nodded toward a picnic table under a sun umbrella behind the Perkins, set there for customers.

"Of course." She slid out of the jeep without attaching Tiger's lead. Tiger followed behind her obediently.

I was worried about what I was going to do when we got back to Blackwater. How was I going to explain to Josh that I had killed his dog and put a low-level demon into it? But the answer was frighteningly obvious: I wasn't.

Inside the Perkins, I got two orders of pancakes, eggs, and bacon, then some extra bacon for Tiger. Did demons eat bacon? I was about to find out. They put the extra bacon in one of those Styrofoam containers that's terrible for the environment, and when I reached the picnic table where Sada was waiting for me, I put the bacon in its environment-destroying container on the ground and waited. Tiger gingerly picked up the container in his big, toothy mouth, jumped up on the bench, and set it down on the table next to Sada before digging in.

Sada laughed. "He doesn't like it when you treat him like a dog."

This...this is not good, I thought.

I thought about asking Sada some more questions about her time with the Children of Endor—then didn't. Did I want to get to know "my protector" better? Sure. I mean, I was curious, but she'd made it clear that she thought I was funny for asking her. Sada could remain an enigma wrapped in a gold burrito.

A few miles outside Blackwater, I finally broke down and made my confession. "Look...I'm sort of...between places at the moment." I couldn't take her back to the shop—Morgana would stab me with an athame—and I couldn't go to David's—he'd just stab me with a scalpel. I was frankly at a loss as to *where* to go from here.

Sada was unperturbed. "Do you know where Berger Hollow is?"

"Sure."

"Follow the road down to Lake Ariel."

I didn't question it because fuck it. I had nothing else going on today. I took the long, winding road that veered around the outskirts of the lake. After passing a series of summer luxury cabins, Sada pointed out a rocky, unpaved dirt road that went straight up. We bumped along for a half mile before the road opened up to a hilltop with an impressive Victorian farmhouse sitting atop it. White with green shutters, summery violets in window boxes, and an attached indoor greenhouse. It even had a cute little rooster weathervane atop the cupola. It was probably in the range of a hundred and fifty years old, but well-maintained—new vinyl siding and a green metal roof had been added. It had a large, paved pavilion, an unattached barn-turned-garage, and plenty of privacy. The nearest neighbors were half a mile down the road.

"The coven's summer house," Sada explained. She presented a key she'd been keeping in her purse. "The magus gave it to me."

I wasn't going to be homeless and sleeping in the rental until everyone stopped being completely pissed with me. I was suddenly very grateful that I'd taken Sada along.

We parked and got out, our feet crunching on the new river stone gravel that made up the circular driveway. There was a fountain here, too, but it was smaller than the one at the Alexander estate: A stone Pan played his pipes with an entourage of maidens dancing about him.

I went around to let Tiger out of the back of the jeep, but even before I reached him, I saw he'd gotten the back door open and was padding after Sada, who was heading up the stairs of the Victorian. I looked at the door he had left open. Yep, I thought, you got some 'splainin' to do, Lucy-fer. Shrugging, I reached inside for my overnight bag.

That's when the kid hit me broadside.

***

I landed hard on my bad arm, which stunned me a little and hurt me a lot. Rolling over, I tried to turn sideways and minimize myself as a target, but the kid moved fast. Too fast. And when I rolled, I somehow managed to roll right into him.

He kicked me hard in the ribs. I coughed out a breath, and kicked out at his shins, but he was...suddenly not there. Another kick—this time to my lower back. I felt my entire body seize up at the impact.

Was he teleporting or some crap?

Roaring, I flipped around and let go of my wings. They slashed him across the face like knives...and I heard him cry out. Yahtzee, motherfucker! It forced him to stumble back a few steps, a hand over his face where it was bleeding all over the front of his shirt. That allowed me enough time to climb to my feet.

"So what corner of hell did you crawl out of?" I asked.

The boy dropped his hand. The tip of his nose had been shaved clean off and looked like hamburger, and there were deep red gashes in the side of his face. He grinned at me nonetheless. "Fuck you, Lucifer."

Now I was good and well pissed. I didn't know the kid—he was maybe eighteen or nineteen—but he fought dirty. And if he wanted dirty, I would show him dirty. I grabbed the athame I kept in my boot and brought it up where he could see it flashing in the afternoon light. "Holy roller, angel, or demon?"

"What?" the boy sputtered with blood flecking the ground at his feet.

"Holy roller. Angel. Or demon?" I repeated more slowly. "Give me a reason why you're fucking up my afternoon, kid."

He did not answer. He roared at me before lunging forward.

I tossed the athame underhand style at him.

It clunked into his right shoulder, snapping him back. I'd had the athame for years. It had been bathed in the blood of enemy angels. Read: Pretty damned badass. And it could hurt things both supernatural and not. In this case, something was definitely all woo-woo with the kid, because the athame began to smoke like a barbecue on the Fourth of July.

The boy grabbed the handle of the athame to pull it loose. Bad move. There were runes carved into it that were just as bad—if not worse—than the actual blade. He began to scream and his blood-slicked fingers slipped off. His hands began to smoke, as well, and he held them out in front of him as if they were covered in flesh-eating acid—which wasn't too far from the truth. Hello, Otherkin.

While he was distracted, I tackled him, trying to bear him to earth so I could get him into a policeman's submission hold. I had him down maybe five seconds, but he didn't stay that way. I was holding him...and then he seemed to just flicker away. When I turned to glance behind me, he kicked me straight in the face, laying me out in the dirt. His blow packed incredible power. Before I could even orient myself, he was on me, the athame—which he had finally pulled from his bleeding shoulder—held high over my head. The handle had burned most of the skin off his hands and the air was full of the smell of roasting pig, but he didn't seem to care about the pain. With a scream, he used both skeletal hands to plunge it downward, ramming the wavy blade deep into the base of my throat.

I didn't so much scream at the impact as I hiccuped. The sudden wash of my blood hit him full in the face, making him shriek some more and rear back. I dropped to my knees on the gravel, grasping the knife half-stuck in my throat, trying to suck in air through all the blood.

Stumbling a half dozen steps, my attacker finally slammed into the edge of the fountain, which stopped him. The creature lowered his hands then, and I saw that my blood had worn the skin off his face in places so the shiny yellow skull peeked out like a Halloween special effect. That pleased me. He looked ready to retreat when I saw him freeze and turn slowly to face Sada, who was standing beside him.

"No!" she screamed and raised her hand. Her magic was fucking strong, because it tossed the kid all the way across the driveway and into a big old elm on the opposite side, near the detached garage. I heard a satisfying crack, and the kid slumped down, his head at an odd angle.

I had given up trying to kneel and was now lying on my side in the driveway, gasping for what little oxygen would slide past the athame and into my lungs. At the angle I was at, I could see the kid's open eyes and gaping mouth. His eyes were black as if someone had sewed buttons in their place. Just shiny black, no irises or pupils. With his skeletal mouth hanging open, something crawled past the remnants of his lips. It looked like a giant, hairless, black tarantula. As it crawled over the kid's bottom lip, it began to dissolve into black mush. In seconds, it was just a black spot on the driveway.

Huh, I thought. That's interesting.

Then I found myself breathing—gurgling—through my own blood and promptly passed out.

| 18 |

Substitutes

I WOKE UP choking, dreaming there was something monstrous crawling down my throat. Panicked, I started clawing at my neck, but someone put their hands over mine and gently stopped me from ripping my throat open.

My fuzzy dream vision cleared and I recognized Morgana's face. It was creased with worry, but at least she didn't look angry with me for a change. "Don't. Let me," she said and proceeded to gently remove the tube from my mouth.

I gasped as I fell back into what appeared to be a hospital bed. A bed I was handcuffed to. Jesus, my mouth and throat felt like they had been paved with sandpaper. I coughed and that made it worse.

Morgana poured me a glass of water from the pitcher on the rolling table beside the bed and helped me sip it. "Sip. Slowly," she said, but I gulped it. My throat was having none of that and I choked it out over my hospital johnny.

"I said slowly."

I raised my hand to wipe my mouth. I tried to ask what the hell had happened, but my throat was too sore to form words.

"Don't speak," she said. "The doctors patched your throat, but it's not healing the way things usually heal on you. If you know what I mean."

Since I couldn't answer, I just nodded and sat up straighter in the bed. Typical Blue Ridge hospital room. Looked like a cheap hotel. Walmart watercolor paintings on the wall. TV near the ceiling. Totally normal...except for the handcuff. Naturally, I yanked on it, but it didn't give an inch. I glanced around, saw there was nothing on the rollaway table to help me communicate, and made a pantomime of writing in my palm.

"One moment." Morgana went to her purse and found the little pad she normally used to write down the herbs she needed to buy from the local farmers' markets. "If it answers your question, your...friend Sada brought you in," she said as she transported the pad and a pen over to me. "Someone put your own athame in your throat. Probably would have killed you, too, if it wasn't *your own athame*. The kid wasn't so lucky."

She ripped the top paper off the notepad and handed it and the pen to me. "Naturally, your prints were all over the athame, so they think you killed him, Nick. They think you... stabbed him and tried to dissolve the body with acid. His name was Brian and he was one of the survivors of the school shooting. He was seventeen years old." She glanced behind herself a moment. "They have a cop stationed outside the room—in case you try anything before they get a chance to question you."

I spotted the uniform loitering just outside the open door. I wasn't overly surprised by this turn of events. I would have done the same to me, had I been investigating the kid's murder.

I wrote in large, scrawling letters *How long?*

"Yesterday. It's been about twenty-four hours." Morgana sank into the plastic seat beside the hospital bed. "When they brought you in...honestly, I thought you were going to die." She took a deep, rattling breath. "What the hell happened at that house? *Did* you kill that kid?"

I ripped the paper away, wrote, *Attacked me.*

Morgana looked annoyed, but I knew that, under all that bluster and annoyance, she was extremely concerned for me. She was just that good of a person. "Why did he attack you?"

Hell, I wish I knew. I suspected the attack at the house and the truck that had run me off the road were connected. But I wasn't about to get into the long, overly complicated story behind that.

Not a boy, I wrote. *Substitute.*

She looked at the pad for a long moment. "Explain. If you can."

I thought about all the things I could write. Too long. Too much. I ripped the paper away and wrote, *Ask Antonia.*

"Antonia? Sheriff Ben's Antonia?"

I nodded.

"What does she have to do—?" Morgana began, but Sada chose that moment to step into my hospital room, interrupting us.

She was dressed in another ankle-length sundress, this one white and designed much like a Greek toga. It was cut very low, showing off the deep, dark cleavage between her gravity-defying breasts. She was wearing a heavy gold medallion on a chain that looked almost Egyptian, a gold brooch shaped like a sun at her hip (to keep the button-less dress closed, I assumed), and huge gold hoop earrings. She was smiling serenely, as usual.

Morgana immediately stood up as if Sada's very presence had ousted her.

I reached out, and even that was a stretch, I grabbed her wrist and shook my head.

"Sorry, have to go. I can see you're in *very* good hands."

She stomped past Sada, but not without giving the woman a brief up-and-down glance that said…many things. None of them good. Morgana was halfway to the door when I got a thought.

I quickly scribbled on the pad and held it up.

SORRY.

She turned to look at me. Her eyes were cold. Fatigued.

The accidents. The betrayals. I had worn Morgana down—who was practically a saint. Now I felt even worse.

Once she was gone, I turned to Sada. I still wanted her. So much so that having a blanket over my lower half was a blessing in disguise. But I was also pissed with myself. Pissed that I had hurt Morgana—the only person in my whole fucking life to have stuck it out with me despite everything. Despite every shitty thing I had ever done to her—and to myself. I started writing a new note to Sada—this not-talking thing was turning into a real pain in the ass—but Sada held up her hand.

"I know what you're going to write, Nick. I'm sorry, but I can't do that."

I had a half-written note in my lap—*Leave me alone.*

Fine. I pointed at the door and shook my head furiously.

"I can't do that, either," she said, hovering at my bedside like some nurse from heaven. Or hell, depending on how you were looking at things. She looked down at me with that infuriating sympathy I was coming to associate with her, then reached out to touch my injured throat, but I slapped her hand away.

Again, I shook my head.

"The magus tasked me with this job, Nick. I can't abandon my post. I can't leave you. Especially now."

I started writing, *You're making my life difficult,* but she answered before I had finished.

"*You* make your life difficult, Man of Sin." Crossing her arms petulantly, she added, "You are reckless and you are stubborn. They warned me about that. They warned me that you would be a good challenge for me, but you should know I'm more than up for the task of protecting you."

I wanted to throw the notebook at her.

Changing the subject, she glanced aside at the open door and said in a low, conspiratorial voice, "Now that you're awake, I'm sure the police will be in to question you." She hesitated to let that sink in.

She had killed that boy for me. But, of course, the police wouldn't suspect her. My weapon. My prints. They wouldn't believe someone like Sada would have the power to kill the boy...the Substitute. The evidence was pretty circumstantial, and I knew none of it would stick in a court of law even if it ever got to trial—which was unlikely—but that didn't mean the police couldn't make things very difficult for me.

The last thing I needed right now was to tango with the police with these Substitutes running all over the place.

Sada senses my thoughts, natch. "Do you want to get out of here?"

Again, I glanced at the uniform on my door. He was turned away, watching a young, pretty nurse in scrubs go by, but I knew that wouldn't last. When he saw I was awake, he would fetch his superior. That would either be Sheriff Ben, if I was lucky, or someone from the FBI, if I wasn't. I turned back to Sada and nodded.

I was, unfortunately, at her mercy.

* * *

Sada turned toward the door and raised both hands, palms up, as if she were beseeching some unseen deity. She murmured under her breath, and I felt the temperature in the room drop dramatically as she unraveled a glamour spell that would make it impossible for anyone in the hallway to look directly into the room. I mean, they could try, but their attention would waver and be drawn elsewhere no matter how hard they tried to focus.

My breath suddenly puffed out in the chill quickly filling the room. This was strong stuff.

She turned back. She didn't seem bothered by the cold even as she began to unclip the ornate brooch at her hip that kept her dress wrapped around her silky dark skin. I closed my eyes, unwilling to subject myself to the sight of her nakedness again, but she palmed my cheek, which just got my attention.

Holy Jesus, girl, why are you doing this to me?

She answered, "Your sin is desire. Desire makes you strong, Nick. Indulge it."

Yeah, well, all that *indulging* was getting me into loads of trouble of late.

"If your brides can't understand—if they are unwilling to support your needs and the source of your power—then they aren't worthy of being your brides." And, saying that, she climbed atop the hospital bed with all the slinky grace of a great cat. I shifted around uncomfortably, but she pinned my legs under her weight. Now, I couldn't move at all. And look away? Yeah, fat chance of *that* happening.

Staring down into my eyes, Sada started chanting in that soft, sweet voice. Angel-speak. She was chanting—praying—in angel-speak. Praying to me. Worshiping me. I thought of the ludicrous nature of power. Gods, angels, demons...they absorbed their power from worshipers. Just normal human beings. But without them...well, all of us Otherkin would probably cease to exist. It was a sobering thought.

But chanting wasn't all she was doing. She was also moving in a primitive dance atop me. A kind of serpent-like swaying motion that went up and down and side to side all at once. She moved her arms in an elaborate sequence like she was drawing cuneiforms in the air over us, and it all worked in perfect tangent with the rhythm of her prayer to me.

I was a pretty normal guy, all told. Naturally, I thought of the few lap dances I had had, but this wasn't like those times. This was primal. Sensual, yes, but far more powerful. The Sun Witch was giving me her worship. She was granting me her power.

The warmth—that good, euphoric feeling—began to bubble up inside me almost at once. I saw her eyes light up when she saw my reaction. How much I was enjoying this. Not like a man, but like a demon. She immediately began speaking faster, moving more furiously—and sensuously. Kind of grinding against me. Good lord, I wanted her flesh...I wanted her power. And she knew it. She made the bed bounce up and down with her snaky little worship dance.

The feeling in me grew...and grew. First an ember, then a flame. Then a full-on fire seemed to lick at the underside of my skin. The pain I felt—my throat, my arm, and my various bruises I'd gotten over the last few days of my misfortune—flared up and hurt more than ever for a moment. It almost made me cry out in response. But then all those places of injury vanquished in one long, trembling cry of angel-speak.

Lord Lucifer, she was saying, head thrown back and eyes mere slits of ecstasy as she literally came atop me. *Lucifer...Lord of Light.*

There was a blinding flash like someone had set off an old-fashioned camera bulb in my face, and I felt the air turn electric and bite like little insects along my skin. It actually lifted my body a few inches, and her atop it. It lasted only a few moments, and, when it was done, I was whole once more.

| 19 |

Alternative Medicine

UNFORTUNATELY, WHILE SADA was giving me her power lap dance, she was unable to maintain the glamour spell. We all have our limitations, and I really couldn't blame her. What she had done was monumental—not something I could have done in my youth, that's for sure.

So, yeah, despite Sada's best intentions, I still wound up with an agent of the FBI standing over my bed. He was a young, cocky pup. Early thirties, he had the kind of pressed, perfect suit and psychotically trimmed haircut I always associate with his type of guy. When I was on the force in New York, we used to make fun of the Men in Black. Always cockwalking across our crime scenes, blasting their badges at anyone who dared question them.

Okay, so maybe I was a little prejudiced. I just didn't like the dude.

"Mr. Englebrecht, my name is Special Agent Kip Murphy. I'm with the Special Crimes Division..."

Kip Murphy, I thought. What a horrible name. His mom must have hated him.

I sat up in the hospital bed and cleared my throat, which hurt a lot less. "How can I help you, Kippy?"

Murphy wrinkled his nose at that, then told his junior associate, a painfully young blond guy, to close the door. That didn't bode well.

When the three of us were alone at last, Murphy started right in on me, asking me what I was doing at the house and the details of the attack. I didn't lie. There was no point to that. Forensics would be able to figure out ninety percent of it anyway, but I left out all the supernatural stuff. Because reasons.

"You threw him into a tree?" said Murphy, sounding unconvinced. "From across the driveway. With a knife in your throat."

I smiled. "Adrenaline is a hell of a drug."

Murphy stopped writing in his notebook and looked up at me with the expression of a man not buying the line of bullshit he was being fed. Myself, I was sort of enjoying this. I wasn't overly concerned about charges. Again, anything the police found would be circumstantial, at best. There was no link between me and the kid. Even if they wanted to bring me up on charges of manslaughter, the judge would throw a case like this out of court due to its sheer ludicrousness.

"Do you normally carry knives around with you, Mr. Englebrecht?"

"It's not a knife. It's an athame. And yes, I carry an athame with me as part of my services."

He made a show of looking over his notes even though I was certain he had done a thorough background check on me prior to arriving. "You're an occultist?"

"I'm a professional witch. I run a herbal remedy shop with my partner."

"An occult shop."

"Alternative medicine. And I do séances. No cults involved." I wasn't telling him anything that everyone in Blackwater didn't already know about me.

"Palm reading. Crystal balls. That type of stuff?"

"If you want."

He glanced at his partner and they passed secret semaphore messages between them with their eyebrows the only way long-time partners can. "So...when this boy attacked you, you used your...athame...to defend yourself."

"It was the only weapon I had available."

Agent Murphy wrote something down. "And then you used acid on him to try and dissolve the body."

"No, I was unconscious at the time. Knife in the throat."

"But perhaps you had your girlfriend do it for you."

"Did you find acid residue on her?" I asked.

Despite what you see on *Law & Order*, it is very difficult to convict someone on a murder charge. You need mucho evidence that there was intent, a written confession, or both. You need evidence up the wazoo. These two chuckleheads weren't getting either out of me because, simply put, I hadn't killed the kid.

Agent Murphy wandered closer and even sat down on the edge of my bed. He smiled in a way that said he was my best friend, but I knew better. His Bad Cop routine was weak sauce. "You're the guy who interrupted the school shooting. You managed to disarm Kenny Johnson."

"I was there. I helped the police."

Again, he glanced at his imaginary notes. "You were also instrumental in discovering the whereabouts of Cassandra Berger, the girl who went missing three years ago."

"All of that is a matter of public record," I said. "Your point, Special Agent?"

He glanced over at his partner and they shared an intimate moment before he continued. "What happened on the night of June 11, 2007?"

I pushed myself up in bed a little more. That was the night my partner, Peter, was murdered by the Arcana. The night he was partially devoured. He died later that night of his injuries. It was also the last day I was an officer with the NYPD. "What does that have to do with any of this?"

"So you're refusing to answer the question?"

"Do I need a lawyer?"

Murphy smiled nicely. "Do you?"

For the first time, I felt real concern. "What happened that night is also a matter of public record. You can read all about it online and in old newspapers."

"I did," said Murphy. "But I'd like to hear your side of the story."

We locked eyes and I felt something move behind his. It felt like a snake uncoiling, getting ready to strike. "My partner Peter and I got a distress call. We investigated. Peter was murdered. The end."

"By occultist." Again, he glanced over at his partner, then back at me. "It's interesting, isn't it? You always seem to wind up in the middle of a fray. People die around you in interesting ways, Mr. Englebrecht. It's as if trouble follows you around."

"Doesn't he speak?" I asked Murphy, jabbing my thumb at his partner. "Or is he just your little sockpuppet?" I glanced over at the big blond guy. "You got a voice, Ahnie?"

"Answer the question, Mr. Englebrecht."

I looked back at Murphy. The thing that was bothering me about him intensified. I was suddenly feeling very belligerent toward him—and I mean way beyond the annoyance of answering an arrogant suit's ten-year-old questions about my failed police career. He seemed...familiar. Not in the sense that we had met before, but in that I knew his type—his *kind*.

It hit me hard, then. A sudden realization. Before I could even think about it, it popped right out of my mouth. "Fuck me. You're Arcana."

For the first time since we'd met, Murphy's smiley "good cop" look vanished and was replaced by good old-fashioned agitation. He stood up suddenly and I knew then I was right. He was trying to hide it from me, and he had almost succeeded, but I could sense Arcana sliminess sweating off of him.

Arcana. The ancient cult that had infiltrated every part of human civilization. Religion. Politics. The police force. The White House. I'd gotten up close and personal with one of their kind in Lancaster while I was investigating the Old Order Amish community that had come under siege by the god Cernunnos. The Arcana leader there, John Knapp, had tried to make a big ol' rare hamburger out of me because the Arcana had this annoying habit of eating angels to absorb their power.

I knew I was right. I glanced over at Ahnie and said, "Do you know your partner here is part of an ancient cult dedicated to cannibalizing people because they think they can absorb their magical powers? Yeah, you might want to watch your back around him. Don't invite him to your house for barbecues anymore..."

"That's enough, Englebrecht," Murphy said, interrupting me. Now he sounded truly angry. "I'm not the one being investigated for murder here..."

I slid sideways out of bed and pulled up the hospital gown so his partner could see the massive, ugly scar that ran along my upper thigh. It was pink and jagged against my skin like a shark had been at me—but the teeth marks were clearly human, not animal.

I saw Ahnie—or whatever his name was—flinch at the sight.

"Murphy's friend John Knapp got pretty enthusiastic toward the end. Started with a knife but ended up using his fucking teeth on me..."

"Ahnie" suddenly looked like he might toss his cookies.

"Knapp thought I was the Antichrist and tried to eat me alive, thinking he would absorb whatever power I had—"

Murphy suddenly decided it was a very good idea to cut this interview short. "We're done," he said, turning toward the door. "But I'm keeping my eye on you. Don't leave town, Englebrecht."

"I have no intention," I told him as I pulled the hospital johnny down to cover the scar. My shadow painted the wall beside Murphy, and it had wings. That drove him back a few extra steps. Evidently, he hadn't known what I was. Now, he did.

"You and I aren't finished," he said on leaving. "I may still have questions."

"Ah'll be back!" I shouted after him.

* * *

Fuck.

The Arcana.

Fuck fuck fuck fuckity *fuck*!

I had more than enough to deal with at the moment without worrying about those clowns, I thought as I dressed in my street clothes. The doctor had finally been in to discharge me. He was frankly at a loss to explain how I was looking so good and talking up a storm, but since my injury didn't seem nearly as bad as everyone thought it was—certainly not bad enough to keep me overnight—they let me go.

I threw my bag into the back of the rental and got into the passenger seat. Sada was in the driver's seat.

She looked over, ever concerned. "I sensed a disturbance—"

"In the Force? Yeah. The Arcana," I answered grumpily. I leaned against the headrest, one eye open, one closed, because I had this throbbing headache behind my eyes that wouldn't give up. I needed some food and some rest, then I'd figure all this out. "I'll get to them eventually. But first, we gotta get to the bottom of these *Substitutes*."

She thought about that for a long moment. "The creature that attacked you?"

"Yeah." I turned my head and gave her my one-eyed, squinty look. "I'm pretty certain they're trying to kill me. I just don't understand why."

| 20 |

The Children of Endor

THE SOUND OF quickly approaching footsteps woke me from a sound sleep.

I opened my eyes, looked around, and almost forgot where I was. The master bedroom of the old Victorian the Satanists owned. Yeah. That was right. The paper on the wall was red and gold damask and the bed was a four-poster monstrosity with red satin sheets and a white fur comforter and veils. There were pictures of Victorian erotica on the walls and a closet full of fancy suits and black leather BDSM gear (which I noticed while looking for a change of clothes I never found). It was like staying in the master bedroom of the Marquis de Sade.

I sat up in bed as Sada walked in, her high heels clicking on the polished cedar floorboards. She was dressed in a simple button-down shirt knotted at her waist and jean shorty shorts with a white chef's apron tied over it. It was hot in the house even with the high-end A/C unit on full blast and she had ditched the long sundresses. Well, it was either the heat or she thought I would find this look more alluring.

She looked worried.

"What's wrong?" I said, digging the crusty stuff out of the corners of my eyes. I'd slept hard, but not long. Maybe a few hours, at most. I still felt like a zombie, and though all my injuries had healed, I felt wrung out, physically and emotionally.

"I tried to make dinner," she said, biting her lip. I noted the tone of her voice was better suited to telling long, epic tales of lost romance and tragic death. "But...it didn't go well."

"No big deal."

"But you must be hungry."

"We'll order a pizza."

She smiled as if that was the best suggestion she'd ever heard. Not for the first time, I got the sharp feeling that this was very much her first rodeo. Despite her age—early twenties, I'd say—she seemed painfully young and almost...innocent. I wondered if she'd ever really been away from the coven for any significant amount of time.

Before she turned to leave me, I said, "Sada?"

"Yes, Nick." She turned about-face, soldier-straight, to smile at me.

"How old are you?"

"Twenty-nine."

That surprised me. She seemed much younger than that.

"And how long have you been with the Children of Endor?"

She looked confused as if she couldn't understand why I would ask her anything so personal. "I...was born into them."

"To one of the girls there," I guessed. "One of the Satanists."

"Yes," she said as she turned to go order the pizza, her cell phone in hand. "Juliette is my mother."

***

The pizza had arrived by the time I dragged my sorry, tired ass downstairs.

Sada had set the table with nice linens and white and red candles. She had set a wreath of wildflowers around some floating candles as the centerpiece. It was almost poignantly romantic—though a scent of burned pasta did manage to waft out of the kitchen, something ruining the overall effect. She seemed happy again as she served me a slice of meat lover's pizza on a delicate bone china plate that felt as if it had been warmed in the oven.

"You don't have to go to all this trouble," I told her. "I usually just eat it out of the box."

She laughed as though she found that hilarious. "But I want to, Nick. I want you to be pleased with me."

I took her wrist and she stopped and seemed to wait. "You are absolutely pleasing, Sada."

To my surprise, she didn't smile as I had anticipated. Instead, she stopped laughing and only looked troubled, a small crease marring the space behind her amazing golden eyes. "But you don't want me. I'm not...beautiful enough to be your bride. Not like the others."

Things started coming together in my head, and my heart suddenly ached for her. I didn't know how to explain this. "That's not true, Sada. You are one of the most exquisite women I've ever met..."

I didn't know how to continue. I didn't know how to explain that I didn't like the fact that Juliette had pimped her daughter out to me to be one of my "brides." But now that I knew...well, absolutely nothing was going to happen between us. Not now. Not later.

I stood up. "Come with me," I said.

I scooped up the box of pizza, took her head, and led her out onto the back patio and toward the beautifully restored vintage wartime porch swing. It was painted white, with soft red velvet cushions. A bug zapper hung on a post nearby, air-frying moths and the swarms of mosquitoes that inevitably got too close. Out here, amidst the hot twittering night and almost full moon, we settled on the swing and together devoured the pizza. We were silent for a long time as we listened to a bullfrog calling.

Sensing my thoughts despite my best efforts to hide them, Sada finally said, "I wanted to come, Nick. I wanted to do this. I even asked Mother."

"And she approved?"

She put a hand on my knee. Not sensual but comforting. "Except for college, I haven't spent any time away from the coven. It's been my whole life. So we both agreed it was a good idea. You needed the protection, and I needed...I *wanted* to do something for the Children of Endor. Show them what I can really do."

Sada fell silent a moment and I wiped at a tear in the corner of her eye. "And..." She hesitated a moment before continuing. "...Mother said I could trust you. That you would also protect me. She wouldn't have let me go otherwise."

"She trusts me that much?"

"Mother says you're a good man," Sada said with complete conviction.

Part of me wanted to laugh at that, given the ludicrous nature of the situation, but the sound of breaking branches out in the woods behind the house made us both sit up straighter. I felt my whole body tense up and a hand went for my boot—then I remembered that my athame was currently in an evidence locker with the FBI. That sucked major balls. If I needed to tangle with another of those Substitutes, things would not go well.

But then a fat, scruffy raccoon popped into the halo of yellow light cast by the bug zapper and waggled his way toward us.

We both relaxed...and Sada laughed. I threw the raccoon some pizza crusts and said, "We need to secure the house against those things. *And* the Arcana, now that I know they're in town."

"I could do a spell," Sada suggested. "I could ward the house. That would stop the Substitutes, at least."

"But not the Arcana," I pointed out.

Wards only worked on Otherkin. To keep an Arcana out would require that the creature be more angel than human—and I didn't feel that Murphy was quite there yet. I thought about the bastard and his friends driving up here in the middle of the night, breaking in so he could make a dinner out of *moi*. It was not a comforting thought.

"I'm not sure," Sada admitted. She stared at her fingers, at the runes on her long, metallic gold nails. "I might not be able to keep one out physically, but I could probably do a spell that would cause it a lot of pain."

Yet again, Sada had amazed me. This was a kind of craft that was a little beyond my level of expertise. I only knew how to do warding with little charms—kind of a haphazard system, frankly. Unfortunately, to do *any* kind of serious warding would require an athame—preferably one bathed in angels' blood.

I asked her if she had one, and she held up her long nails. "These work the same."

"But are they bathed in angels' blood?"

Her shoulders slumped. "No."

Mine was—but mine was currently with Agent Kippy.

I stood up. "Road trip. Go get Tiger and meet me back here. Ten minutes."

That made her brighten considerably. "We're going with you?"

"Well, I'm not leaving either one of you behind."

| 21 |

The Queen of Tarts

AS WELL AS checking out that boyfriend of Vivian's, I'd also been kind of Facebook-stalking him. I wasn't proud of that, I did learn that that rich schmuck Mike Bartholdi had bought and renovated The Loop in East Stroudsburg a couple of years ago.

The history of The Loop was shrouded in mystery, booze, and rap sheets. During the Nineties—before my return to Blackwater—it was a black-lighted haven for aging punk Gen-Xers, and one of the bigger outlets for the local drug handlers to peddle their wares. Club drugs and pansy wine coolers were the in thing. The Loop sold a lot of Zima and ecstasy—sometimes together. A lot of kids OD-ed. Police were called in on a nightly basis, yada yada.

It changed hands at the turn of the century, flopped, and then shut down for about ten years. The Fairy King had snatched it up on the cheap and re-opened it as a crunchy-granola-hipster juice bar to service kids who wanted to drink mocktails and listen to terrible local talent and pretend they liked it. It was only barely squeaking by, not really turning a profit because, hey, this was East Stroudsburg, which is only a little larger than nearby Blackwater, and we're not exactly bursting with crazy ravers here in the mountains.

Then two years ago, that changed. Bartholdi again renovated the dump, The Loop got its black lights back, and they started selling fancy shmancy club drinks with names like Absinthe Friend, Blood of Dracula, Barbed Wire, and the Virgin's Cherry—all of which were just glorified wine coolers with a lot of food coloring in them.

The Loop had come...full loop. Except that now, Vivian was involved. Partial owner, as I understood it. She and the Fairy King were running a gothic nightclub in the mountains. It was so cute. Not.

The old, decrepit brick building squatted in the very center of the sad, forgotten urban disaster zone that was essentially our local answer to Black Harlem. Well, just not that nice. Not that well kept or celebrated. And not really that Black.

This being the weekend, there were a lot of out-of-towners lurking around. I told Sada to lock the rental tight and stick close to me as we crossed the big, crumbling parking lot behind the club.

Sada, holding Tiger's leash, followed me toward the employees' entrance behind the club, where the big blue Dumpster lived. I'd been here once before when I first learned that Vivian was working nights. This was only a short time after we'd broken up. I'd bought her flowers and gone in the back door, ready to apologize and try and make amends. I wanted to be—not her lover, of course, but her friend. But after crossing the narrow, dingy hallway that connected the storage room to the kitchen area, I'd changed my mind. I'd caught a glimpse of Vivian unpacking wine coolers and chatting with another employee. She looked...happy. Frankly, happier than she'd ever looked with me. And it was then I knew I had to let her go.

"You can't let that dog in here," a server said after the pneumatic door thumped closed behind us.

"He's a service dog," I pointed out. I'd taken the time to put Tiger's blue work apron on that said as much.

The server looked divided, so Sada reached out, all too casually, and touched his forehead with just the tips of her gold-painted fingers. "There is no dog," she said, and the server suddenly blanked out and looked confused, his brow wrinkling as if he had lost his train of thought before moving on.

"Neat trick," I said.

Sada shrugged, her beautiful white Grecian dress rippling sensuously. "Glamour is very useful."

This was the first time I was seeing the main floor. The cathedral-sized space had been polished and refurbished. The walls and ceiling were paved in reflective pink and purple bricks or covered in neon glyphs, and there were posh seating arrangements around the outer edges of the dance floor, table seating along the catwalks, and a DJ in bondage gear spinning remixed trance and darkwave beats in the loft. A sea of bodies in shiny black fetwear writhed along with the lighted motion-detection panels that covered the floor. Strobe lights flickered across the club, picking out the big, glossy horror movie posters on the walls or the giant glass chandeliers hanging from the ceiling. A glass-topped bar ran the length of the club, though I noted Vivian wasn't the bartender on duty.

Clubbers checked us out as we passed. Sada grabbed my arm. I looked over and saw she was practically transfixed by the sight of the place. Surprise, horror, or fascination, I couldn't tell you.

As was typical of my situation these days, several of the dancers abandoned what they were doing to follow behind us a few steps. They seemed unperturbed by the fact that Sada and I were a little too old to be hanging out with this crowd—or the fact I was standing here in ragged, unwashed jeans and a dull black T-shirt with SORRY I'M LATE I DIDN'T WANT TO COME printed on it. I'd gotten the shirt at the Dollar General since I refused to wear the suits hanging in the closet in my room in the Victorian. Many belonged to my dad, Sada had informed me. Reason enough not to wear them.

When I felt that familiar twinge in my witch's mark, I turned my head and spotted the subject of my visit as she passed through a curtain of chains separating the main floor from another hallway on the opposite side of the room. Vivian was dressed in another one of her little club dresses—a shiny black number with buckles down the front and over-the-knee hooker boots with corset backs. She wore her athame in a garter holster—entirely visible and now part of her outfit, though I'm sure everyone here assumed it was a prop. Her long, rusty-red hair hung loosely down to mid-back and the subtle backlights of the club made it look like her entire head was on fire.

She looked at me and frowned.

I swore under my breath. "Here we go."

Sada's grip on my arm intensified.

"What are you doing here?" Vivian said when she had reached us. She was uncharacteristically reserved, making it sound almost chummy, though her eyes kept shifting toward Sada, who looked scared half to death. She was still pissed with me but trying not to make a scene of it.

"I have to ask a favor of you. It's important." We had to shout to be heard over the DJ. "Can we go somewhere private? It won't take long."

Vivian was now staring directly at Sada. I could tell she knew something was up with my companion. Witch radar—if you will. "You. But not her."

Sada seemed to crumple inward at her dismissal.

Tossing her hair, Vivian gave me a cold, direct look before turning on her heel and stomping back across the floor and through the curtain of chains.

I put a hand on Sada's, trying not to spit nails. Naturally, I didn't like the idea of leaving Sada on her own, but she surprised me by saying, "It's all right, Nick. I make her uncomfortable."

"I don't care. You're coming with me."

She pulled her hand away. "Don't, Nick. We need that athame."

I turned and took her by the hands. At some point, I had become extremely protective of her. Not in a girlfriend-type way, but like she was a naivete child in need of my guidance. "Sada—"

"No. It's all right," she assured me with a sad little smile. "I'd...I'd like to be on my own for a little while anyway. I've never been in a place like this before." She nodded toward Tiger, who seemed to be checking out a hot girl in pink spandex stalking past us. "And I have a demon. I'll be fine!"

* * *

Vivian led me into her private office. It was small, about the size of a glorified broom closet, but soundproofed. It sported a desk and two filing cabinets to either side—all the furniture that would fit. No windows. A battered-looking spider plant sat atop one cabinet. It looked in dire need of watering.

I felt a wave of relief when she closed the door and turned to face me. I could finally stop playing nice.

"Who is she?" Vivian asked, cutting right to the chase.

That bolstered my mood. It amused me that she would ask. It helped my badly wilted ego to know she was concerned. "Her name is Sada."

"Sada what?"

"Just Sada."

"What is that, her pop music name? She's a witch."

"Astute."

She folded her arms across her ample bosom, obviously not amused. "But that's not *all* she is."

By now, I had begun moving restlessly around her tiny office, picking at random things like the stack of forms on the chair behind her desk and the droopy-looking plant. Annoyingly enough, the whole office smelled of her perfume. Viva la Juicy. That was what she wore.

I really didn't want to be here. "She's also a Satanist."

"Witches don't believe in Satan."

I turned and offered my hands. "And yet...?"

She sliced the air, cutting me off. "Why are you here, Nick? What do you need?"

Telling the whole sordid tale was going to take too long. But I needed to trust she would believe me. "It's the Arcana," I explained. "They're in town, and I need to borrow that athame I gave you for Yule. Just for a few days."

That unbalanced her. "Arcana?"

Suddenly, she was a lot less angry with me and far more concerned in general. That incident at the Amish community with the Arcana who wanted to make a juicy cheeseburger out of ol' Nick? Vivian had been there. She'd seen. And if she hadn't saved my bacon, we wouldn't be having this conversation right now. "They're here? In Blackwater?"

"Afraid so. And there's this big galoot who has it out for me. I need your athame for a warding spell."

"What happened to yours?"

I didn't want to get into the story of the Substitutes. "It's...let's just say it's out of commission at the moment."

She was giving me some serious side-eye. I could tell she believed me, but she sensed I wasn't giving her the whole story. The curse of the witch's marks. "So what does Beyoncé out there have to do with the Arcana?"

I shrugged and stuck my hands in my jeans pocket. "She's my protector until all this blows over..."

She gave me a *yeah sure* look. "Didn't let any grass grow under your feet, huh, Nick?"

"We're not involved," I told her, and, for once, I was telling the absolute truth.

"Do you have a witch's dating app on your phone? Swipe left for Satanists...?"

I cut her off. "Mike Bartholdi. Hello? Pot, meet kettle."

"Oberon isn't a witch," she said, stepping up to look me in the eye. Her voice was rising in octaves and the air suddenly smelled like a summer storm as the lightning gathered.

I took a step back. Long ago, in a galaxy far, far away, an angry young Vivian made her cheating boyfriend burn at approximately the temperature of burning jet fuel. I wasn't about to push *that* button. Instead, I took a deep breath and tried logic instead of emotion, which was hard where we were concerned. Vivian and I had always been all about passion, even when we hated each other.

"You being a witch makes you infinitely more dangerous to him than I am to Sada. You know this, Vivian."

That made her stutter on a response. "I wouldn't hurt Oberon."

"His name is Mike Bartholdi, Viv. He's the son of a mobster from New York City. And he has no business getting involved in all of our witch shit."

I recognized she was about to say, *You've been checking him out?* But I didn't let her continue. Instead, I advanced on her, which caused her to step back, her butt hitting the edge of the desk. "I taught you, Vivian. You know better!"

Vivian folded her arms and glared hatefully at me, but there were tears in her eyes.

Now I felt like crap, like some creep who had stepped on a puppy.

"I was lonely," she finally said. "Sue me."

"Dump him before he gets hurt."

"It isn't fair, Nick!"

"It isn't fair. It is lonely!" I shouted back. "Get over it!"

She turned around and bowed her head so I wouldn't see her crying.

I looked around the office and spread my hands. "What happened to you, Viv? You were graduating. You were going to go into business with that friend of yours. Queen of Tarts. What happened to *that*?"

When we were together, we didn't always talk about witch stuff. We also talked a lot about Vivian's dream of opening a bakery and catering business. She'd had the degree, the smarts. She even had a business plan. Queen of Tarts. That's what she'd planned on calling it, and she used to laugh that it would be the first bakery that Blackwater had had in decades. One night, we went to peek into an abandoned Polish deli at the corner of Main Street. Vivian said if she could only get the venture capital, she'd have the Queen of Tarts up and running within a year.

She stared at the floor between her feet, refusing to look at me.

"Vivian…"

"You happened!" She turned. I saw—not tears of pain, I realized. But tears of anger. "*You* happened to me."

"What do you mean?"

"Do you have any idea what you did to me, Nick?" She took an unsteady step toward me, making me back up his time in this crazy, embittered dance of death. "Before I met you, I had everything going pretty well—a shitty day job, sure, but at least I was headed in the right direction. I was getting there, slowly. Then you trained me...but you also *changed* me."

She had me up against the wall. She looked up at me, her tear-stained face contorted with rage. "You never told me I couldn't bake!"

"I don't understand," I told her honestly.

She gestured wildly at everything and nothing. "You never told me that witches can't make cakes rise. Did you know that? It's how villages in the Middle Ages determined there was a witch among them. The cakes and breads wouldn't rise. And, sure, most superstitions are total shit, but not *that one*." She stopped and sniffed, her hands clenching and unclenching at her sides. "So before you ask me what I did to *myself*, why don't you ask yourself what you did to *me*?"

I hung against the wall, kind of stunned.

In all my days, I'd never dreamed of this scenario. Sure, I'd dreamed of us screaming at each other, accusing each other. I'd dreamed of us fighting and never talking to each other again. I'd even dreamed of us making up. But this...this, I was unprepared for.

I tried to say something, but nothing made sense.

She must have seen something in my face, because, slowly, the lightning cleared from her bright, sea-green eyes. "You didn't know, did you?"

"About this?" I said, appalled. "No one ever told me about this. Do you think I'd set out to sabotage you, Viv?" I had to swallow and find the right words. "I taught you magic to *protect* you. I didn't know..."

I couldn't do this anymore. Fuck the athame. I turned to leave, but I felt her hand on my shoulder. Her touch sparked all along my back as if she were setting my skin on fire—which she could do, by the way. I turned back around, my back to the door, and saw the anger and the pain draining from her face, replaced by something far more familiar to me.

"You really didn't know?"

"I swear on my life, Vivian," I whispered. "I didn't know."

Her hand bunched in the wrinkles in my shirt, spreading a warmth out from her fingers. "God damn you, Nick," she said and pulled down so we were at eye level and she could kiss me. I sighed at the familiar taste of her lips, the scent that was her—bitter and sweet. She tasted like ozone. Like burning. Like magic. I slid one hand along the curve of her hip, gripping her tightly through the kinky little dress as her kiss intensified and she first nibbled and then bit my bottom lip. Hard.

She moaned against my mouth and her hands moved down my back to my ass. It ignited my lust in a way nothing else could.

Her other hand wrested my jeans open and slid inside. Christ. I growled in response and slid my hand beneath the hem of her dress, finding to my extreme delight that she wasn't wearing any underthings. She began rolling her hips in response to my touch.

This was wrong. So very, very wrong. But my concerns and all my worldly worries were quickly swept away by the tide of my desire for this woman. We were the same. We were mates. We were one.

She clawed at my jeans—no sweet, passive damsel was Vivian Summers. During our time together, she used to ride me like a trick pony rider. Our mouths clung in a kiss as she writhed against me while simultaneously ripping my pants open. Pressure within me built and built and, soon enough, I cupped her bottom so she had the leverage to impale herself upon me.

I didn't fuck her so much as I was fucked *by her*. My shoulders hit the door in a series of harsh thuds that rattled my bones with their intensity. Vivian's luscious mouth was contorted into a passionate snarl and her eyes looked black and wild and inhuman—no better than mine, I suppose.

"Show me," she growled through her teeth suddenly gone a hair too sharp behind her red, red lips. "Show me, Nick."

I knew what she wanted. I let myself go.

My wings slashed outward, knocking the dead plant off her filing cabinet. She didn't care. I knew the sight of those damned wings turned her on as nothing else could. With a cry, she wrapped her legs tightly around my waist, pinning me in place so she could take total control of me.

She bucked against me, each thrust pushing my back up the wall and making me gasp with the sheer power and ferocity of her rutting. I rolled my head back and my mouth yawned open, my tongue dancing over the horrid, hook-like angel teeth in my mouth. She was my demon lover, my succubus, my bride, my one true heart...

I didn't mind being her sex toy. She used me roughly. It was fucking heaven. Everything I wanted. Everything I needed. Her eyes shone with love and lust and anger as she pounded us both to climax. Breathing roughly and kissing hungrily, our fanged eyeteeth clicked together.

| 22 |

Hocus Pocus

SADA WAS UNUSUALLY quiet on the trip back to the house. I'd expected anger, tears, accusations—surely she knew what had happened behind that closed door. I mean, she seemed informed of everything else about me. But she barely looked at me.

"Did you enjoy yourself?" I asked to break the claustrophobic silence hanging between us.

Sada glanced up from her fingernails and said, "Yes. I talked to one of the bartenders."

I thought back to last night. I'd left her at the bar in the company of a woman I knew. Kara. One of David's friends from college. A stunning Asian witch with red streaks in her black bob of hair. I'd partied with her once, along with David, Vivian, and David's roommate. Good times. But, more importantly, I trusted Kara to be nice to Sada.

I waited for Sada to elaborate. She didn't.

"So, did you get Kara's number?" I asked and Sada's head bounced up. She had underestimated my powers of observation.

"No."

"Why?"

Sada shrugged.

"Because she's a woman?"

She didn't answer, so I turned back toward the road. "Your mom wouldn't approve."

"She's not like that," Sada snapped, getting defensive. "We believe love is love."

Sada went back to studying her fingernails.

"Ah. It's because she's Wiccan."

"I don't want to talk about it, Nick."

"Fair enough."

Back at the house, I started the workings of a circle. Sada helped by undressing and calling the four corners. Once finished, she moved to the center of the circle where I stood with the unsheathed athame that Vivian had let me borrow. There, she knelt and began praying in Angel-speak. That warm, good feeling began surging somewhere under my breastbone. I lifted the athame and started working the spell while Sada fed me her loyalty, her love, and her worship.

The athame began to glow faintly. I could feel my power extending outward as if I were holding a lightning rod full of unspent power. My magic touched all the walls, windows, and doors in the house, making them impregnable to even our strongest enemies. The power crawled the walls like small, branch-like cracks full of black light. My father's light is bright, blinding white, but mine—perhaps because my blood isn't as pure—is darker, more muted. I saw the dark light flicker and fork up the damask wallpaper and around the doorway and windows, warding the entire house.

This was powerful stuff, even by daemon standards. Part of it was Sada's worship, of course, but I knew that another part was the sex I had shared with Vivian. Vivian's power was elemental and sexual. I had absorbed it during our coupling like a second-rate incubus. According to Sada, sex acted as a battery for me.

There was a terrific buildup of raw, sexual power in the house. I felt the itch of it along my skin and knew there would be no rest for me tonight. I'd definitely be abusing the ol' witch stick. One of the mirrors in the hallway cracked. Sada threw her head back and touched herself. But I knew she was thinking of Kara, not me. I was okay with that.

The light grew brighter, almost blindingly so, before flickering out, leaving behind the vague aroma of burned sugar.

It was done. The house was warded like a motherfucker. Anything supernatural that dared enter this dwelling without my permission did so at its own peril.

* * *

After all that, I was pretty zonked. It took Sada coming into my bedroom and shaking me out of a sound sleep before I heard the persistent knocking at the front door.

She was standing over me, dressed in a robe she had clutched at the throat. Despite the warding and its protections, she looked worried. "You don't think it's them?" she whispered, and I knew what she meant.

Arcana.

I sat up and threw back the covers, then realized I was pretty naked under there and pulled the covers back up nicely, but not before Sada noticed. "Somehow, I don't think they'd knock politely on the front door," I said, thumbing the corner of my eye. "But don't answer it to be on the safe side. I'll be down in a minute."

Sada nodded and left the room so I could quickly throw on last night's clothes.

Downstairs, I drew the athame—because, hey, it's still a knife, and the only weapon I had—and moved closer to the front door.

The knocking was fierce and insistent—banging now. I felt my heart jump with each impact.

Standing on the stairs, Sada gave me a worried look. There were long windows on both sides of the front door, but the glass was frosted, preventing me from seeing more than vague movements, and there wasn't a peephole to be found, which disappointed me bitterly.

I put my finger to my lips and she nodded. Without saying a word or giving away my location, I slowly undid the chain lock and grasped the doorknob.

Squeezing the hilt of the athame to reassure my grip on it, I pulled the door open an inch. A man immediately wrapped his fingers around the edge of the door and tried to force it the rest of the way open.

I stopped the door's progress with my foot and swung around to face our visitor head on, the athame up and ready to be plunged into his throat if I didn't like his face.

"Nick!"

I felt a wash of relief at the sound of the voice and quickly lowered my arm, tucking the blade away safely in the back pocket of my jeans. "Josh," I said, modulating my voice so I didn't sound like I was about to put a knife through my ex-girlfriend's brother's face. "You're back."

"Yeah. It was a short trip," he said, sliding off his travel shades. There was an edge to his voice. "Mind if I come in?"

"Sure. Of course."

As he stepped into the foyer, he lifted his head slightly and focused his attention on Sada. He could smell her perfume, I suppose. "Sorry if I'm interrupting anything. Didn't mean to. I went to see Viv and she gave me this address." He then turned his head to me and said with a smile, "What are you doing way up here in Pooh-pooh Land?"

Pooh-pooh Land was the (admittedly juvenile) slang we townies use for the pricey, modern lake houses surrounding Lake Ariel. They're mostly owned by Wall Street gurus who came up here on the weekends to play golf, pretend hunt, and hone their silly zombie survival skills. "It's...a long story."

"Make yourself at home," I told Josh, meaning it. "I'll go put coffee on and we can talk about what you're doing back so early."

Sada already had the kettle on for tea. I fiddled with the fancy electronic Mr. Coffee machine until I got it to start squirting out the black gold Josh liked. By then, he'd taken a seat at the island in the kitchen and sat hunched over.

He looked haggard and exhausted. "Where's Tiger? He usually can't wait to see me."

Oh, no. I wasn't sure how to explain that. The last time I'd seen Tiger, he was in his room upstairs, stretched out on the cot bed, paging through a Playboy magazine. Given this was the second time Tiger was indulging his baser interests—the first time being last night when he insisted on following girls around The Loop and sticking his head up their skirts—I was starting to fear that what was inside him might be some kind of incubus. At the very least, a pervy demon.

"He's sleeping, I think," I said.

"He's not sick?" said Josh, concerned. "You didn't feed him something weird?"

I put a mug of coffee down in front of him. "I think he's just tired from all the dog things we've been doing. I've kept him busy."

Josh, caught up in the web of his own concerns, seemed convinced as he stared down into the dark depths of the coffee mug.

"So what happened to the surgery?" I asked. I leaned my butt against the kitchen counters. "Maybe I can help."

Sada had fetched me a mug for my coffee. I smiled a thanks to her.

It took Josh a long moment to align his thoughts. When he finally looked up, I felt my heart jump a little. He really was a cute guy. Who was I kidding? He was sexy as hell. Charming and adorable in that tired little boy way, but still masculine as hell.

He shook his head. "You can't help, Nick. I just...I didn't qualify for the program."

I felt a spike of outrage. "How could you not?"

He raised his hands helplessly. "They said it wasn't a life-saving medical procedure in my case. In other words, I'm doing just fine without my sight, so fuck off."

I could hear the anger in his voice. I could feel it. The house was probably concentrating it, the way it had concentrated my sexual energy last night.

"American healthcare," Josh murmured as he raised his mug in salute. "Ain't it grand?"

"But you're a vet. You're entitled." I let out my breath, which was steaming a little. I was getting too angry and told myself to calm the hell down. "So they had you fly all the way out to L.A. to tell you what they could have said over a phone?"

He shrugged. "It wasn't a complete loss. I got to see some old friends in the L.A. music scene. They introduced me to this club owner." Josh sat up and his voice lifted just a little. "He asked me to put a tune together and said he liked my singing, said I could have a permanent gig, so...maybe that's the window opening when God slams the fucking door in your face, eh?"

"But in L.A."

He made a vague gesture. "Not like I got a life here, man. I mean, I'm practically livin' out of my car, as it is."

I sipped my tea. "You're not staying with Vivian?"

He wrinkled his nose. "She offered, but *he* kept dropping by. Odin or whatever the hell his name is..."

"Oberon," I offered.

"Yeah, him. And he's a creep. Can't explain it."

I set the mug down. It took me only a moment to decide. "Stay here with me."

I cringed. Like that didn't sound creepy. "I mean, crash in one of our many bedrooms upstairs until you figure out what to do," I said, trying to make it sound funny as if he'd won a prize on a game show.

Josh frowned "Is this your place?"

"It's Sada's…family." I almost said *coven* but changed it at the last minute.

"I don't know, man. I don't like crashing pads when there's a couple involved. Third wheel and all—"

"Sada isn't my girlfriend. We're just friends." I had to think quickly. "She's my student in the…you know."

He nodded as he caught on. "The hocus pocus stuff."

That's what he called it. Hocus pocus. I never got the impression he believed in witchcraft, either mine or his sister's—and that was just fine with me. He didn't have to believe it because he wasn't part of this. I didn't want him to *ever* be a part of this. Friends don't let other friends get involved in the craft.

"Yeah, exactly," I told him. "You're welcome to stay here, Josh. I won't take no for an answer."

Maybe it was the spell and the atmosphere of the house making me all feely feel, but I wanted him to stay. Then again, it could just be my stupid libido. Wouldn't be the first time.

| 23 |

Lord of Hell

JOSH DECIDED TO stay "Just for one night."

I checked with Sada to make certain she was cool with that, but she was preoccupied with making dinner for her house guests and didn't seem to even hear my question. During Operation Spaghetti Dinner 2.0, she even managed to burn her hand while she was straining the pasta into a colander. I wound up fetching the first aid kit from the upstairs bathroom and carrying it to the kitchen counter so I could bandage her hand while she sat there patiently and looked miserable.

"Why don't you call her?" I said.

Sada's mouth wriggled. "She wouldn't want to talk to me. Wiccans don't believe in the Devil."

"So what? That doesn't mean you can't see her. I mean, you're not planning to debate theology with her." I smiled as I finished pinning her ace bandage into place. "Go call her. Now."

"All right. All right!" She grinned like a little girl as she bounced up and hurried up the stairs to her bedroom. I wondered if this was what it was like having a teenage girl around. Although, if I was, in fact, her father figure, I probably shouldn't be driving her into the arms of suitors, right?

I looked at the half-made meal she had prepared. Somehow, she had managed to decimate the kitchen with a bottle of Ragu and a box of Ronzoni. There was burned pasta sauce on the stove and congealing spaghetti filled the sink. I got the saucepot off the stove as quickly as possible before it set off the smoke alarm, but the reek of burned stuff was still filling the whole kitchen. I finally found something that resembled blackened garlic toast in the oven, got that out, and tossed it into the sink to join the alien mass of spaghetti.

Sighing, I cracked a window to air the kitchen out and went upstairs. No loss. I wasn't particularly hungry tonight, and tomorrow I had to do things that I wasn't looking forward to. I decided to call it a day, switched off the light, and collapsed onto the bed.

Maybe I got an hour of sleep. The music woke me.

"Now what?" I said to no one and got out of bed. I padded down the hallway in just my jeans, the gentle lilt of an expertly strummed guitar leading me on. When I reached Josh's room, I stopped.

He was sitting on the bed, playing chords of Led Zeppelin. But he stopped when he recognized I was standing there. "Sorry. Didn't mean to wake you."

"I wasn't sleeping well," I said, rubbing my eyes. Wasn't lying. When I did sleep, I usually had these weird David Lynch-inspired dreams that didn't make a whole hell of a lot of sense. It wasn't that they were nightmares, exactly, but I always seem to be working so damned hard in them—either trying to find someone or save someone. It was exhausting.

Josh's head turned toward the window. I'd heard it, too. A light tapping.

Somewhat concerned, I stepped into his room. I still had the athame in my back pocket from earlier that day. Liberating it, I crossed to the window. The house sat on a few acres of semi-cleared virgin forest. Oak and maple trees dotted the landscape, and wedged between them was a lot of untrimmed grass and some thorny bramble bushes. Tall hedges of forsythia and overgrown shrubbery bordered the backyard on one side, near where an abandoned, unpainted chicken coop squatted. The other side was made up of a neglected flower garden that had run wild, with a stone path that snaked through it to the fence on the edge of the property.

I watched a pine tree growing just outside the window sway in the light breeze of what felt like an oncoming storm, its needles ticking against the upper part of the open window. I breathed a sigh of relief and looked back at him.

Like me, he was shirtless on this sticky, humid night, dressed in just some carpenter pants that looked a little too large for him where he sat cross-legged on the bed. He had one of those deliciously whippy builds, and the sweat on his chest made his skin shine invitingly as he breathed deeply in and out. He was staring out the window, but he didn't seem to be breathing.

"Josh?"

He didn't answer. I went up to him and repeated his name while waving my hand in his face. I got the same vacant stare even though I was inches away.

"Josh. Joshua."

Nothing.

Maybe it was the house or the spell I'd cast. Maybe it was having some latent effect on him.

I certainly wasn't prepared for it when he reached up and laid a hand on my chest. I wished he hadn't done that, because the moment he touched me, I felt a spark skip across my skin and got some of the hardest wood ever. *That* monster had been getting me into more trouble than I was prepared to deal with at the moment, so I started withdrawing, but he moved his hands up to my face and slid the pads of his fingers around my neck. The guitar-callused tips rubbed deliciously at my muscles, making my skin hum and sending a delightful shiver down my back.

His lips were slightly parted as if he were trying to ask me a question. I honestly wasn't strong enough to resist them. I leaned down to slant my mouth across his. Kissing him was like heaven—or a nice, cozy place in Hell, at least. He tasted like whiskey and smokes and honey. Ah, damnit. Delicious.

Josh seemed to like it. I heard a sensual moan rise up in his throat. It was a siren call to me and, seconds later, I was on top of him in the bed, kissing and nuzzling the side of his neck, trying to pleasure him. Trying to make it good for him. I didn't feel the raw, violent lust I had for Vivian. With Josh, I wanted to go slow. Tease him. Make him shivery with desire. The delightful scratch of his beard made my blood sing, and my desire for him, for this beautiful man, vibrated inside me.

He grappled my jeans, trying to undo them, and even got the first button open.

God, how many times had I fantasized about this? Tasting him. Moving inside him like some slow dance.

I couldn't stop kissing him. I wanted to eat him whole. But when my wings came out while we continued to claw at each other, I knew something was very, very wrong. I wanted him too badly, with a sharpness that hurt to endure. I knew he felt the same, and it was making him frantic. The whole room was suddenly suffused with our lust...and that wasn't Josh. I knew Josh. Slow, cool Josh...

I pulled back. It was an effort because his hands were tangled in my jeans. I did want him. Just not like this.

"God, you're hot," Josh said, voice dreamy and slutty and definitely not-Josh. It sounded like someone was speaking *through* him, and that just raised more alarm bells. He arched his whole body up invitingly. "Fuck me, Nick. I want to feel that fat cock inside me."

I squeezed my eyes closed, my heart thudding in my ears. "Josh..."

"Fuck me. Just fuck me, my Lord! Like Vivian. Like David!"

Yeah. Okay. I managed to wrench myself free.

Josh suddenly convulsed as if he was suffering a seizure. The stench of magic surrounded him. Ozone and burned sugar. I grabbed Josh by the wrists, using my whole weight to hold him down, and calmly talked him down until he segued into a kind of half-sleep. His eyes fluttered and his head writhed on the pillows.

I checked his pulse. It was a little fast, but he seemed to be okay.

"Nick," he said a few moments later in his usual whiskey-burned voice. "Nick, wha—?"

I realized this looked a little weird, so I said, "I checked on you. You were having a bad nightmare. I had to stop you from hurting yourself." I climbed off him and quickly re-buttoning my jeans.

"Jesus Christ." He sat up and put his head in his hands. I knew he had bad PTSD dreams from his time in the military. "Didn't mean to wake you or nothin'."

"It's no problem. I was already up."

"Sorry..."

"Don't worry about it, man. Just go back to sleep."

Seething, I went downstairs and out the kitchen door and into the backyard. It was speckled with moonlight. The houses were spaced far apart here, and there were no lights except for some security strobes attached to the side of the house shining out into the road, so it was as black as an abyss at night, but I could just make out the even darker shape of the figure standing at the end of the property near the broken-down chicken coop. I was too angry to be afraid of it.

Marching barefoot down the garden path, I didn't even feel the sharp stones poking at the soles of my feet. "Motherfucker..." I whispered and stopped inches away from the property line. I spread my wings wide and looked at Dr. Theodore Lamb standing there with his arms clasped behind him, dressed in his long habit, smiling, and the light of the moon reflecting white in his small, square spectacles. He was observing the window of Josh's room, but after a few seconds of silence, he turned to look at me.

His smile never slipped and his eyes were all light and mischief.

"Fuck me, my Lord. Fuck me," he said in a high, singsongy voice. Despite the smile, there was no spot of malice in his whole countenance, though I did sense a drive in him. A kind of agenda. It infuriated me to no end that I *knew* he was evil, but I couldn't *feel* it. His power—his charisma—was too strong.

"He really does want you, you know," Lamb announced. He said it in a conspiratorial whisper as if we were two old chums gossiping at the bar. "I can feel it. *He* just can't see it." Lamb smiled with that boyish charm that was so infuriating to see. He chuckled. "Get it? Can't 'see it?' With Josh being blind and all?"

I didn't answer him.

He stopped chuckling but the wholesome, apple-cheeked smile remained. "You know, I didn't have to do a thing to him."

"You did something to him," I said, my voice so low it was barely human.

Lamb pinched two fingers together. "Just a little push."

I glanced around the backyard. "How can you compromise my wards?" I was genuinely interested in hearing his answer to that. "You should be in pain right about now."

"Your...wards?" He reached out to me, crossing the land's boundary. I immediately saw the tips of his fingers smoke. He jerked his hand back, tendrils of smoke drifting off his fingers, and looked at it with interest. "I...didn't know."

He looked up at me. "I don't know much about what I am," he confessed. "Bad childhood. Lots of foster homes. No one ever taught me the rules of the game."

I wish I could tell if it was genuine or not. Lamb was this huge enigma to me. I knew he was either fucking with me or he was genuinely so powerful that even my wards couldn't keep his influence completely out of the house.

You know what? I didn't fucking care. "Leave Josh alone. Leave all my friends alone. They're off-limits."

Lamb's smiley eyes glinted in the dark. Even now, he looked friendly and fatherly and helpful. Nothing to be concerned about. I was looking into the eyes of the Beast of Revelation, and I didn't feel even an iota of fear. There was something wrong with that.

"You want him," Lamb stated matter-of-factly. "I understand. He's very handsome. Very desirable. So why don't you take him? Force him?"

"The way you force people…Therion?"

That didn't even rattle him. "I don't force anyone, Officer Nick. I only let them be their true selves."

"Oh, fuck off, Lamb."

"But you want him. And you always get what you want."

His charisma wasn't affecting me at the moment. I think my wards were protecting me. But they couldn't seem to fully stop his charisma. Even now, I wanted to go back inside and up the stairs to Josh's room. I wanted to wake him up, kiss him, and have my way with him. I could do it, too, and make him forget later on. It would be as if it never happened. The desire was so powerful, I could taste it in the air.

Lamb just smiled on and on. It was probably his thoughts I was picking up on.

"No," I stated.

"Some lord of Hell you are—"

"What are you doing here, Lamb? What do you want from me?"

Lamb glanced around even though it was far too dark to see anything. "I was in the neighborhood. I wanted to stop by. I heard you just got back into town—"

"They warned me about you," I interrupted him. "The Satanists. They really got your number, Lamb."

He turned his head and looked at me. For the first time, I saw a crack in his mask—the annoyance on his face. "*They* are children playing games they have no control over."

"And yet..."

"You don't belong with them. You belong with me."

"Really," I laughed. This was getting interesting. Finally, I was digging through the many layers of the man's lies and subterfuge and craft and getting to the good parts. Something I could use.

Push his buttons, I thought. Push his fucking buttons.

"They tell me you beat children. Is that how you get yourself off, Lamb?"

He looked insulted at last. "I don't 'get off' in any such way."

"That's not a denial, you piece of shit."

"Oh, I'm not denying anything." He again looked harmless and beautiful and welcoming. I felt the intense need to cross the property boundary. I didn't. "I discipline my children where it is needed. And if that discipline is harsh, so be it. I'm a good disciplinarian."

"And you expect me to believe that."

"The humans need it. You know this. You were a police officer, Nick. You know how terrible they are. How...undeserving of forgiveness they are."

"You hit your children because you think they deserve it?"

His face was utterly blank and empty when he leaned close. He showed me his teeth. Hooked teeth. There they were—his angel teeth. "I hit them because they are bags of human shit and deserve to be treated as such."

I didn't even get a chance to open my mouth before he added, "You don't believe this because you are the Great Satan. Put upon the Earth by your God to maintain free will and balance. You bring the darkness because that is what the world needs. *They* need to respond to it."

Raising a finger, he added, "But make no mistake, Officer Nick, if they have the chance to crucify you, they will."

"Nice speech," I said. "Now get the fuck off my property."

Smiling again nicely, Lamb started toward his car, parked across the road.

He was halfway there before I called out, "Send any more of your Substitutes to kill me, and I'll fucking kill you first, Lamb."

Lamb stopped and turned around, stunned by my warning.

Finally, I had gotten to him.

Yeah, he thought I was stupid. Most people do. They think I'm some uneducated punk without two brain cells to rub together. That I can't put the pieces of a complicated puzzle together. And maybe that's the impression I give. I don't know. But I do know that people—and Otherkin like Lamb—chronically underestimate me. Call it my superpower.

"I know you sent them," I told him with a wry smile of my own. "I know you're working with the Thin Man. That you control him in some way. That's why you gave me your books. To suck me into this. To control me. And you shouldn't have done that, Lamb. You shouldn't have invoked me. You have no idea what I'm capable of when I'm good and pissed." I grinned and I think he shivered just a little. "But you will."

| 24 |

"They Disappear."

HONESTLY, I DIDN'T make the full connection until I saw Dr. Lamb at the property line. Sure, it ticked away in the back of my brain somewhere—the sudden attacks on my person coinciding rather wonderfully with meeting Lamb for the first time. It had seemed pretty random at the onset. But that's the power of glamour, you see—to make you see what you *want* to see. Randomness. Naturalness. *Safeness.*

When nothing was random, natural, or safe.

Well, the blinders were coming off, and it was all starting to come together. I'd thought the mine was the linchpin holding everything together. Now, I knew better. I wasn't sure how he had done it yet, but, somehow, Dr. Theo Lamb had harnessed the Thin Man like a beast of burden for his own dubious purposes. That was…impressive. Even as a daemon, he should not have been capable of such power. Being half-demon doesn't automatically make you Superman or Master of the Universe. It gives you an affinity for the craft, that's it. Maybe it gives you some weak-ass X-Men powers. But to control the Thin Man and his Substitutes?

Yeah, that's some impressive woo-woo, right there.

Unsurprisingly, I spent the rest of the night wide awake in bed, keeping vigil and reading through the books my enemy had provided. It was mostly the history of the Lucky 8 Mine, but it did mention the Thin Man, a "shadowy presence that reached through a wall and touched a miner's shoulder. When he turned around, he saw a thin, gaunt creature hanging upside down from the ceiling."

Sometime in the early hours of the morning, I closed all the books, lay against the headboard, and stared up at the ornate tin ceiling, contemplating my next move.

I wish I could talk to Morgana about these things. But that train of thought quickly took a turn off the mountain. Morgana loved an early morning romp. I never understood it, myself, and I had never really appreciated it until it wasn't there.

I missed her badly. Not just her wisdom, but her. And I missed David. Not just the sex, but the togetherness. The comfort of them. I didn't like the way I had left things between me and Morgana—and me and David. As I lay there, my mind bounced between my two brides (as Sada had called them), and I slowly realized something.

I wanted them both but for different reasons. Both filled something in me, something that had been lost—or something I'd never had in the first place—so choosing between them was impossible. Having them both? Yeah, that was impossible, too. David was willing to share, I knew, but with Morgana, it was all or nothing.

I reached over for my phone. But, coward that I was, instead of calling her, I texted: *I'm sorry. Can u try & forgive me 4 being an ass?*

It took a few minutes for her to text back. *I don't know Nick.*

Fair enough.

Can't handle this. You. Wearing me down.

I get it. I'm bad.

You're not bad.

Suck at boyfriending.

It took her a moment to respond. I entertained myself with the idea that she was, at least, chuckling over my message. But, in the end, she sent me a broken-hearted emoji. Didn't make me feel any better about being a shit.

I shouldn't have seen David. Was weak.

Another long pause. And then she texted something very surprising: *Do u need a guy?*

I frowned. *Not about that.*

Then what?

By now, my thumbs were getting sore from texting, so I decided to stop. It wasn't as if I had any answers for her anyway. *I'll take the store today. Let you go rest. Maybe talk later?*

A few tense seconds passed, and then a simple, noncommittal *OK* came through.

* * *

I left a note for Sada on the kitchen table explaining my sudden disappearance, then went out to the unattached garage, hoping to find a car or bicycle. Sada had taken the rental last night and wasn't home yet. I imagined she was still enjoying sexy time with Kara. And I only knew that because she'd texted me that she would be back late in the morning.

There was no car, but there was an old Schwinn bicycle with soft tires hanging on the wall.

I found a bicycle pump in a corner near a workbench and got the Schwinn in good working order. The ride from Pooh-Pooh Land to inner Blackwater didn't long—it was maybe four or five miles in total—but it was hilly and hot. Even a five-minute rain shower did nothing to alleviate the endless heat baking the highways and pebbly back roads.

Morgana hadn't opened the shop yet. I used my key and set things up for what I expected to be a long, hot, boring day. I'd brought one of Lamb's books along to read, but I finished it even before the first customer came in—a little old lady who planted herself in one of the back aisles so she could peruse the collection of how-to occult books we sold.

An idea struck me and I went over to the bookshelf. Sure, we had books on the Wiccan lifestyle, tarot reading, crystal healing, and spells, but we also had a bunch of books published by local, small-press publishers, mostly related to the folklore of the Pocono Mountains. Touristy stuff. I'd never really looked it over because I always figured it was bullshit, but now I wasn't so sure. And I was curious.

"That's a good one," the old lady said, pointing to the book in my hands. "I have that one at home."

I looked at it. It was a big, fat tome entitled *Ghost Stories of the Lehigh Valley*. While the customer continued to pick out her purchases, I went back to the front and started thumbing through the pages. I found a whole chapter on Knockers and Cousin Jacks—small, malformed people who supposedly lived in the mines, stealing food and tools from the miners. That was weird enough, but I found it even stranger to learn that in the olden days, some people had lived in the mines year-round—mostly those who were mentally ill, deformed in some way, or who worked as prostitutes, according to the book. I assumed these were the origins of the "haunted mines" legends that dotted these mountains.

"Are you reading about the mines?" the old lady asked as she brought her purchase up. Two books and an ornate Ouija board.

"Yes, ma'am," I said, ringing her up.

"They always been trouble, those mines," she told me with a frown. She had the broad, rugged Pennsylvanian accent of a lifetime townie. "Don't know why no high-fluent millionaire would wanna open them up. People keep dying down there like bugs."

"How so?"

"They disappear. I remember dis time in the seventies when it was last open. I was much younger—and handsomer!—and my friend Bettes went in on a dare to call on the Thin Man."

"You know about the Thin Man?"

"Everyone knows about the Thin Man." She patted her bright blue hair. "Or they used to. You go into Lucky No. 8 and do this little ceremony. Spin around three times and say:

"Hickory, dickery dare,
The Thin Man touched your hair,
Neither witch nor man can bring you back,
Hickory, dickery dare."

She followed it up with a string of foreign, Germanic-sounding words I couldn't follow. Maybe something from out of the traditional mountain hoodoo ceremonies that used to be so popular around here.

I found all this very interesting. "And kids back then used to do this?"

"All the time. Maybe they still do. I don't know."

"I thought people always came back. Isn't that the story?"

"They do, but it ain't them. Bettes wasn't Bettes ever again." She leaned in close, happy to share her wisdom. "That thing? It just looked like Bettes. But Bettes was deader'n toad in a road."

After she left, I kept thinking about the Thin Man and his Substitutes. Maybe somehow, the mine had become his point of origin in this world. His birthing spot. A thin spot that he—and Theo Lamb—were exploiting for their own purposes.

I'm not especially claustrophobic, but creeping around a closed-up mine was *not* my idea of an ideal afternoon. Small, closed-up space, with something malicious in it? Something that liked abducting humans and turning them into pod people? Something that had tried to kill me twice?

Yeah, fuck that noise. I wasn't taking the party to the Thin Man unless I had no choice.

* * *

Around noon, I closed up the shop and walked down the Strip to Mike's Pizza on the corner. In the blossoming noontime heat, I could already smell the fresh Stromboli coming out of the oven and my stomach growled in anticipation. As is typical of me, I had gotten so wrapped up in researching my enemies, I'd forgotten to eat anything today.

If my enemies wanted to kill me, they just needed to throw a puzzle at me. I'd starve myself to death while they stood there, chuckling their asses off.

A few minutes later, I was savagely attacking the broccoli and cheese Stromboli on my paper plate and watching the local news channel on the little TV in the corner above the sports bar. A pair of local drunks like to hang out here most of the day. They were like Miss Marple gossips, just with coveralls, baseball caps, and beer bellies.

The TV was down too low to hear, but as I watched, the broadcast cut from the studio to a country road maybe five miles west of here. Shelley Preston was talking into a microphone while a banner ran underneath her. *Kenny Johnson, suspect in the June 11 shooting of Holy Name escapes custody...*

Leaving the Stromboli behind, I got up and walked to the bar. I called over to the female barkeep, "Can you turn this up?"

The young, college-age blonde in Daisy Dukes smiled widely at me. "Sure thing, sugar." Grabbing the remote off the top of the coffee machine, she made Shelley's nasally and perpetually annoying voice boom through the bar area.

"...isn't known at this time, but police suspect he may have been just lucid enough to evade his captors." Shelley turned to indicate the road behind her. "To recap, Kenny Johnson was found staggering down this road this morning in a fugue state. Eyewitnesses have indicated that he seemed to be talking to himself. He was not armed. Once police officers arrived and examined the suspect, Kenny announced that he was on a mission, the nature of which is still under question."

My stomach bottomed out and I was suddenly no longer hungry. The Thin Man had gotten Kenny. And, yes, he was on a mission, and I knew exactly what that mission was.

He'd been sent to kill me. To shut me up before I told anyone about the Substitutes.

"Some shit," one of the old-timers bellowed into his beer. "Kid's probably a terrorist."

"Fucking millennials," another one said. "Can't trust 'em. They all liberals."

I turned to the two old drunks, trying to keep my temper in check. "Do you know where they took Kenny?"

"Hopefully out back to shoot 'im in the head like one of 'em sand niggers," one old bastard muttered his breath.

Deep breaths, Nick.

"Seriously," I said, trying to get them back on track. "Is he back in the county lockup or did they take him to a hospital?"

"Back to the hospital, she said earlier," Daisy Duke provided, pointing at the TV before moving to help a new customer.

Meanwhile, one of the drunks looked me up and down with his small, piggy eyes. He wore a bright red cap atop his tiny, bald pinhead and a white T-shirt under his plaid jacket. The T-shirt had a screaming bald eagle on it. "You that fag Satanist?"

The other chuckled at his friend's wit.

I'd had enough of these two. I scooted down low to look him in the rheumy eye. "Which fag Satanist would that be?"

"The one that runs that shop where my wife spends all my money." His tiny eyes narrowed further as if he was seeing me for the very first time. "Your kind needs to go back to the city where you belong."

"My kind," I said. I admit a part of me was intensely curious about this ongoing distaste for my presence in this town. My mother had been born and raised here. My family, the Wodehouses, had been a founding family. I had every right to be here, the same as every other townie. Maybe more so.

He dropped his voice to the smallest of whispers. *"Homosexuals."* He stretched the word out as if this was the first time he was saying it aloud.

I never blinked. "That's fine. I'm not a homosexual."

He subtly mimed flipping a light switch. I knew what he meant. "What's the word, Earl?"

Before Earl could help him out, I put in, "It's called None of Your Damn Business."

Fuming, the old-timer raised his hand to stick his finger in my face. "Look here, young man..."

I put my hand atop his. The rush of images only took a microsecond. I didn't turn it on; it just happened. As is typical of me, my mouth ran before my brain could catch up. "What those boys did to you wasn't right. And what happened after...the way your parents blamed you...called you a liar...that wasn't right, either, Francis.

But you have no right to take your anger out on anyone else. What happened isn't their fault. It isn't *my* fault."

The beer in Francis's other hand slipped through his fingers and exploded into shards on the floor.

I stood up—mechanically. A part of my mind was still with Francis and would be for hours afterward. It wasn't a good place to be and I hated this. Forgetting all about the Stromboli, I walked out of the shop.

| 25 |

Blackity-Black

I SHOULDN'T HAVE done that, I thought as I furiously biked out to Blue Ridge. Francis hadn't deserved the pass. But, honestly, I hadn't felt like I was in control—something to do with my talents as the new Lucifer, I think.

I'd always likened it to being a high-paid, swanky prosecution lawyer. Lucifer's job was to bring humans to justice and uncover the truth behind their lies and anger. A job I had to admit I was particularly suited for as an ex-cop. Not that that sat well with me, because it didn't.

Gritting my teeth, I skidded the bike to a halt in the Blue Ridge Hospital parking lot. I figured the hospital staff would in no way allow me to see the kid I had helped arrest, but it certainly couldn't hurt to try.

As I looked over the building, I realized I was growing *way* too familiar with this place, of late. Before I went in, I checked my phone for the hundredth time. A half an hour had passed since I'd left the shop. Morgana didn't like long absences, and I was already in the figurative doghouse, so I would need to make this quick.

I experienced my first wave of luck when I stepped into the lobby. The courtesy desk was empty with a *Be Back in Five Minutes* sign on it. I glanced around, noticed no security guards—honestly, security was pretty nonexistent at Blue Ridge, as we weren't exactly Newark, New Jersey—and slid behind the receptionist's computer. She'd left it unlocked—oh happy day. I got Kenny's room number and was across the floor and stepping into the elevator just as she wandered back to her computer.

Blue Ridge was relatively tiny, as hospitals went. Only twelve floors. It didn't even have visitation hours. You just came and went when you wanted, and the nurses left you alone, so long as you didn't make a nuisance of yourself. Still, there was no security in the corridor as I moved toward room 704—and *that* I found odd. Blackwater had a tiny police force—just Sheriff Ben and two deputies. But I'd anticipated that at least one of the deputies would have been put on Kenny's door. As it was, there was no one to stop me as I approached the door and knocked on it. This was almost too easy—and that made me nervous.

"Come in," said a male voice that was not Kenny's.

Inside the hospital room, I made the not-so-great realization that Special Agent Kip Murphy (seriously, did his mom hate him or what?) had beaten me to the punch and was already interviewing Kenny, who was sitting up in the hospital bed, smiling and nodding as he spooned green Jell-O into his mouth.

Agent Kip was alone this time. I guess he'd ditched that human wall he'd been dragging around with him. Or maybe he'd eaten the guy. Who knows? He turned to look me up and down. I could tell he hadn't expected me. "You," he stated coldly, eyes narrowed and a hand shifting incrementally closer to the gun in his pancake holster. "Get out."

His tone of voice pissed me off. To serve and protect, asshat. "Make me."

"This is a police investigation, Englebrecht—"

"And you're not police." I stepped forward. "You're fucking Arcana, which is about as far from police as you can get." I nodded toward Kenny Johnson. "And you're only interviewing him because he's connected—however tentatively—to me—"

It didn't take a flippin' genius to figure all that out.

Agent Kip lunged at me. I hadn't expected that, frankly. The Arcana were usually more composed than this. He must have really been hungry.

I'd forgotten how strong they are. Not angel-strong, exactly, but stronger than a normal human being. And when Agent Kip sank his hands into my shoulders and spun me around in his attempt to get me down on my knees and properly cuffed, I went with his momentum. We wound up smashing against the wall beside the door. My back hit it so hard, I was afraid a nurse or two might come running, but the hallway beyond the room was empty. That was good...and bad.

Agent Kip leaned in close, pressing me hard against the wall. His teeth were slightly pointed, noticeable only at this proximity. It was obvious he'd downed a few angel chasers in his time. I was almost certain he was going to bite me. He'd knocked me into the wall in an attempt to prevent me from using my wings, so I reacted defensively and with the good training I'd received at the Police Academy and kneed him hard in the balls.

Kippy dropped to the floor like a sack of flour. He grabbed his damaged junk in both hands and I heard the whoosh of his breath as he leaned over, trying to compartmentalize the pain. I gave him a few seconds because whatever else I am, I'm not some monster. In the meantime, I liberated Vivian's athame—just in case. Finally, after getting himself back under a semblance of control, Kippy

Skippy looked up. His eyes had turned all angel blackity-black, but after a few tense seconds, they turned back to their usual baby-shit brown color.

"Get out," I told him, and that made him flinch, which was incredibly satisfying to see. I flipped the athame in my hand, catching it by the handle, in case he got any ideas into that tiny, black Arcana brain of his. From the look on his face, I'm sure my eyes were all blackity-black, too, and my teeth all pointy-scary. He knew I meant business. "And stay away from Kenny Johnson and everyone else in this damned town."

"Or what?" he moaned.

"Or I'll gut you like a fucking fish, Arcana, and use your head like a basketball."

Admittedly, that sounded both silly and overly dramatic. Oh, well, too late now.

Surprisingly, Kip the Asshole Arcana chose not to challenge me. He didn't even rub his hands together like a Saturday morning cartoon villain. I found that disappointing. His look did say, *Soon, motherfucker.*

"Yeah, fuck you, too," I said as Agent Kip picked himself up and shambled out the door with his family jewels still in hand.

I turned to Kenny—or, rather, the thing that Kenny had become. He—it—had witnessed the whole lewd exchange. He was staring at me, a spoonful of green Jell-O lifted to his mouth, but frozen now as a wide, unnatural smile spread across his face.

** * ***

"Hello, angel."

Well, this is awkward, I thought. I'd saved a monster...from another monster. I wasn't sure where to go from here, so took a step toward Kenny, the athame at the ready.

"Really?" it said. The handcuff on its left wrist jangled as it sat up straighter in bed. "What do you think I can do to you, angel?"

I didn't know how to answer that. "I don't know. What *can* you do?"

It tilted its head slightly as if it was calculating something. It never lost that chillingly unnatural smile. "You're...tainted."

It took me a moment to follow what it was saying.

"A nephilim."

That impressed me. "You know what a nephilim is?"

"I know many things." A pause while it seemed to orient itself like a newborn robot. "But not a white nephilim. You are dark."

"Yeah, well, you're pretty fucking dark yourself, buster," I said, venturing a step toward the bed. "What are you?"

It seemed to consider. It even looked down at its spread hands. "Human..."

"No. What are you *really?*"

Its eyes rolled up to meet mine. It lost its smile and opened its mouth. I spied the spider-thing peeking out. Then it closed its lips and the smile returned. "Your destroyer," the thing that used to be Kenny told me.

* * *

I left that hospital with a new perspective. And a new mission.

I'd foolishly hoped I wouldn't need to enter that mine. That I could fight this thing on my own terms. But that was impossible now. I realized that. If I killed the thing that had once been Kenny Johnson, the Thin Man would just send another. And another.

And if I ran...?

Well, fuck that noise. I wasn't the running type.

I was going to need to get in front of this thing. And sure, this thing was like a runaway locomotive now and was more likely than not to crush me under its wheels.

As I biked back to the shop, I made an itinerary in my head.

1. Find the Thin Man.
2. Stop him.
3. Get the girl back. Or the boy. (I was pretty flexible there.)

Of course, that meant going toe to toe with a monster—in the dark, in its place of hiding.

It'd stopped the Arcana. I'd busted the chops on some angels. I'd even defeated a god once.

How hard could this be?

Well, yippee-ki-yay, cowboys. Here we go.

| 26 |

Grunches

BY SOME MIRACLE, I managed to get back to the shop before lunch was over. Sometimes I even surprise myself.

By early afternoon, the heat was virtually unbearable, and the A/C unit we'd had fixed only a few days earlier was once again unfixed. I took one look at it, slammed the door of the fifty-year-old unit, and went out into the shop and started turning off lights to try and conserve what little coolness the space had trapped. It might give the impression we were closed, but I wasn't overly concerned about that. No one was coming in, anyway.

I ducked into the backroom where Morgana kept the more important books—and a few grimoires she had collected over the years—and gathered them up, taking them with me out to the counter so I could spread them out. Despite what you might assume, I was a poor spellcaster. That was more Morgana's shtick. She knew exactly what pinch of what she needed and what to say and how to gesture to get the effect she wanted. I was more of an idiot savant—emphasis on the idiot part. If I did something right, it was entirely accidental.

I mean, I'm not stupid or incapable of learning. I just don't have the patience to be a good witch. And to be a good witch demands patience.

"What are you doing?" Morgana asked as she stepped into the shop. She was back from the fair in Germantown she'd been attending and carrying a heavy tote bag with her. She loved to shop for charms and little magical treasures, many of which she stumbled upon accidentally.

There was no point in lying. She was already aware I was investigating the school shooting. So I looked up from the huge, handwritten tome in my lap—it had belonged to Morgana's Aunt Lydia, a powerful conjurer, by all accounts—and said, "I'm trying to solve a problem like a proper witch instead of stumbling around in the dark the way I usually do."

To her credit, she wasn't at all hostile. "What kind of problem?" She set the tote on the floor next to the counter. "Maybe I can help."

I looked her in the eye. I could tell right away we were not going to discuss our private issues right now. That frightened me a little. It meant this thing was bigger than I'd first anticipated.

"I went to see Kenny in the hospital today."

"Kenny Johnson," she clarified. "The school shooter?"

"He wasn't trying to shoot students," I explained, turning a page of Aunt Lydia's book of shadows. "He was shooting Substitutes." I thought a moment before continuing because I knew she would ask. "Like pod people in *Invasion of the Body Snatchers*. But it got to him. It turned him into one of...them. I think it's taking or murdering anyone who knows what it is."

"It?"

"The Thin Man." I went on to explain what I thought it was. Not that I had a great understanding of it—yet. Some shadowy being hiding like a coward inside the bodies of dead or disappeared children. Something that didn't want its secrets revealed.

She glanced at the book in my hands, an invitation to go on.

"A few months ago, a developer reopened the No. 8 Mine. Kenny and a few of his friends went inside on a dare. They did a ceremony—a silly conjuring spell. But I think it's connected to a thin veil there. I think it let something out."

I stopped to let her absorb that. Her lips moved a moment and then she said, "Something as in...what?"

"I don't exactly know." I cleared my hoarse voice. "Something out of Heaven. Or Hell. Or...I don't know. The multiverse. But I don't think this is the first time—"

"It's going back and forth," she finished for me.

"Would seem so."

Morgana made that moue thing with her mouth that she did when she was thinking about a myriad of possibilities. "Why did Kenny shoot up his school?"

"He thinks...he thought...this thing...whatever it is...has been kidnapping kids involved in the conjuring and replacing them with something calling Substitutes." I watched her eyes to see if she thought I was insane. "He wasn't trying to kill his friends. He was trying to kill the Substitutes."

She looked at the floor a moment before shifting her attention back to me. "Do you think he was telling the truth?"

"He was autistic. I don't think he would deliberately lie."

"You saw him in the hospital—"

"*That* wasn't Kenny."

I told her briefly about what I'd experienced while talking to the Kenny Substitute, and then what happened several days ago with Brian. I told her how he had died with that alien creature crawling out of his mouth.

I saw her put it all together in her head. "You told me to talk to Antonia."

"Did you?"

Shaking her head sadly, she said, "I thought you were...overreacting."

She'd meant to say *lying* but had changed it at the last moment.

Morgana held out her hands. I placed the heavy grimoire in them. It took her maybe fifteen seconds to decide on the proper spell. She turned the book around and showed me her aunt's careful scrawling across the pages. It was in English and looked like nothing more than an elaborate recipe. "Use this to pierce the veil on your own terms."

I reached for the book, but she drew the book back. "This isn't black magic by nature, Nick, but keep in mind that in your hands...well, it could go sideways very easily."

Nodding, I took the book and looked at Aunt Lydia's spell. I took no offense; that was no hollow warning on her part. Lydia's grimoire had been written for human witches, not the daemon flavor alternate. That was a whole other ballgame.

"It's also not something I can't help you with," she explained. "It's grunchy."

"Ah."

"Grunchy" was the term Morgana used for spells that had a habit of blowing back onto the conjurer. Some of the clients we received had "grunches," or the residue of failed spells clinging to them like toilet paper to the bottoms of their shoes. Essentially, they had cursed themselves, either due to the nature of the spell itself or their sheer incompetence. She telling me this did not bode well. She was saying the worker of this spell could very well end up cursing themselves, and if she believed that even *she* wasn't strong enough to control it, then I was certain I'd fuck it up big time. Except, of course, I was cursed already. Damned, at the very least. So spells—and curses—never really stick to me.

In other words, my life couldn't get any worse than it currently was.

I looked up over the book. "Thanks."

She didn't look angry, just sad. I could tell that in the time we'd been apart, she'd come to some hard decision that was leaving her in mourning...and that worried me. "You're going to get involved in this with or without my help. It's better that I help and...minimize the damage if I can."

"We still need to talk," I reminded her.

She nodded once. "We do. But not now. Just go save the world, Nick. I'll be here when you get back."

***

I hiked through the woods by the light of a full blood moon, a heavy gym bag slapping my side and the troubling, orangey light shining down from above and illuminating the tangled path of half-flattened grasses ahead of me. The ground hummed with insect life and bullfrogs frantically calling to each other in a nearby marsh. An angry-sounding screech owl called in a tree above.

"Nice touch," I told the owl. It was all almost poetically pretty in an early Halloween-type of way except for the fact that I was about to do something immensely stupid that might kill me—or, at the very least, leave me grievously wounded.

The mine lay ahead, down a steep gravel trail. I remembered the way because I'd been here once before when I had volunteered to look for a lost hiker. I'd spotted the mine, but I hadn't gone in. By then, my familiars had picked up on a trail leading in another direction.

They joined me now as I cut a steady path down the hill to the entrance of the mine. I couldn't see them, but I could feel them pressing in on my conscious mind in small, subtle ways. I was also there when I caught a familiar scent and then heard the snap of a twig behind me. They had surely done that on purpose just to mess with me.

"I know it's you, Brownie," I said, turning to glance behind. To my surprise, two fauns were standing on the gravel path about a hundred feet away. I recognized the big one as Brownswick, my longtime familiar. But the second one was lanky and barely larger than a teenager.

Despite them being my animal to call, I've never been extraordinarily fond of fauns. Having two of them following me was...concerning, to say the least. Not that I was going to let them know that.

"Brought a friend, hey?"

"My lord." With a formal little head bow, Brownie moved toward me, virtually gliding soundlessly over the ground. A large male in his prime, he stood at least two feet taller than I did, which was saying something, and his full rack of antlers gave him an additional two feet. His eyes glowed faintly blue in the strong moonlight.

The young one, less experienced, made more noise as it followed his lead. It looked up at me with some trepidation. It had no antlers, just soft, triangular ears laying flat against its nearly human skull. Although it was smaller than Brownie, it still stood nearly my height.

"And who's this?" I asked.

Brownie swept the young one forward. "My lord, may I present to you...Honeycutt."

When some of the shadows came off the young one, I saw it was female. Slender, coltish legs, softer pale fur, small, budding breasts. She surprised me. I'd never seen a female faun before. I hadn't believed they existed, even though that was ridiculous. When I'd visited the Amish community in Lancaster that had been haunted and terrorized by the god Cernunnos, I'd learned that fauns were the unfortunate offspring of the god dallying with the women of the colony—the malformed newborns not disposed of by midwives. There was no reason not to believe some of those babes were female.

The young faun looked up at me with large, wet doe eyes. "Greetings, my lord," she said in a light, breezy voice and bent down in something like a clumsy curtsey—if curtseys were done on little cloven feet.

I was instantly smitten. I didn't like fauns, but I couldn't deny her effect on me. It was like looking at a lost little puppy that needs you—that can't live without you. As ridiculous as it sounded, I loved Honeycutt immediately. And that annoyed me to no end. I shouldn't have fallen head over hooves for anything like her so quickly.

"Approach your lord, Honeycutt," Brownie commanded the young one and gave her a harsh shove forward.

She stumbled, then stopped herself and turned to look at him with a worried expression on her little face. A shiver ran through her body and her hand went to her mouth as if she were thinking of sucking a thumb.

"Honeycutt."

"Yes, Baba."

She turned to look at me. She looked terrified, the moon reflected fully in her huge eyes. Now, she did stick her thumb in her mouth, but Brownswick snorted and she immediately put her hand down.

I wanted her to not be scared of me. That was very important to me. At the moment, it was the most important thing in the world. So I went to one knee and held my hand out to her as you might a sick or wounded dog. "It's okay, sweetie."

She shuffled closer to me, her big eyes never leaving my face. I tried to imagine her life. Surely, she had been born in the colony. Her horrified mother had rejected her with a scream, but a compassionate midwife had decided against ending her poor little life. But what had happened to her after that? Perhaps they had crated her off, or put her in the barn with the other animals. Maybe they just left her in the woods to live or die on her own, hoping nature would do what they could not, and Brownie's wives or some other fauns had found her. I had never given it much thought until now.

Desperate, I reached into my jacket pocket and found half of a 3 Musketeers I'd been hoarding as a little pick-me-up. I broke off a piece and offered it to her. That brought her to me. She seemed hungry.

A few seconds later, her belly full and her sweet little face smeary with chocolate, she knelt in front of me and seemed to think a long moment. I imagined her trying hard to remember what Brownie had probably taught her.

Frowning, she finally said, "I am yours, my lord. Please command me."

| 27 |

The Spell

BROWNSWICK AND HONEYCUTT escorted me to the mouth of the mine. Somewhere along the way, Brownie's wives had decided to join us as well, so that by the time I reached the tracks of the railway, I had a veritable entourage of Otherkin tagging along.

I looked over my little entourage, wondering if they were here because they could sense my intention, or if they had other reasons. Maybe they knew that tonight would be a good one for a working. Of course, the dryads licked their full lips as they slithered through the trees surrounding us. Once I was in the dark, I would need to keep a close eye on them.

"This is going to be dangerous," I told them while I watched, slightly mesmerized, as the three wood nymphs shedded their bark and assumed more humanlike forms, complete with soft female skin set aglow by the light of the moon. The Weird Sisters stood there, looking at me hungrily, and I shivered inside. "It's best if all of you stayed here."

"We come," Brownie stated only.

"I plan to pierce a veil tonight," I explained, shaking the bag I'd brought. "There could be consequences."

"The working will be stronger with us. We come," Brownie again stated in a way that suggested the subject was not up for debate.

"Baba..." Honeycutt said worriedly, trying to take his hand.

"You, too!" Brownie ordered and pushed her again, almost knocking her to her knees.

"Cut that out!" I shouted at Brownswick, but he just snorted dust in response.

Honeycutt moved closer to me. I wrapped an arm around her and she immediately snuggled into my side as I stepped onto the track. There were signs all over the place suggesting that the corporation that owned the mine was not responsible for accidents happening outside of work or tour hours. I ignored them as I rummaged through the bag I'd brought and pulled out a powerful LED Maglite. The light was substantial, but the yawning black hole in the earth that was the Lucky 8 Mine seemed to suck it right up.

I didn't see that as a good omen.

The Lucky 8 didn't look like something you might see in a western on TV. The entrance had been cement-blocked into a rough arch reminiscent of a train tunnel. "No. 8" had been chiseled into the cement so long ago, that the characters were practically illegible when I skirted the light over it. Along both sides were long lists of names roughly scratched into the support cement—the names of the men and women who had lost their lives to the mine. The list was fairly extensive.

"This'll be fun. Not," I said and took my first step inside.

The railway led down into a large underground space ribbed with timber and lined with overhead electric lights. There were more lights strung along the walls, and probably a power box somewhere that controlled them, but I didn't want to switch the power on. I figured it was likely rigged into a grid controlled by a security firm in town since, along with the lights, there were also close-captioned cameras set up. I wasn't supposed to be here and didn't need any security guards busting in and interrupting me.

As a group, we moved into the center of the underground cavern. I moved my light all around. I could smell the mold and age and hear water ticking down from somewhere distant. At least it was minimally cooler here than it was outside. That was the only plus. I prided myself in not being a coward, but this place had what it took to send a chill into my bones. I wasn't a big fan of being underground where it was dark and close, making combat that much more difficult.

"Huh," I said when my light splashed over a corner of the cavern. Dropping my utility bag, I took a few steps toward the wall where my light had picked out some engravings. I touched them while Honeycutt continued to shadow me. "Pretty," she said, seeing them better in the dark than I ever could.

"They are pretty," I said, touching them. Runes. Someone had cut runes into the walls. And no, I couldn't read them. They weren't Celtic or even ancient Germanic. They were something else. Cut into the wall by that bastard Lamb to help him harness the power of the Thin Man? Hell if I know. They could be gang graffiti, for all I knew.

Pretty, I thought. And probably very, very bad.

My shivers were increasing by the moment. I quickly returned to the bag and knelt to remove the tools of my working, suddenly needing to hurry. I had brought stocky white candles for the calling of the four quarters, some packets of herbs carefully selected by Morgana, different colored chalk, and a leather satchel of black salt to contain the working. Taking up the sack, I found a mostly clean space and kicked away as much of the sand as I could. I didn't draw a pentacle on the floor—that wouldn't have worked for me, anyway. Instead, I drew a circle with the sign of my father's house in the middle. One long line bisected the circle with a little curl at one end and two forks at the other. The Morning Star.

When I had finished, I stepped back to look it over. I thought about Morgana's warning as I retrieved a piece of black chalk and began to draw runes with the circle. Because this was me, and I would be calling on the power of the House of Lucifer, a lot of untoward things could happen.

"Go big or go home, eh, Brownie?" I said as I knelt there, finishing the last of the runes I had memorized from out of Aunt Lydia's grimoire. They would, theoretically, help me concentrate the spell. The fauns and dryads had drifted back just far enough to lend me their power as familiars without interfering with the actual spell.

Almost as soon as I had finished drawing the boundaries of the circle, the salt and chalk began to glow faintly with a bluish light similar to what I had come to associate with myself. My wings glowed a similar color. I hoped that was a good sign.

That done, I set the candles at the four quarters and sprinkled the herbs around, then removed my borrowed athame—seriously, I was going to have to get Vivian some flowers for allowing me to corrupt her athame like this. I hesitated a moment—because ouch—and then gritted my teeth.

"Suck it up, princess," I said and cut the upper part of my forearm, careful not to bisect any important tendons. The blood that bubbled up and over my pale skin was a blue so dark it looked like shining tar. I used it to mark the four quarters and call down the elements one after another. The circle completed, I moved so I was standing dead center and pulled the T-shirt up and off my back.

Naked to the waist, I held the athame out and took a deep breath before committing to this. This was the part I'd been dreading all night.

Angling the athame toward me, I rested the razor-sharp tip against my Adam's apple and said, "Lucifer...you've risen and fallen a thousand times. Michael drove you down into the pit, but you rose again, great dragon. Gabriel sent you into the mountains, but you returned stronger than ever."

While I spoke, I drew the athame down over my skin, from throat to groin, drawing a rough approximation of the Morning Star. It was not a pleasant feeling. I felt like I was unzipping my flesh for all to see the twisted and unnatural things lurking inside of me.

"I have not lost. I cannot lose. What is light without dark? What are they without me? I can never be defeated. In war and in peace...in darkness and in light...in life and in death...I will rise again."

My skin split along the rune I had drawn over my own body and light spilled forth, briefly illuminating the whole subterranean cavern. The fauns and nymphs took a lurching step backward as I revealed my true self to the waiting darkness.

***

The spell hurt like a bitch.

My eight archangel wings slashed forth. My long hair writhed like golden serpents over my shoulders. My skin felt like it was a few sizes too small and cracking apart on my bones. The pain nearly drove me to my knees on the floor of the cavern.

I forced myself to straighten up, every motion an agony, and saw my hands were clenched around...not an athame, but a long, slender staff in burnished gold, with a jagged, two-pronged fork at the end of it. The Morning Star bident. The spell was on my lips before I even thought about it. I spoke it aloud in Angel-speak. At the same time, I raised the Morning Star over my head, turned the prongs so they were aimed at the floor, and drove the sharp points down into the earth at my feet with every ounce of my strength as a man and as a Lucifer.

The whole cavern rocked side to side, and stones and dusty debris rained down all around me. I felt the raw, flaming power of my father's house as it was forcibly sucked out of my familiars—those who stood with me here tonight, as well as my worshipers miles away in Philadelphia. Even Sada, currently snuggling in bed with her new girlfriend, sat up, her mouth yawning open as the power was ripped violently from the center of her being. Every creature I was connected to stiffened and cried out as I wrenched the magical energy from their very bones for my working. It all went exactly to plan. Better, in fact.

After that...well, that's when things got really interesting.

* * *

I'd taken an already weak spot in time and space and run a hot knife through it, ripping it forcefully open. Well, not a *knife*, per se. More like a sword. Or maybe more of an IED bomb. Yeah, real "I came in like a wrecking ball" shit. Regardless, I took a soft spot and blew it wide fucking open.

I bombed the hell out of a doorway into another time or place, but before I could stop to congratulate myself on a job well done, the Thin Man noticed. Because of course he did.

And, call me crazy, but I don't think he liked that one bit.

* * *

The stone floor rippled and opened up in front of my feet as if I were looking at the surface of a black lake with a massive boulder dropped into the water. The candles fluttered in the sudden, hot gasses that seemed to fill the room, and the air trembled and suddenly stank of ozone and heat. I had to work hard to keep my fear and excitement in check.

Something—some *thing*—was being drawn up through the vortex in the floor. It was black and gangly. Huge. The candles were slowly being snuffed out one by one, leaving the faintly glowing Morning Star the only source of light in the cavern. As a result, it was difficult to puzzle it together. It looked painfully thin, and there were far too many legs, but the head was strangely humanoid as though there had been some nightmarish attempt by a long-forgotten deity to make it seem at least passably human, but the two huge, fang-like tusks and the assortment of round red eyes all over its head made it seem anything but.

The moment the Thin Man saw me, I made a weird warbling noise of displeasure and pressed its two huge front legs together much as a praying mantis might while on a hunt. Those legs looked serrated and as vicious as blades. From the front view, with its legs pressed prayerfully together and partially obscuring its misshapen head, it did, in fact, look almost human. I thought about all those kids who had seen this thing in the last few seconds before they were taken. It was a terrible thing to witness in your final moments.

Once landed, the creature started to struggle against the binds of my working, but he could not move outside the circle. However, that didn't mean it could not move *up*. And it did. Despite its impressive size, maybe ten feet from tip to tail, it moved with ephemeral grace, as though the creature were made entirely of air and nightmares. Within seconds, it had jumped to the ceiling and turned itself upside down.

"Angel," it said in a surprisingly soft—almost feminine—voice. It shivered with anger. "Why have you summoned me? I have no quarrels with your kind."

"Perhaps. But I do."

"You seek me, but I am not your enemy, Lucifer."

It could not break my circle...and it was under an obligation to answer all my questions for the time I held it. I opened my mouth to demand more information when I realized that neither of us had said a single word. We had been conversing in some other way and in some language that neither of us understood. I assumed it must be an empathic language—maybe the most basic language of the working universe.

"You must answer my question for the duration that this circle holds," I reminded it.

It agreed—but reluctantly. I could feel its insult like a wet cold slime on my skin.

"Why are you taking the children who call you?"

It shuddered, trying to resist me. I held the Morning Star up. Its minimal light touched the creature's monstrous face and I heard it scream in my head.

"They called. I came."

"Where? Where do you come from?"

"The other."

"What is the other?"

"Not here."

I realized there was no approximate word for what it was trying to explain. Wherever—or whenever—it came from, it was a place alien to human existence.

I skipped trying to puzzle that out and asked, "Who controls you, creature? Who holds your bit?"

"Him."

"Tell me, creature."

"Him!"

"Lamb?" I shouted at it in my mind and held up the Morning Star. "Does Lamb command your fealty?"

Shivering. Screaming. The whole mine shuddered.

The sudden earthquake knocked me off my feet, and, as I fell back, I realized I was crossing—and breaking—the circle. But there was nothing I could do as I tumbled down on my ass. I grunted and sat up, but the creature was already free and crawling across the ceiling toward me. It moved with terrifying speed, its big, mantis-like arms reaching out hungrily for me.

I lashed out at it with the only weapon I had, but it knocked the Morning Star away as though it were a toy.

"Stupid little Lucifer," it said in that sibilant, almost whispery-sexy voice. "You know nothing of what is or will be." It lunged, eyes ablaze with insult.

Morgana warned things might go sideways. Well, she was right.

I tried to kick out, but its thorny mantis arms sank into my flesh like spikes, dragging a real-life scream from my throat as it lifted me off the ground and dragged me to the ceiling of the mine with it. I tried to fight it off. My wings beat at it. But I was just a giant moth caught in the web of this hideous cosmic spider.

The Thin Man laughed at me as it hauled me close enough to see my reflection in its many blood-red compound eyes. I smelled it—a hot, dry, rotten smell like carrion rotting on a burning desert floor. It smelled like death. It smelled like hell.

A gust of hot air opened up beneath us like someone had thrown open an oven door. A door, yes, I thought as I helplessly continued to lash out at the monster—to no avail. A doorway into its place. Its homeworld. I continued to struggle, but it dragged me effortlessly down into that godforsaken place.

***

Somehow, the vortex had managed to flip us over in mid-air so I was on top and the creature was beneath me. The screaming wind filled my ears. I still hadn't managed to uncouple myself, and now its many arms were all around me, creating a kind of thorny cage as we fell through scorching, bone-dry air. I immediately found I couldn't breathe. The air all around felt like it was made of fire, hard to suck down into my lung. And that made me fight even harder. I punched and gouged the creature until, with a cry, it let me go, the fierce wind ripping the thing far, far away into the horizon and leaving me falling through a burning, sulfuric red atmosphere.

For a few seconds, I seemed to float on a wave of hot, sulfuric wind. During the course of it, looked down at the landscape beneath me.

There was little to see, but all of it was frightening.

A scorched red planet, barren and hostile, stretched out in every direction. No plants, no animals. No trees. Just endless grey, cracked rock and dunes of red sand and not a drop of water in sight. The sky was just as painfully red and void of life, though occasional cracks of searing white lightning seemed to break through the scudding clouds at times. If this had, at some point, been a real world full of real living things, it had long since been glassed by some unmentionable disaster. What I was seeing was an alien landscape of wind and rock and storms and nothing else. And I was headed right toward it.

I lifted my wings, veering slightly to the left. It didn't exactly save me, but it slowed my momentum enough that when I dropped the last hundred feet, I didn't break every damned bone in my body. But make no mistake: The ground, as soft and sandy as it was, still hit me like a hammer blow, most of the damage to my hip and shoulder as I crash-landed.

The impact knocked the wind out of me, leaving me groaning and gasping, my long hair blowing all over my face as I dug my fingers into the parched sand and pushed myself up. Flares of pain kept me from doing much more than that. But when something under the dead earth grabbed my wrist, I suddenly found the strength to jump to my feet.

A hand. It was a human hand sticking out of the soft red sand. I hadn't planned it, but the sight of it surprised me so badly that I leaped back a few steps and my wings beat frantically at the ground as they carried me back. That blew the sand off the person buried there.

I had no idea who he was. Some human boy. Maybe one of the kids who had been taken. Or maybe he was a kid from some other plane of existence. It was hard to tell. His skin was desiccated from lack of moisture so he looked like a fire-burned corpse. Somehow, though, his flesh had *grown* into the rocky earth, and vines were spiraling up his nose and down his throat. One had even grown through the socket of one eye. His fingers grasped at the open air —opening, closing, opening—but he was entirely unable to move. Most of his bones and organs were fused into the earth. I could see his heart fluttering inside the open cage of his ribs, feeding arteries of blood and nutrients into the dead earth.

The gory sight startled me so badly that I cried and opened a portal to Dis involuntarily. I fell through it like some trap door and landed hard on the floor of the throne room.

Baphomet, who had been sitting nearby, drinking tea and reading a newspaper, looked up and tutted. "My liege?"

| 28 |

Spiders from Mars

YEAH, SO, THAT didn't go well.

Out of my league? You bet.

Was that going to stop me?

What do you think?

I woke, shirtless and in jeans, in bed in my room at the Victorian. I hurt all over. I mean, I'd been in fights. I'd won fights, and I'd had the shit kicked out of me in fights. Though I was not a fan of pain, I was intimate with the fucker. This surpassed all that. I wished I had a few more of those oxy/Tylenol bombs the hospital had prescribed me, but I'd taken the last one last night when I'd gotten in. My head swam and I had the kind of thudding all-over headache that makes you want to puke. Every inch of my skin felt like I was suffering the worst sunburn of my life, my muscles felt like I'd been lifting weights for ten hours straight, and I felt generally wibbly-wobbly. I thought about moving but gave up after flexing a few fingers.

Sada turned over in the bed beside him and carefully placed her arm over me as if she was afraid I might spring up. Fat chance of that happening. "Don't try to speak, Nick. You're seriously depleted."

No shit.

She moved her hand up my bare chest, the tips of her elongated fingernails drawing ideograms I couldn't see. Under different circumstances, I would have found that immeasurably pleasurable. As it was, her fingernails, carved with runes, actually hurt as they skated over my poor, scorched skin.

"I can't fix all the damage, but I can make you functional again," she explained.

As she spoke, the runes on her nails glowed with dim white light. She leaned in close and added, "That was incredibly stupid. And *reckless*. Your coven exists as an extension of you to lend you power willingly, Nick. You don't need to steal it."

She punctuated the last with a jolt of energy.

I gasped at the sensation of cool relief seeping into my skin and muscles like a Noxzema balm. She was right, of course. I'd acted like a jerk during my spell work. I'd anticipated borrowing strength from my familiars—from Brownswick and Honeycutt, respectively—but it hadn't been enough, and I'd wound up siphoning power from the Satanists and they'd noticed. My bad.

Half an hour later, I dragged myself out of the shower and looked into the smeary mirror above the sink. My wet hair was way too long—some grunchy backwash from my spell work the night before, I guess—and it hung to my elbows in long, ridiculous golden waves that made me look like an elf reject from *Lord of the Rings*. I'd need to get to a barber sometime soon. But my eyes frightened me more. They looked blasted, too wide, and red-rimmed. For the first time in my life, I looked truly traumatized. This Lucifer/angel/hero bullshit was for the fucking birds.

After a quick shave, I spent a good five minutes brushing my teeth and spitting with Listerine several times to wash the taste of hell-desert out of my mouth. Sighing, I changed into fresh clothes—Sada had thoughtfully laid out some grey carpenter's pants, a white tank top, and a short-sleeved red and black cotton plaid shirt, everything with tags on it because she knew I hated the clothes they had provided in the closet. That made me feel even worse about what I'd done to her last night. I tied my stupid hair back—that made me look...well, not exactly *human*, but more Nick-like, at least—and went down to the kitchen.

I was surprised to see Juliette standing at the stove, shoveling blueberry pancakes off a grill, with Sada sitting at the breakfast nook near the back door, her face down and half-buried in a cup of coffee. Juliette was giving her daughter shit for leaving me to my own devices last night, but she immediately shut up when I stepped into the room.

"Don't talk to Sada like that," I said grumpily. "She's doing the best she can."

Juliette looked over at her daughter. She gave her no quarter. "I don't need Sada doing 'her best.' I need her doing what's expected of her."

"Then what you're expecting is too much. Let the girl live her life, for chrissakes!"

Juliette looked shocked I would speak to her so she reconsidered who she was speaking to and quickly changed the subject. "Are you hungry, my Lord?"

"No," I said, gruffer than I'd intended. "What are you doing here, Juliette?"

Juliette pressed her lips together hard while she digested that. "My Lord, this house belongs to the coven. It belongs to all of us."

She owned it. She and her brother. I should have figured that one out on my own.

I sighed, seriously off my game. Kicking myself mentally, I went to sit in the breakfast nook on the bench opposite Sada. Sada looked up from her phone and gave me a grateful little smile.

Juliette wasted no time rushing a cup of tea over. It was doctored exactly the way I liked it—no cream, but a lot of sugar.

I rubbed my temples where the headache was still socking me in the skull with big, soft clown hammers, making my thoughts muzzy. Jesus, that spellwork had sucked it out of me, big time. "Look, I'm—"

"Not a morning person. I understand." Juliette nodded and her eyes drifted to the ceiling. "I told your friend Josh that you went out drinking last night and that you were hungover pretty badly. You were sick in the middle of the night and he was worried."

I could barely remember. I know I had stumbled into the house and that Sada, already there and waiting for me, had dragged me upstairs. God only knew what state I was in. I had blacked out after that.

I was starting to feel pretty terrible about the way I'd been treating Sada, Juliette, and the whole coven. They'd given me this house. They'd lent me their power last night. Sada had done her best to patch me up. They had even let Josh stay here despite him not being one of them. Juliette had rushed down here from Philly to see to me after last night's fiasco. I had no right to be cross with any of them.

Reaching out, I touched Juliette's hand. "Sorry. The last few days have been a literal hell."

"I understand," Juliette said with a nod. "That was big spellwork you did last night, Nick. You're lucky the Simulacrum didn't come across and stay here. That would have been…well, let's not discuss that."

I sat up straighter. "It has a name?" In the back of my mind, I'd started thinking about it as the Spider from Mars.

She took the seat across from me and folded her hands, letting the pancakes burn on the grill. This was more important. "I don't know that it has a name, per se. But that's what we call it."

"She means the Thin Man," Sada mumbled as if I wasn't making the connection. "It's *not* a god...whatever you may think. It's more like a copy of a god. A caricature. *A Simulacrum.*"

I thought about the creature...the things it had said. It had acted godly...overbearing and egotistical, but I had managed to hurt it. "It talks a tough game, that's for sure, but I don't think it's as strong as it lets on." Else, why would it prey on some dumb kids? "And that other place..."

Juliette sucked in a sudden breath and looked over at Sada, who quickly picked up her smartphone without being asked. I could tell she was eager to please her mother after last night. Juliette asked Sada to check on a book in their library, *The Picatrix*.

Sada's head went down while she consulted her phone. I thought that was pretty amusing, that the Satanists had dedicated their books to electronic format. They probably had their own website, Facebook, and Instagram sites, too.

After a few minutes of searching through their digital library, Sada finally said, "Its world is called The Red Planet. *Not* Mars. *Not* any place in this known universe." Her head bobbed up. "It's hard to find any real information about it because almost no one has ever returned from there."

Juliette, the magus, nodded. "Tell us what you can."

"The Simulacrum is known to steal victims and take them back to its homeworld, the Red Planet, a world that is understood to have been destroyed by a global cataclysm millions of years ago. Its mission is hitherto unknown. But to maintain balance and not alter matter in this universe—and, thus, cause any cracks in time and space—it must replace the missing matter. It does so by cloning the original." She looked up. "Essentially, creating more Simulacrums." Looking down again, she concluded, "As to what it does with the originals—no one knows that."

"I do," I told her, feeling sick. I remembered the boy planted in the ground. "I saw what it does with its victims."

I was acutely aware of their collective curiosity, but I shook my head. I had a feeling this was my burden alone to bear. "Don't ask. I don't want you to know. I don't want anyone in this world to know."

Juliette must have seen something in my face, some shadow, because she didn't press. She just reached out and brushed a long strand of blond hair out of my eyes. "I'm sorry, Nick. You should not have to carry this burden alone."

Story of my life. I swallowed down the rest of the tea. It helped my parched throat. I organized my thoughts and said, "I'll tell you this. All of this has been going on for a while. A long time."

Juliette nodded. "So how is the Beast tied into this?"

"Him," I said, sitting back. My voice sounded so bitter. "I don't think he is tied into it. All this started when a group of kids accidentally opened up a soft spot in the veil. After that, someone at Holy Name just passed their suspicions about the Substitutes onto Lamb —maybe during a counseling session. Who knows. It was probably all more of an accident than anything planned on his part. He's just exploiting it, is all."

"Do you think he's controlling the Simulacrum?"

I had to think about that for a long moment, pick through the psychic rubble in my brain. I thought of the runes in the mine. "I don't know. I think it's more they have an accord. An understanding." I glanced over at Sada to include her. "I do know he's a Daemon. He has the power to hurt it. He doesn't. He just lets it do its work."

"So what does he get out of it?" Sada asked.

I thought about my encounter with the man in the garden. God, he was such an enigma. "I don't think he's getting a damned anything out of it." To Juliette, I said, "You said he loves chaos and pain. Maybe that's enough."

Juliette stared at the table for a long moment. "Or maybe he's biding his time...hoping the Simulacrum makes a mistake? Unbalances the order of the universe?"

I snorted. "Blows everything up? The whole universe? And himself with it?"

Sada looked appalled.

Juliette's eyes flashed dangerously. "The Beast is a sadist *and* a masochist," she explained. "I believe he is far more dangerous than anyone suspects. And he has his agendas. He always has."

"If that's true, why involve me?" I asked. "Why clue me in? Surely he knew I'd try to stop him."

"Maybe he wants to watch you try and fail. Or..." She stopped, looking even more troubled than ever.

"Go on," I urged.

"The Beast is the servant of the Dragon."

"Yeah, well, fuck that noise." With servants like that, I don't need enemies.

She looked up. "Maybe he's trying to save you. Maybe he has some escape hatch plan in place and means to take you with him. You think he wants to hurt you, Nick, but he could be deeply in love with you."

Thinking about the possibilities was making me feel sick. The whole house suddenly felt claustrophobic. I got up and paced to the back door and looked out through the panes of glass. I could see the old chicken coop and the garden from here. Opening the door, I re-walked the path I had taken that night, wending my way through the overgrown garden to the edge of the property—the place where I had faced Lamb and seen his true face, even for only a second, for the first time.

I stood there a long time, puzzling over the man's intentions. I still couldn't make heads or tails of him.

When I heard the grass shushing behind me, I stiffened up, then noted it was Juliette standing behind me. She had followed me. "I talked to my brother just now. We will be fast-tracking the mine's closure. Demolition will begin tomorrow afternoon."

"For what good that will do. It already has access to this world. It'll just find another point of entry. It's not like the veil doesn't have soft spots all over."

"So what are you thinking?"

I contemplated that. I kept trying to work up a reasonable and safer solution, but I realized the direct route was the only way to be sure. Too much, quite literally, hung in the balance. "I have to destroy the Spider from Mars." I hesitated a moment before adding, "However that works. You said it's not a god. More like a...photocopy of a god?"

"We *believe* so." She looked down at the tall, uncut grass as it brushed the palm of her outstretched hand. "I don't know, Nick. Much of this stuff is as esoteric to us as it is to you. It's not part of our *ways*..."

"But it could probably be destroyed." From hard experience, I knew that gods could not be destroyed. Not by my hand, anyway. But a photocopy of a god? I felt that was doable.

"Anything is possible, of course."

I turned and walked up to her and took her hand. That surprised her. When she looked up, I saw something in her face, something I don't think I have ever seen in anyone's face before, except maybe Morgana's.

Concern. Juliette was worried about my well-being.

"Sada said something this morning," I said as we stood there together, baking under the early morning sun. "She said by doing that spell, I acted pretty recklessly."

Juliette shook her head. "Sada is young. She doesn't unders—"

"She was right," I said, cutting Juliette off. "It was reckless. It was stupid. *I'm* pretty reckless. *I'm* pretty stupid—"

"Nick..."

"Listen." I let my breath out in an exasperated puff, but I wasn't exasperated with Juliette. I was raging mad at me. "I've never really been responsible for anyone but myself. I'm not...very good at this coven type of thing. All this is new to me..."

"My Lord, your will is our will. Whatever you need of us...whatever you need *from* us...is yours already." She sounded so sincere it nearly broke my heart. "You don't need to make any excuses."

Maybe she felt that way, but I didn't.

Juliette sighed as she looked at her hand, which I was still holding. "You're young. And in many ways, you're much like him, Nick."

I didn't need to ask who she meant. "Selfish."

"Stubborn." She nodded with that sage wisdom she seemed to possess. "And that's good. I suspect it's saved your life more than once. But you're going to have to learn to give yourself time to grow and adjust to this."

"I don't know what 'this' is," I told her honestly. "You shouldn't have that much faith in me. You shouldn't have that much faith in anything, Magus. It's bound to hurt you. Disappoint you, at the very least."

She pressed her lips together in a severe way. "Let me explain things to you this way, young Lucifer. You're imperfect, yes, but you're here. You get involved. You care. That's more than anyone can say for the God of Abraham."

"If I screw this up"—*when*, a tiny voice whispered in the back of my head—"everyone...everything...could die. I could wind up killing the whole fucking universe." Just saying it made me want to throw up. "I'm so not the Chosen One, Juliette, it's not even funny."

Juliette reached out and boldly put her hand on my cheek. The gesture touched me in a way I thought I couldn't be affected any longer. "You'll do your best, little Lucifer. And that's all any of us can do."

| 29 |

Lights Out

JULIETTE ASKED ME to sit in a chair in the center of the living room with a small hand mirror resting in my lap. She said I should concentrate on it while keeping the Thin Man in the back of my head. That wasn't all that difficult, considering I couldn't get him out of my head.

"What's this going to accomplish, again?" I asked, modulating my voice so I didn't sound like some sarcastic ass. I was honestly interested in accomplishing something here today.

Juliette sat facing me in a chair a few inches away, our knees nearly touching. Sada stood behind me, her hands resting heavily on my shoulders.

"You are going to scry by looking into a suitable medium in the hopes of detecting a significant message or vision about the future. But you will be using *my* power to do so—*not* your own." She nodded at her daughter. "Sada will act as your conduit to me."

"Okay," I said, sounding nervous even to myself.

A small smile touched her lips. "You're a witch and you've never scried? Never even tried it?"

My father had a scrying pool in Dis, I knew. But I'd never tried it. I'd never really seen the point, to be honest. I had enough trouble just dealing with the present. But I didn't say that. I didn't need Juliette knowing I operated on that level of incompetence. Instead, I just shrugged. "Have *you* tried everything in the witches' how-to manual?"

"Nearly everything."

"Yeah, well...I'm still fatigued from yesterday," I huffed.

"You won't be using your power, Nick. You will be using mine."

I gritted my teeth. It hurt my ego that I was the crowned prince of Hell but I had to be instructed by Juliette as if I was a newbie witch still wet behind the ears.

Juliette, of course, sensed my dilemma. "Stop getting in your own way, Nick. Just close your eyes and drift."

"Drifting" is what she called it—read: Use the Force. She said I had to let the craft have its way with me. I was fighting too hard to try and control it. I closed my eyes, acutely aware of the warmth of Sada's hands on my shoulders, and tried to relax my mind, which was harder than it sounded. Every time I tried to settle my thoughts, I'd think of the Thin Man and what he'd done to those children. What he was doing. How the hell could I relax when all I was feeling was outrage?

"*Drift*, Nick," she reminded me. "You are doing this for them. And you'll never understand the Thin Man if can't see what he's capable of."

Sada's hands seemed to grow increasingly warm. I dropped the tension from my shoulder and tried to relax. I forced myself to drift like hell.

* * *

"Nick, open your eyes."

I did.

I could see the Angry Red Planet reflected in the mirror in my lap. The hellish landscape stretched on and on—an infinity of red emptiness broken only by yellow, sun-bleached shards of bone sticking up through the sand. Whether they were animal or human, I couldn't tell. In the distance, several volcanoes appeared to be coughing red-hot molten rock and grey ash into the already thoroughly poisoned atmosphere. Some jagged glass structure loomed in the distance, half-buried in the always-present red sand. The dim light of the dying sun was reflected in its broken windows, and it was surrounded by dark mountains of unidentifiable debris. It looked like the sad remnants of a building...a civilization...gone. Destroyed. Dusted.

I squinted to make out more details, but before the image came clear, the mirror fogged over and changed to a room somewhere. Dim and dingy, with arcane graffiti crawling over the grey walls. A young girl was standing with her back to me, but it was too dark to see any significant details. Like the previous vision, I felt this one was just as important—if not more so.

"Turn around," I begged. "Turn around."

And, to my surprise, she did.

It was Antonia Oswald. Her eyes were wide and full of terror and light. Her mouth dropped open in a soundless scream,...and then a shadow swept over her from on high and she was gone from sight, though I heard her scream in my mind, echoing into infinity.

I jerked upright and dropped the mirror. The surface cracked on the floor at my feet and the vision vanished. My hands were shaking and my fingers flexing open and closed where they hovered in front of me. I could still hear Antonia's shrill, helpless scream echoing in my head.

"Nick," Juliette said from the chair in front of me, snapping my attention around to her. "Nick, what did you see?"

I had to force the words out. "An-Antonia." I sounded hoarse as if I'd been screaming for hours. "She's next, Juliette." I slowly lowered my hands to my lap. "It's coming for her next."

***

Ben's house was located at the end of Oak Street, in the newer part of town. A towering, grey and white remodeled colonial set behind an honest-to-god white picket fence. I parked the rental on the street out front and got out, following the brick walkway to the front door, which sported a summer wreath made of dry lavender and green grape leaves. Lavender traditionally represented refinement, grace, and elegance. I knew Brenda, who ran the local rotary club and various church suppers and did Toys for Tots every Christmas, had chosen it.

"Nick," she said, sounding concerned as she opened the front door. I couldn't blame her. I'd spent the last few minutes frantically banging on it like some madman. She glanced up and down the street as though there was some obvious emergency. "What's going on? Ben's not here right now—"

"I'm not here for Ben, Brenda," I said, interrupting her. "I need to talk to Antonia."

She frowned. "Toni? What's happened?"

I swallowed to compose myself. I didn't need a lot of questions from Brenda Oswald. If I'd had Antonia's number, I would have called ahead and bypassed all this, but I'd never had any reason to put her on my phone, and I didn't want to ask Ben. He'd just pummel me for answers as any concerned dad would. "Please. It's important, Brenda."

"Toni's not here, Nick. She bartends the juice bar at The Loop three days a week."

"She's there now?"

"Should be. What's all this about?" she demanded. But by then, I was halfway back to the rental. Brenda shook her head and went back inside while I was turning over the engine, so she never saw what happened next.

I always thought the backseat ambush trope was TV cop show crap. But Agent Kip had managed to pull it off. I spied him in the rearview mirror in the moments before I pulled out. My cop brain immediately identified the captive bolt pistol in his hand—a large, black, mean-looking thing generally used to stun cattle for slaughter.

The coward. Couldn't even use a human taser, I thought.

"Fuck!" I said as he pressed the gun to the side of my neck.

Instant lights out.

| 30 |

Wake-Up Call

"WAKE UP, ASSHOLE!" something shouted just before a pail of freezing cold water hit me full in the face.

I jerked awake with a start. I was sitting in a hard-backed chair in some stuffy, dusty storage room somewhere, my wrists handcuffed behind my back. There was a ceramic bowl on the floor, sort of half-tucked under the chair. And I was in far more pain than I should have been, given the situation.

"Ughk," I said because it felt like someone had put giant fishhooks into my flesh all over and had attached them to massive, weighted balls. I felt my entire body bow under the painful, invisible pressure and had this weird fantasy of my skin being pulled off my bones in a kind of full-body degloving if I moved too fast in the wrong direction.

"I said fucking wake up!" someone said angrily before hitting me in the face with the pail next.

The metal smashed into my nose and upper cheek and bounced away, the bucket making a sharp *clank* as it hit the floor. The pain was searing and instantaneous. With a shout, I sat up, almost toppling the chair. The bucket in the face was pretty bad, granted, but that was still small potatoes compared to the invisible weights in my flesh. I screamed like a little girl as I sat up.

My head was swimming with pain and the whole room was going all teeter-totter around me. It took a few seconds for everything to settle down and for me to get my breathing under a semblance of control. The pain lessened somewhat and I tried my best to work through it and assess the situation.

The room was tiny and unfamiliar. Random clutter filled the space—white storage boxes, racks of choir robes, some sports equipment, Christmas decorations (including a life-sized, light-up nativity scene), and what looked like random stage props. There were posters on the wall for church suppers and the local food bank hosted by St. Peter's Church. And crosses. Lots and lots of crosses on the walls everywhere I looked. No wonder I was in such pain.

"Jesus Christ, man!" someone said from behind me where I couldn't see him. "You're gonna kill the bastard."

"He can't die," said the man in front of me whom I finally identified as a thoroughly pissed-off Agent Kip. "At least...not easily." He was wearing black slacks and a dress shirt, but his jacket and tie were off and his nice pinstriped shirt was open at his throat. He'd rolled his sleeves up, and I took a moment to ogle his rather muscular forearms. I felt sorry for any suspect he'd ever decked during an interrogation.

I tried to say something, but I think he'd dislocated my jaw with the bucket. It came out all garbled nonsense.

"Welcome back, Nick," Kip said. "Have a good sleep?"

My muddled brain began to form connections. Looked like we were in a storage room of the rectory at St. Peter's, the isolated little Catholic church just outside Blackwater. This was confirmed when I tried to straighten up and experienced one of the worst pains of my life. At first, I thought maybe the creep behind me had stabbed me in the back with a long, dull knife, but as I screamed and jerked spastically in my seat, I caught a whiff of the smoke coming off my exposed skin. Throwing back my head, I caught a quick glimpse of the ginormous plastic crucifix suspended over the chair, undoubtedly scrimped from the nativity scene. And fucking plastic. But it was a cross and this was a place of faith. For something like I was, it was like being hit in the back of the head with a mallet with nails embedded in it.

I screamed loud enough that my jaw clicked back into place and the jerk behind me screamed in response.

"Jesus-fucking-Christ, man! What the fuck, man?" he bellowed. "I never fucking touched him!"

Despite my pain, I laughed at that.

Agent Kip said, "He thinks you're funny, Mike."

"Oberon," the creep intoned, walking around the chair so he could look at me from the front. I found myself staring up at Vivian's boy toy. I still didn't like the fucker. "Holy shit. Is he on fire?"

"Something like that."

I was peripherally aware that smoke was drifting off my head and shoulders like a vampire at the end of a Hammer film. I could see it swirling around me like a wreath. It made me want a cigarette. "Miiiike," I managed, my voice dry and raspy.

"Oberon, fuckhead!" Mike Bartholdi screamed. He squatted down so he could look me in the eye. I noted his fucking stupid eyebrow piercing. Pussy. "You look like dog shit, man, you know that? Not such a pretty boy now."

He glanced up at Kip. "So the fucker's a vampire?"

"Daemon," Agent Kip provided. He was busy with a large gym bag he was setting down on a nearby table. I was trying to wrap my brain around the idea that these two knuckleheads were working together and failing horribly at it. "Half human and half demon."

"Hard*core*."

"I doubt Nick's thinking that at the moment."

"So he's like a dhampir or something?"

Kip rolled his eyes and gave me an exasperated expression. "No, Mike. He's *half demon*. Tell him, Nick."

"Fuck you," I spat at him. "Do I look like Wikipedia?"

Agent Kip walked over and grabbed me hard by the ponytail and jerked my head back. That hurt and forced my swollen lips apart. "You see teeth, asshole?"

"Well, yeah."

"Angel teeth—not vampire teeth."

Mike watched me burn at a low simmer while Kip explained that I was a glorified meat source. Through me, he could ascend. Consume my flesh...consume my power. Level up to archangel status.

Mike's eyes slowly widened. "And Vivian's the same?"

"Yes." Kip released me so he could cross back to the table. Reaching into his bag of tricks, he extracted a pair of brass knuckles and set them on the table—except they weren't brass. They looked like they were made of silver. "But we'll take care of the little Lucifer later. Right now, we're going for the big kahuna."

Mike swallowed as if he was rethinking this whole thing.

"Go stand over there." Kip pointed to a corner and Mike obediently shuffled out of my line of sight.

"Recruiting?" I said as Kip approached me, pulling on a pair of black leather gloves.

"Always. But I'd worry less about your ex's new boyfriend and more about what's going to happen to you in the next few minutes."

"I don't give a shit what you do to me," I spat, meaning it. "Just leave Vivian alone. She doesn't even have a soul for you to take."

"I'm aware." Agent Kip put his leather-glove-clad hands on his knees and crouched down. "And what did you do with that, I wonder?"

"Sold it on eBay," I hissed out while smoke continued to swirl around us. It was starting to remind me of bacon cooking on a hot griddle. "Let's just get this shit over with, Kippy."

"Big talk for a guy about to be eaten alive." He reached out and grabbed my upper thigh, giving it a harsh squeeze. "Not much on you. You surprise me, skinny, considering all that sugar you binge. Good metabolism."

"I'll give you diabetes."

He chuckled at that and moved his hand up to grab my long hair, which was hanging down in ragged loose ropes over my chest. He used it to yank my head back.

That left me looking up at the cross hanging over my face. That hurt. A lot. It was just white plastic, the kind you light up on your lawn at Christmas, but it seemed to be burning like a small sun in the center of the room. I could feel it singeing my face. I screamed right on cue.

"I like you, skinny. I'm going to make you a deal. You ask me to end you and I will. You don't...well, we'll see how far you go."

He let me go and my head fell forward, my skin tight and pulsing with waves of dizzying pain. Mike continued to swear up a storm behind me. I figured I was probably approaching the shade of a boiled lobster at this point.

"Dead or no deal?" Agent Kip asked.

"Go fuck yourself," I said through cracked and burned lips.

"Get his shirt off," Agent Kip said to Mike. He sounded agitated as he took a step back and picked up the silver knuckles, sliding them over his gloved fist.

Mike came around to rip open my shirt while Agent Kip punched the knuckles into his open palm a few times to warm up.

For about half a second, I considered asking Mike for help. Then I saw his eyes. He was feeling a bit put off by the current pageantry, sure, but there was a definite glint of pure evil glee there. I wasn't getting rescued by him anytime soon.

"What the fuck did she ever see in you?" Mike said as he analyzed me up and down. "Fucking Beach Boy. Vivian likes goth dudes."

I laughed at that.

Agent Kip laughed, too. "Old Nick's about as goth as you can get."

"I just don't get it," said Mike, stepping back as Agent Kip took his place in front of me.

I looked up at Kippy Skippy playing tough guy with his stupid silver knuckles. "You gonna beat me up like a two-bit goon, Kippy?"

Agent Kip smiled. It was a very dead Arcana smile. "Consider it more...tenderizing the meat." He admired the knuckles as if he were a gangster admiring some pricey bling.

I should have known this was coming. I'd embarrassed him back at the hospital, and hell hath no fury like an Arcana emasculated. Mike made a little noise as Agent Kip stepped forward, his eyes traveling over my naked chest as he considered his first move. "I can say with absolute authority that this will hurt you far more than it's going to hurt me."

"Stop talking me to death and fucking do it already."

In the end, he landed the first blows to my face. He started slow, with a series of carefully placed punches to my cheeks and jaw. I could tell he had experience. Probably worked out three days a week at Planet Fitness, maybe with little extracurricular at some boxing school he slummed at. Pop punches. The kinds that blacken your eyes and leave your ears ringing. But the knuckles, man...they hurt more than they should have. It was like being punched with a hot branding iron.

After a few minutes of grinding my teeth against my skull, Agent Kip stopped shadowboxing my face and grinned at me. There was blackish blood on his knuckles. He licked it off, making a lascivious show of it. "How do you like my baby, Lucifer?"

I spat out some blood clotted in my cheek. "Charming."

He rubbed his "baby."

"Vatican silver. She packs a helluva punch, doesn't she?"

Blood drooled past my lips and down my chin, and penny-sized drops plinked into the basin at my feet. The punches hurt, sure, but not as much as the cross above me. That was the real bitch because the longer I sat there, the weaker I felt. The weaker I became, the harder it would be for me to recover from whatever Agent Kip threw at me. I wasn't going anywhere, and that cross was slowly killing me where I sat.

"Weaksauce."

He punched me in the mouth for that. I felt the jarring pain all the way down my spine. "We'll see who's weaksauce after this." Crouching low like a prizefighter, he went to work on my solar plexus. The first good punch knocked the air out of me. The next few built on that, driving my breath out too fast for me to catch up so I wound up hyperventilating in the chair, which made my already dizzy head spin like a top. The cuffs clattered loudly against the chair with each blow, filling the room with a sound I knew I would forever associate with this moment for the rest of my life.

Kip was good. I'd give him that. All his blows were well calculated to land with optimum pain but also with the kind of blunt trauma that wouldn't damage me too badly. The knuckles hurt more than the actual impacts—and seemed to be getting hotter as time went by.

He kept it up for about a good five minutes before dropping his fists and stepping back. He was sweating and panting and walking in circles.

I grinned. It gave me a perverse joy to see how this little workout was taking a toll on him. Weaksauce, as I said.

I spit some blood onto the wooden floorboards while Agent Kip went to the gym bag and grabbed a bottle of coconut water and twisted off the cap to take a long slug.

Coconut water.

"Fucking pussy," I said, though my words came out all mush-mouthed.

Agent Kip turned and gave me a small, mean-spirited smile. "Thirsty?" He walked up to me and squirted the nasty-ass water in my face. More darkish, unnatural-looking blood dribbled down the front of my body and collected in the bowl on the floor under the chair. I'd finally figured out why it was there.

Done, he turned back to the gym bag. All that blood had made him talky and he started to instruct Mike in the archaic ways of the Arcana. He sounded like a college professor explaining an esoteric concept. "Every part of the Daemon is of use to us. Never let anything go to waste. You can even boil the bones for broth." He turned and approached me with a pair of nasty-looking shears.

I admit it—a part of me jumped inside at the sight of them, but he casually went about the process of stretching thick strands of my hair out before clipping them short to my head. It was pretty much the worst haircut of my life. He yanked my head this way and that, pulling brutally on my hair as he hacked it off in long gold strands that fell to the floor at my feet.

"Pick up *every* strand," Agent Kip instructed, and Mike hurried to bag everything in these Ziploc freezer bags with the little zipper closure.

"Damn," Agent Kip said when he grazed my scalp hard enough to draw blood. "Sorry about that, skinny."

I hissed through my teeth at the brutal way he was treating my hair. I hated it, too, but it didn't deserve this.

Once he had hacked it all off and Mike had dutifully Ziplocked up every strand, Agent Kip went back to the table and exchanged the scissors for the holy silver knuckles. He walked back over to me and leaned over, grabbed the ragged hair at the back of my skull, and dragged my head up. "Ready?"

I spat blood in his eye.

I thought that was pretty funny. Kip didn't think so. Holding my head in place, he rammed his silver knuckles at my face...but stopped two inches away from hitting me. When I finally wound up the courage to open my eyes, he proceeded to plow two fingers past my swollen mouth and down my throat. I choked hard and started to gag and struggle. I rattled in the chair as my body, suddenly deprived of oxygen, started to panic. He didn't let up and even smiled as he slowly suffocated me. After a few seconds, I started to froth at the mouth and darkness started leaking into the corners of my eyes.

At that point, Agent Kip finally yanked his fingers out of my mouth and shoved me back into the chair so hard that it toppled over and I landed hard on my back, knocking the air out of my sore and tired body.

"You talk a good game, tough guy. But we'll see what you're made of when you're all carved up." He stood over me, his face stony and full of hate. "Go on and scream. I want to hear it. I want to hear you beg for death, Satan."

I didn't scream, but I did laugh. Nothing was funny and everything was fucked up and I was probably going to die here tonight, but the ridiculousness of the situation was hilarious. Of all the types of dying I had contemplated and feared in my admittedly messed up life, I hadn't seen this one coming.

Agent Kip didn't see the humor in the situation. My laughter seemed to make him even angrier. Gotta love a sociopath. He leaned over the overturned chair. "Beg!" he screamed, his snarling, red-faced visage filling my whole field of vision. "Beg me to end your godforsaken life, you infernal piece of shit!"

I just laughed and laughed.

With a roar, he punched me across the face. That made my head bounce against the back of the chair. I moaned in pain.

That pleased him more. Reaching between my legs, he grabbed the front of my cargo pants and undid the button. When his hand slid inside and he grabbed that part of me, I bucked my hips, trying to dislodge his grip, but the overturned chair had me at a disadvantage. I couldn't move or even fight while he groped me. Despite this being another miserable rodeo I was used to, I found I didn't like it one bit—hated it, in fact—and a little whimper escaped my lips, making me ashamed.

"You know what I'm going to do with you, tough guy?" Agent Kip growled, leaning close so his face was almost against mine and I could see every little vein popping in his forehead. "First, I'm going to cut off your arms, and then I'm going to cut off your legs. After that, I'm going to cut off that big dick you're so proud of and fuck the hole that's left behind."

Letting go of my pants, he stepped back and raised his foot, slamming the toe of his shoe into my crotch and against the edge of the seat so he could right the chair. The blow to my scrotum was enough to make me blow out a breath and try to suck it in at the same time, which didn't work. The pain made my brain wheel away to some dark place.

"Any more witty comebacks?" Agent Kip barked.

I was running on empty at that point. I gagged and spat out more blood...and I think a loose tooth. It pinked into the bowl.

We went back to the silver knuckles. I guess he was tired of my face because we concentrated on my solar plexus and the lower muscles of my abdomen. The blows were sharper now, more concentrated to drive the force of each punch all the way through my body. I could feel the power of his rage and malice as he worked on tenderizing that muscle group before working his way downward—perilously close to the family jewels. I coughed, heaved, and gasped with each blow. Once again, he forced me to suck in breaths far too fast for my own good, and it wasn't long before I started to hyperventilate and a disconcerting wheezing noise started to issue out of my lungs.

He took a coconut water break after that and went back to his bag of tricks.

Mike came around and scooted down to look me in the face, though I couldn't lift my head anymore. I was left staring at the wooden floorboards where my blood was regularly plinking down like bloody pennies while Mike said, "Holy-fucking-Jesus-H.-Christ. Not such a pretty boy anymore, huh? Wish Vivian could see you now, hotshot."

Mike saying her name pissed me off. I somehow found the strength to lift my head a few inches. "Fucking poseur," I said, spittling blood across his face.

"Fuck you, man." He punched me square in the face and that was it.

Lights out again.

| 31 |

A Good Catholic Boy Never Would

I CAME AROUND sometime later. When, I don't know. I had no idea what time it was or what day.

It was worse now. My skin felt about two sizes too small, my lungs seemed to be full of rocks, and every breath made me feel like I was sucking glass shards into my body. I could only see out of one eye, and my entire face was numb—which was better than the alternative, I suppose. Every part of my exposed skin felt boiled and peeling. Sitting up caused a cramp of agony to flow through me that was so bad, I started heaving onto the floor.

"Fuck, man!" Mike yelled, jumping to his feet. He'd been sitting in a chair wedged back against the wall, and he nearly broke his damned neck as he sprang up.

Heaving made it worse, somehow. My whole body seemed to be locking up on me. I realized the repeated blows to my face and head might have done something to my brain because suddenly I couldn't seem to control myself as my body started to rock and roll in the chair. Even the giant cross couldn't keep me in place, and I felt the whole room tilt sideways as the chair with me tied to it slammed sideways onto the floor. My body spasmed for a few seconds more and I lost control of my wings, which sprang out and started beating the air and floor around me in a kind of spastic panic.

Mike continued to swear as he danced around the room, trying to stay clear of my wings. Thankfully, the seizure only lasted a few minutes, though it left me feeling even more exhausted than I already did. I lay there, moaning deliriously until Agent Kip commanded Mike to get my chair upright.

"I ain't goin' near that...that freak!" Mike shouted as if I had leprosy or something.

That left Agent Kip to get my chair up while trying to stay out of the path of my wings, which were shuddering of their own accord. "Get the fucking feathers, genius!" he barked.

That led to a hellish hour of Mike tentatively plucking flight feathers off my wings and jumping back each time my body shuddered in response. I didn't feel much of that. I was too sore and depleted to even feel any new pain.

After my wings had been plucked over and the feathers properly bagged, Agent Kip returned to the bench to retrieve his cursed silver knuckles.

"Oh, come *on*, man," I moaned, hating the wounded, pitiful sound of my own voice.

"Beg for death, black-winged Lucifer, and it's all over," Agent Kip reminded me. "No? That's okay, too. I like you this way—broken and obedient." He drew his arm back, ready to land the first blow to my face.

I closed my eyes...but the blow never fell.

When I opened them again, Agent Kip laughed.

Fucking kill you, I thought.

Smiling and chuckling, he moved around to where Mike was emptying the bowl of my blood into a plastic milk jug via a red kitchen funnel. Agent Kip waited until Mike screwed the top on securely and then told him to go put it in his bag along with the hair and feathers.

"Sure, man," Mike said. He wasn't sounding so enthusiastic about this operation anymore, not since my seizure. He sounded weary of it all, but he obediently carried the jug to the table and started placing it in Agent Kip's bag.

Agent Kip looked at me, raised his eyebrows, and put a finger to his lips. *Shhh...*

Picking up a baseball bat resting against one wall, he crept up behind Mike. I hated the little poseur. I really did. But I couldn't just sit here and do nothing. Problem was, the sound I made was little more than a hiss of air through broken and parched lips.

Mike, sensing the presence behind him, turned around. He even raised an arm in defense, but it wasn't enough. Agent Kip landed one solid blow to Mike's face, cracking it like a dinner plate. Mike squealed like a pig being slaughtered. The blow drove him back and into a wall of shelves, knocking some random boxes down. Old VHS tapes of animated Bible stories flew out of a damaged box and across the room, some of them unraveling in the process. But Agent Kip wasn't finished. He took a step back to gain some space and momentum and started pummeling the kid over and over into the floor, the blows focused and fast, aimed to kill.

I'd seen some shit, let me tell you. But watching Agent Kip destroy Mike with a concentrated series of blows that broke every bone in his face was something else. Something even I didn't need to see. I was no fan of Mike Bartholdi, but his muffled, kitten-like cries of agony ripped up and down my spine. I felt a tremendous wave of relief when Agent Kip finally drove the broken particles of Mike's nose into his brain and ended his torment forever.

I was trembling in my seat when Agent Kip stood up, the baseball bat—bloody, with some bits of Mike's scalp still stuck to it—in his hand, breathing roughly but looking supremely satisfied by his work. He turned and gave me a smile and a wink as he threw the bat aside. "Well, angel mine, where were we?"

***

He managed to punch me so hard, the handcuffs broke and I wound up spilling like liquid Nick to the floor. He had to pick me up and put me back in my seat and tie my hands and legs to it with some clothesline he'd found in the room. I let him do it. By then, I was too weak to sit up straight, never mind fight him.

I was beyond pain. I looked up at the cross hanging above—the thing sucking out every bit of my strength—now almost fascinated by it as it swayed gently above me, burning layers of skin off my face. Agent Kip thought that was interesting.

"What do you see, skinny? Your past? Your future? Do you even have a future?"

He was playing with a long black feather with a white tip, twirling it in his hands. But when I didn't answer his question, he threw it aside and stepped up to me. He plowed a few more brass-knuckled kisses into my guts until I threw up, then returned his attention to my face.

Blood, drool, and teeth poured out of my mouth as he strategically rearranged my jaw. By then, he was drunk on his own power—and probably my blood. He stopped to take a few gulps of it from the plastic milk bottle and flexed his fist a few times—his knuckles were raw and the skin split and painful-looking—before putting on the silver knuckles once again.

I couldn't look away from them. They were so strangely beautiful. Turning about-face, he gave me a blood-slathered smile as he approached. "Hail Satan, motherfucker!" he said and then punched my lights out for the second time.

* * *

"Nick? Nick, wake the fuck up, man."

I opened my eyes. I was still tied to the chair, but I wasn't in pain any longer. I felt weak and tired, but, thank whatever gods remained, there was no more goddamn pain.

The room was dark. Agent Kip was gone, but he'd left a candle burning on a shelf across the room. It didn't throw much light, and what it did was sallow and chancy, but I could still make out the vague outline of a man sitting in the chair that Mike had been using before he'd been murdered.

"Nick, man. You awake?"

"Y-yeah," I answered, my voice hoarse and unrecognizable. "Peter."

"You remembered."

I felt a lump form in my throat. My heart suddenly hurt in a way I hadn't felt in a long, long time. "How could I forget?"

"I never know with you, man," Peter said. He was backlit by the candle and I couldn't see his face, but from the familiar way he was sitting there, I could tell it was him, all right. "An enigma wrapped in a burrito. Remember?"

I laughed at that. That was something Peter used to say about me. I was an enigma wrapped in a burrito. "Yeah." I couldn't believe he was alive, but it filled my heart with relief and happiness that he was. That I'd been wrong. He hadn't died. He'd been alive the whole time.

"I looked for you, man," I told him. "I went to fucking Hell to look for you."

Peter laughed. "I know I wasn't perfect, but...Hell? Really, Nick?"

"I thought maybe...I don't know. Is it really you?"

He moved subtly in the chair. I still couldn't see his face, but I recognized his blue uniform. An NYPD badge was pinned to his jacket.

Happy tears filled my eyes. "I've missed you, man."

"Don't get sappy." But I thought maybe he was smiling. "What in hell happened to you?"

"A lot. *Hell.*" I laughed at that. "Hell is exactly what happened to me. But it's all crap, man. It doesn't mean anything." I thought a moment. "You remember that time at the policeman's ball when I got drunk and you had to walk me out of there? But I threw up on the commissioner's wife's dress and you were all like, 'It's the salmon thingies over there. They're bad.' And then we got the hell out of there and we thought for sure we'd get busted down to crosswalk..." I was babbling and he knew all this, but my head was just so full of memories, some good, some bad...most of them ridiculous.

"Yeah, and we went to that little cop shop with the hot little waitress, and you bet me twenty bucks she'd be all over you, but you were drunk as hell..."

That was the night I was just drunk enough to tell Peter how I felt about him, but then I chickened out. A few days later, we got a distress call from an old brownstone in Brooklyn. The night Peter...

I stopped and just stared at him. "This is bullshit, Peter. You're dead." I nearly choked on that admission. It hurt more than all the pain I had endured in the last few hours. He was gone. I had lost him forever. "Why are you here?"

Peter tilted his head to the side. I turned my head and saw Agent Kip standing at the table where he'd had his gym bag. The bag was gone. He had a butcher board set up now, with a collection of wicked-looking knives resting on the board. He was sharpening the largest butchering knife in his arsenal.

"Aren't you worried?" Peter said.

"Not sure I can do anything about it."

"So you're just going to sit there like a great big dummy and let him do it to you?"

"I think I deserve it," I told him truthfully. "I've hurt so many people over the years."

"But I didn't deserve what they did to me." Peter was starting to sound angry. "What *his* kind did to me."

The memory hurt so much. What the Arcana had done to Peter. The precise way they had butchered him. He was right, of course. I needed to fight this. I needed to fight *them*.

"I can't move, Peter. I can't do anything with that up there," I confessed, nodding toward the giant cross hanging above our heads.

Peter—a good Catholic boy—looked confused.

I didn't want to tell him, but I realized I had no choice. "I'm not what you think I am, Peter."

"A hot mess? I've always known that."

I shook my head. I didn't know how to explain it.

"Oh," said Peter. "That." He was on his feet, closing in on the wall...where a rope securing the cross overhead was tied to an anchor. Agent Kip had suspended it from a hook in the ceiling, one likely used for a hanging lamp. The rope was just a clothesline like the stuff he'd used to tie me to the chair. All I needed to do was to untie the knot...

* * *

"Talking to your imaginary friend?"

I jerked awake suddenly. Pain flowed back into my body, the full force of it making me sick. Peter was gone and Agent Kip had turned away from the cutting board where his knives were lined up neatly next to it to speak to me.

He was wearing a white butcher's apron now and he was smiling. "What did he have to say to you?"

You're an asshole, I wanted to say, but it was just bloody mumbles that probably sounded like delusional nonsense. A bloody tooth dropped out of my mouth.

He picked it up off the floor and put it in his breast pocket like some kind of charm. "I'll be back for the main event after I get rid of our friend here. He's starting to smell in the heat and he's ruining my appetite. Don't go anywhere, skinny." He grabbed my bicep and seemed to measure it before moving to where Mike was lying in a puddle of congealed black goo in the corner. Picking him up by the feet, Agent Kip dragged the kid unceremoniously to the door and stopped to open it before dragging him outside. He slammed the door closed and I heard it slam into Mike's cracked and deformed head.

I canted my head a little to peer around the room, but Peter was gone. I was alone again, looking at the rope that Peter had shown me.

My body hurt so, so much. I probably had minutes—if that—before Agent Kip got back. Taking a deep, shuddering breath, I did my best to throw my weight sideways. The whole chair went over as it had during my seizure. But this time, when it hit the floor, the dry, old rickety thing snapped in several places. It was just enough impact to break two of the legs off and for me to get my legs free of the rope. The back of the cane chair had snapped, as well, but it took a bit more fiddling to slide my bound hands loose from the rails of the seatback.

After that, I had to lay there on the floor for several seconds and work on my breathing. Between the cross and my injuries, it felt as though I was swimming through pain molasses. Every little movement hurt, and I thought my shoulder might have been dislocated in the fall.

I looked at the door to the storage room, trying to gauge how much time I had left before Magical Hannibal Lecter returned.

Not much, Peter's voice seemed to whisper to me. *If you don't move now, asshole, you're going to die alone on this filthy floor.*

After I got my breathing under control, I tried pushing myself up—and almost screamed at the pain that lanced through my half-broken body.

God, you're such a pussy, Peter would have said. *Suck it up, princess. The whole world is counting on you to keep your shit together. Antonia is counting on you...*

Pushing against the floor with both hands to gain some leverage, I was able to get myself up into a half-sitting position, but my wrists were still tied behind my back with rope. God, I sweated through the pain. My wrecked shoulder was making it almost unbearable to move.

Some Lucifer, I thought as I resorted to pushing myself along the floor on my side like an inchworm. It seemed to take forever before I reached the wall. And that was just half the battle. When I finally got there, I realized I would need to push myself up into a half-crouch to reach the rope. I didn't think I could handle doing that, not with the weight of the cross bearing down on me like a cartoon anvil.

There was a stack of cardboard boxes pushed against the wall. They were full of cheap, locally grown communion wine. I rested the upper portion of my body against them. That hurt a lot as I aggravated all my sore muscles and pulverized ribs. My head swam with red, raw agony, and there was a frightening moment where I was sure I'd pass out. I had to bite my tongue to get my head to focus. Turning sideways, I wormed my back against the wall so I was finally sitting atop the boxes with the rope in the anchor about two feet above my right shoulder. By now, my body was screaming at me to cut this shit out. Red and black speckles were invading the corner of my one working eye. I knew I was on the verge of passing out if I didn't get this done soon.

Out there, somewhere in the building, I heard a door slam shut. Shit, he was on his way back.

Ignoring the pain and darkness infusing every inch of my body, I pushed myself up the wall. I felt the whole room tilt slightly, but, by then, I'd managed to get a hand around the knot of the rope anchoring the cross. I weaved dangerously as I pulled on it, but it didn't seem willing to budge. Gritting my teeth to hold in a scream of absolute agony, I pulled again, this time too hard. Lost my footing and my balance, which was crap anyway from the beating I'd taken.

I went down hard on the floor but kept my grip on the knot. Someone somewhere must have been looking out for me because it loosened the rope enough that the cross came banging down on the floor beside me.

The moment the cross was down on the floor and not upright, I felt that tremendous, elephantine pressure lift and my ability to mend started kicking in. I was still in a house of God, so there was no way I was going to operate at full strength, but not having that burning cross bearing down on me like a ship anchor certainly helped.

By the time Agent Kip threw the door open and stepped into the room, I was already partially mended. But because I was against the door by the communion wine boxes, he didn't notice me at first. Swearing under his breath, he walked to the center of the room where the broken chair lay and bent to pick up a length of rope, then switched his attention to the giant cross that had fallen to the floor and stared at it as if he couldn't believe it.

"What the hell—?" he growled, turning around to scan the room.

He never finished his statement because, by then, I was upon him. And at that moment, I was not myself.

* * *

I have no clear memories of what happened next—and that was for the best.

Agent Kip had damaged me badly. And, at that point, my body had switched to automatic pilot. It needed to heal. And something about what he was—Arcana—made him an exception to the normal rules of the working universe. I hadn't been able to hurt McCarty, even though I sorely wanted to. But Agent Kip Murphy was just angel enough to be fair game.

I remember being hungry. The kind of hunger that tears at your mind and body and sanity and makes you want to rage at the whole world. Most people don't understand that kind of hunger. But I did.

My mind latched onto a memory. I was eleven years old. There was this pizza joint in downtown Brooklyn. Spinelli's. When my foster dad got rough and drunk, I'd stay out all night. There was always some food in the Dumpster behind the shop. You'd be surprised what people throw out.

One night, I saw a handwritten letter taped to the edge of the big blue container. It read, *You're not an animal. Come around to the side and we'll give you something to eat, my friend.* One of the staff, a large black man in cook's whites and a stained apron, was waiting with a white bag "You the one? Kind of skinny."

"I'm not skinny," I told him as I took the bag.

He laughed. "I'm Sherman."

I didn't give him my name.

He smiled anyway. "Okay, kid. Come 'round tomorrow night and I'll give you another bag."

It became our routine for a few weeks. Sherman kept me fed until the boss caught on. Then Sherman didn't appear at the back door any longer. Maybe he'd lost his job over it. I don't know. But that was when they started spraying Dumpsters with bleach to keep scum like me from digging around in them. Not long after that, I learned I could get an even better meal if I just spent some time with lonely, rich older women.

I gasped as I pushed myself up and back. My whole world was colored red and there was thick, choking foreign stuff in my mouth. It felt like hot Jell-O and it tasted like shit. I dropped to my hands and knees, gagging noisily on whatever was clotting my throat. I felt a convulsion rip through my entire system. Shuddering, shoulders bunched, I tossed my cookies all over the floor. Chunky red and black steamy stuff. The moment I saw it, I threw up again, this time all blackish liquid like ink or motor oil.

I sat back on my knees, panting through the goop on my mouth and dripping off my chin. I rubbed at it with my sleeve while my eyes drifted down to Agent Kip.

What remained of Agent Kip. His scalp was twisted sideways on his head, and an eye was gone, replaced by a gaping black hole into nothing. His molars showed on the side of his face where the skin had been peeled back in a flap. He stared up at me, wide-eyed and almost comically surprised, his jaws open in a scream he'd ever had the chance to utter.

"Shit," I said and turned away to throw up one last time.

This time, it didn't come easy. Something was stuck down my throat. My body kept convulsing, but I couldn't seem to loosen whatever was in my throat, blocking my windpipe. I resorted to sticking two fingers down my throat. That helped. I fingered something and started pulling it slowly up and out of my throat.

A long, bloodied white feather that looked like it'd seen better days.

"Are you *shitting* me?" I asked no one in the room.

But Agent Kip had eaten at least one angel. And I'd eaten Agent Kip.

It was the fucking circle of life, man.

| 32 |

Bogey in the Bathroom

I STAGGERED OUT the back door of the church and into the parking lot. It was after nightfall. Hot. Soul-sucking heat. God, I hated the heat. I hated the night heat even more. It never seemed to end.

I leaned my back against the brick wall by the slowly closing pneumatic door and worked on catching my breath and working through the remainder of the pain. I needed to find the jeep. Needed to get to The Loop and make sure Antonia was all right. There was no question of that. I just wasn't sure if my body was going to cooperate even after what it had done.

The thought made me sick all over again. I was a "day-old pizza for breakfast and Doritos for dinner" kind of guy. I didn't subsist well on long pork. After heaving one last time—which was painful on my now empty stomach—I found myself sliding down the wall to the asphalt. I breathed in and out, in and out, then raised my head and scanned the parking lot.

The jeep was in a parking space a hundred feet away. I tried to force myself up, but the whole world went sideways on me and I wound up collapsing to my side, instead. My body had done a magnificent job of healing the worst of my wounds, but as of ten seconds ago, it was done. Kaput.

I needed help from this point on.

I fumbled along the sides of my pants, working through the various pockets on the cargo pants, hoping against hope that Kip hadn't taken my phone. Turned out, he hadn't—probably because I had stupidly put it on silent and he never knew it was there. There were a dozen texts from various exes asking where the hell I was and if I was alive. I wasn't sure if they were kidding or not.

I scrolled through speed dial.

Morgana? Pissed as hell.

David? Same.

Vivian? Yeah, okay, you're hilarious.

In the end, I chose to text Juliette. She was about the only one left speaking to me.

HELP ST PETERS

It was all I could manage. No sooner had I hit Send, I felt my brain slip away and the phone dropped out of my open hand and clattered down on the asphalt of the parking lot. My body shut down so fast that I hardly realized what was happening.

When next I was aware of a presence, it was still dark out, but Juliette and Sada were standing over me and there was a sedan running with doors open behind them. The headlights were making smeary halos of everything.

"Back the car up and help me get him in." Juliette was calm and organized, as usual, and between the two of them, they managed to drag me into the sedan—no small feat.

Juliette drove and I lay in the backseat, my head in Sada's lap while she ran her magical fingertips over me in a non-sexy way and wove a spell to hurry along my recovery. It wasn't perfect, but it certainly helped—whether it was an actual spell or she was doing her worship, I wasn't sure and didn't care. After a few minutes of whispered prayer, I was able to sit up.

"Don't say it." My head was pounding and there was a taste like something had died in the back of my mouth. Glancing down, I realized I looked like a victim of the zombie apocalypse. Sada kept staring at my blood-streaked upper chest.

"I'm not saying anything," Juliette said. "What happened?"

"Arcana."

Juliette frowned in the rearview mirror. "Who are they?" the magus said as we rumbled along the back roads. The famous Pennsylvania potholes were doing little for my queasy, sour stomach. "Give us their names, and I promise you we'll hunt them down and punish them all."

She meant it, too.

I shook my head. "Took care of it."

I saw Juliette flinch and her eyes widened. I had a feeling she didn't think I was capable of it.

I looked at Sada. "Water...?"

Sada quickly leaned between the seats and reached for a bottle of Polar Springs sitting in a cup holder. And I swear that was the best water I've ever drunk. I spilled it over my chin and down the front of my chest as I chugged it down. The last few hours had been a literal hell on earth and I was dehydrated as all get out.

"We'll get you back to the house in Philly," Juliette insisted. "We can treat you there."

Thankfully, the water helped jump-start my brain. "No," I commanded my little coven. "I need to get to The Loop. Now."

***

Vivian's club was jumping when we arrived.

The ravers had come out en masse to see the live band, a semi-successful local act comprised of a bunch of dudes in tight black pleather and melting face paint screeching into their microphones. Clusters of kids sweating badly in club gear were moshing around in a rough horseshoe around the band, making it hard to see past them.

I pulled the too-small cotton plaid shirt Sada had given me over my naked chest as I strained to see above their heads, looking for Antonia. Sada had done her best with the remains of the water and some paper napkins from Dairy Queen that she'd found under the seat of her mother's car to clean me up and get the blood off my face. And she'd given me the shirt she was wearing over her tank top because she'd run out of water and there was still plenty of gunk over the rest of me. So, yeah, I got a few odd looks from the ravers as I passed.

Sada pointed and said something I couldn't hear over the blasting death metal agitating my ongoing hammer-and-nails headache, but I followed where she was pointing and saw the object of my concern.

Antonia was standing at a table, serving drinks. She was wearing a two-piece bodycon dress of the kind that Vivian used to favor before she started spending most of her nights in the office—a short halter top that was a glorified black bra and a tight wrap skirt decorated with steel rivets. It was sexier than I'd expected and I wondered how Ben felt about his daughter's new gig. All the guys at the table looked her over as she walked away.

"Nick!" she said when she spotted me. Her eyes, outlined in smoky cat-eye makeup, widened, and her mouth dropped open. "What happened to you?"

I moved toward her and took her shoulders. "Not now," I said. "We need to get out of here."

Trying to pull her toward the exit proved useless. She dug her big, chunky heels in and shouted over the band, "Why did my mom call me about you looking for me?"

The band was getting louder and my headache was getting nastier. I knew if I forced her, she'd probably make a scene. "Can we talk someplace quieter?"

She steered me toward the nearest quiet room—the ladies' bathroom near the bar. Sada followed us in, looking over her shoulder for any trouble.

As soon as the door slammed closed, Antonia pulled her arm away. "Can you please tell me what the hell is going on?"

After the dimness of the club, the fluorescents were incredibly bright and dazzling. I still wasn't fully recovered and the light felt like an ax buried in my brain. I weaved suddenly and Sada caught me and pushed me upright, using a wall for support.

"What happened to Nick?" Antonia asked Sada, looking at the bloodstains down the front of my body. She sounded genuinely frightened.

"Nick's had an accident, but he's all right now."

Turning, Sada reached out and put her fingertips to the center of Antonia's forehead. I noticed a faint glow at the point of contact, and her touch seemed to settle the girl. Leaning down slightly, Sada said in a soothing, reasonable voice, "Something's happened, Antonia. We think you're in a great deal of danger and we would like you to come with us." Sada smiled. "My mother and I will keep you safe."

The girl blinked and the pupils of her eyes dilated as if she was suddenly on some hardcore drugs. "Danger? What kind of danger?" She seemed to consider that, the thought line between her eyes deepening. "Does this have something to do with Kenny?"

"Yes," I managed, pressing my shoulders against the bathroom wall to keep myself upright. I was getting tired of feeling like a useless raggedy doll. "It has to do with what happened in the mines when you, Kenny, and your friends did the ritual."

Her frown deepened as she remembered. "The summoning spell?" she said, sounding confused. "That's just a game. Everyone does that just before they graduate..."

Antonia started to babble while the fluorescent buzzed angrily above us. There was a whole colony of moths in the lights, and their panicked wings were throwing flickering shadows against the far wall. It highlighted some graffiti that looked oddly familiar. Something in the back of my mind ticked away worriedly. It took me a moment to search my rattled brains, but when I did, I realized it was the same graffiti from my scrying session with Juliette...

My heart jumped up somewhere near my throat and I blurted out, "Hypnotize her, Sada. We need to get out of here. Now!"

"It doesn't work that way, Nick," Sada barked. "I can't make her come with us!"

"Then try—"

I never finished my statement because the lights flickered and went down, plunging the whole bathroom into absolute darkness. My worry went up several notches. At the same time, the room temperature dropped about twenty-five degrees in three seconds. I had a bad feeling about that and pushed myself upright, not that I was going to be much help.

Antonia swore. But then, after a second or two, the lights came back on.

I was facing the two girls, so I saw the creature in the far corner of the bathroom before they did. Like a smudge of feces on the wall. The manlike thing warbled with annoyance and pressed its two front legs together prayerfully, partially hiding its fanged mouth and some of its many eyes. I shouted a warning, but the girls had heard the sound, as well, and both turned to face it.

The lights went out again.

"What was that? What the fuck was that?" Antonia screamed.

Sada recited the words of a simple spell and each of her fingertips began to glow like candle flames, which at least afforded us a dim, bluish light. It illuminated the look of icy horror on Antonio's face as she slowly tilted it upward. I followed her example and saw the Thin Man hanging upside down off the ceiling only a few inches above our heads.

It warbled and then began to screech.

Using every ounce of strength I had, I tackled Antonia to the floor—well, more fell on top of her—and tried to shield her with my body. Sada, standing above us, raised her candlelit fingers and shouted out another spell. The Thin Man cried out—whether from the spell or Sada's light in its face, I don't know—and lashed out with one inhumanely long arm that resembled a serrated scythe.

Its strength was unbelievable. The stunning blow knocked Sada back and into the sinks. I heard the sickening clunk of her head hitting the porcelain basin, saw a splash of dark, blackish blood on the floor, and heard her delirious moan as she sank to the floor, arms out and the fingers of her hands still glowing, but now slowly fading.

I started getting up to wring the bastard's neck with my bare hands, but it was too fast. It reached for me and I felt its arms stick in my flesh the way it had last time. Slowly, it dragged me toward its fanged mouth.

"Angel," it whispered, voice dripping with venom. The spikes in its arms seemed to sink deeper into my flesh as if it was deliberately growing them longer just to fuck with me. I cried out at the pain and jerked my arms back, but that only made the pain worsen.

"Enough play," it said, its many eyes squinting at me in its version of an angry face. That was the last thing I saw as the room went dark again.

***

I wanted to cast a spell of some kind, but I had never been good with this stuff on the fly. Not like Sada. And it wasn't as if it gave me a chance, anyway. It just yanked me upward like a toy, aggravating all my half-mended injuries and bruises.

It shook me hard like a child having a temper tantrum with one of its playthings. That was bad on my already weak stomach and when I opened my mouth to curse it, I basically just heaved on myself as it let me go, grabbed me by a leg, and dragged me upside down toward the ceiling. The Thin Man moved swiftly, scuttling across the ceiling with supernatural speed and dragging me along with it.

My whole body was inflamed with pain. But that was the least of my worries because we were headed for the far wall. I tried to kick out, but it was like being dragged by a hydraulic machine on full throttle, and all I managed to do was slam my still tender shoulder against the hand dryer as we zipped down the wall and to the floor.

I groaned as I hit the tiles on my back. It landed atop me and I found myself pinned under the thing's weight, its spiky long arms clicking together inches above my nose as if it was sharpening knives.

"More weaksauce," I said.

It screeched with insult and raised its serrated arms high as it prepared to slash them through my body. A good witch would have been able to set the thing on fire or freeze it on the spot or something equally badass, but I'd never been talented that way. I regretted my lack of academic craft skills as it tried to eviscerate me now. I swore to Christ that if I survived this fucking mess, I'd study the hell out of the craft.

Thankfully, even though I was a lousy academic, I was good in a fight. Reaching up over my head—honestly, more in an attempt to deflect the blow than anything planned—my hands fell on the edge of a metal wastepaper can. Okay, sure. Let's work with that. I gripped the edge tight and brought it up and over my head. That emptied its contents—tissues, wet wads of paper towels, and a few used sanity napkins—over my face, but I didn't care as I brought the metal can crunching down atop the Thin Man's head as hard as I could. The smashing blow echoed around the bathroom. The can, now grossly dented, bounced off the Thin Man's spider-like head and fell into the dark.

The creature screeched and jumped back—more in surprise than anything else, I'd wager. But it gave me room to sit up. Fuck me...I was hurting badly in every place I had and a few I wasn't even aware of. But I was also running on adrenaline, and that helped. As I scooted back, I found my feet, winding up in a low crouch on the bathroom floor. I kept my eye on the creature, which, at present, was scraping its face with its long arms.

I needed a plan. A decent weapon, at least.

"Fuck it," I said and raised my left arm to summon the bident as I stood from my crouch. When it doubt, stab it with a stick.

My father's weapon came to flaming life in my clenched hand and burned with cold blue flames. I was much closer to Antonia than I'd realized, and the blue light of the bident carved lines out of her terrified face and made her eyes look like they were burning from the inside out. Her mouth was open in a wordless scream, and there was steam pouring out of her mouth. The bident had dropped the room temperature another twenty or thirty degrees.

I felt sorry for Antonia, but I would explain later. Taking the spear part of the bident in both hands and turning the prongs outward, I wasted no time lunging at the Thin Man, who was hanging against the wall of the washroom, its long, gangly arms over its eyes as if the light was burning them. I used the weapon like a Korean dangpa and thrust the sharp tines into the creature's thorax with every bit of remaining might I had.

The Morning Star had been bathed in the blood of fallen gods. It could destroy angels, gods, and monsters—and the Thin Man was at least one of those three. The tines slid in like a knife through soft butter, creating two pinpricks of light as if the thing was a crazy Lite-Brite lightbox.

The Thin Man roared, shaking the whole room with its pain and its rage. It raised its huge, scythe-like arms toward the ceiling. With a grunt, I set my footing and lifted the bident higher, widening the hole substantially. More light spilled from within its misshapen body. Huh. I hadn't expected that.

The creature continued to scream, hurting my ears and cracking the mirrors above the sinks, but it also seemed to be melting under the bident's vicious, bloodthirsty teeth. Leave it to the Morning Star to eat through it like a virus. I had gotten it ripped almost in half before the light became too blinding to look at any longer. With a final screech, the thing collapsed to the floor in a puddle of sulfuric sludge.

A second later, the lights came back on and I found two disasters waiting for me.

| 33 |

Into the Void

ANTONIA HAD RETREATED into a crouch in the corner of the bathroom and looked a bit like a mental patient in desperate need of care. She had seen way too much in the last few minutes, and that concerned me. But it was Sada who was my primary concern. She was lying on the grey bathroom tiles in a slowly spreading pool of her own blood. Her eyes fluttered slightly. I wasted no time moving to her side to check for a pulse. It flitted against my fingers, but I wasn't taking any chances. This woman had become far too important to me.

"Antonia, I need your help!"

Antonia turned her head and looked at me with big, sightless, dead-deer eyes.

I snapped my fingers, which seemed to startle her. She gasped and slowly rose from her crouch, but looked confused.

"I can't move Sada in this state. Call 911!"

Finally, her eyes snapped downward at the phone in her hand. I suppose she'd taken it out to use as a flashlight when the lights went off the first time, but now she blinked down at it as if she didn't recognize the device.

"Antonia!"

"Yeah...all right," she responded suddenly as she speed-recovered and started jabbing keys. She surprised me. Her explanation to the dispatcher was remarkably calm. The dispatcher told her to stay on the line and that an ambulance was on its way.

We both said nothing. I just held Sada's hand and Antonia stood there, staring down at black dust on the floor of the bathroom that was once the Thin Man. She looked traumatized by the whole experience. I was about to ask her if she was all right when the lights buzzed again and went out, leaving Antonia's stunned expression bathed in the blue light of her cell phone.

"Nick..." she began. I saw her breath puff out as the temperature dropped once more. "Nick, what...?"

She never finished her statement. The lights snapped on again...and I spotted the Thin Man—or, rather, *another* Thin Man—standing behind her. He was grinning at me. Or, at least, the closest thing he could manage with that wretched mouth full of oversized, tusk-like fangs.

"No—!" I cried and pushed myself to my feet, but they were too far away.

The Simulacrum made a warbling laugh as it wrapped one huge, weapon-like arm around Antonia's shoulders, making a display of it so I saw. Antonia stiffened and opened her mouth to scream, but the lights snapped off again. The last thing I heard was her cell phone smashing to pieces on the tiled floor and her scream echoing for a long, long time after she'd been dragged away.

* * *

Juliette stayed with Sada while I took her keys and rushed out to the parking lot. I must have looked pretty fucking grim because

Juliette never even tried to stop or advise me. Ten minutes later, I was pulling into the parking lot of Holy Name High School. I had no logical reason to believe Lamb was here, and if I were thinking with a clear head, I'd probably conclude he was home at this hour, wherever that was. But I was operating on autopilot now.

Stop getting in your own way. Just drift.

I drifted.

The school was locked tight, but I found an unlocked window in the basement easily enough and headed straight for his office. There was a light peeking out from under the door.

Raising my arm, I bounced the door open so hard that it crashed back against the wall.

Dr. Theo Lamb was sitting at his desk under the sallow light of a banker's lamp, pasting cut bits of news stories into a journal. I wondered what the news stories were. Something about missing children? Some disaster somewhere? What did sociopaths scrapbook about?

"Officer Nick," he said pleasantly without looking up. He was so calm and collected you would have thought that incident in the garden behind the Victorian never happened.

I was exhausted and hurting and so angry, it took an enormous act of will on my part not to materialize the Morning Star and run it through his fucking head. But I needed the fucker. I needed what he could do. Marching forward like a soldier, I grabbed the edge of the scrapbook and tossed it against the nearest wall, knocking over a standing lamp, which crashed to the floor with the pop of a bulb. Bits of paper fluttered into the air like confetti.

He sat back in his seat and smiled. Unperturbed. Nothing to see here, folks.

I leaned over the desk and grabbed him by the front of his cassock and dragged him halfway across the ink blotter while my wings unfurled behind me like black sails, filling the room. His eyes grew large, but I don't think he was afraid. Just the opposite. He looked thrilled to be witnessing me in full Lucifer form.

"Tell me why I should not end you," I whispered, dragging him close enough to see the different colors in his blue irises. "Convince me."

It took him only seconds. "You don't know who I've charisma-ed. It may be someone you love. It may be you. And if you kill me, they will never recover."

I hated him. I showed him my teeth. "Call it!" I growled and threw him back in his seat. "Call the Thin Man or I swear to god, Lamb, I will tear your heart out by the roots and hand it to you!"

* * *

"What are we waiting for?" I barked from the corner of the office.

Lamb was standing in the center of the office, looking over the spell to call the Simulacrum. It lay in one of his many books. His own personal Book of Shadows, I suppose. After I'd threatened him, he'd just smiled, made a quick phone call on the antique rotary phone on his desk, and then stood up as if nothing was amiss. He'd tossed aside the throw rug in front of his desk to reveal runes carved right into his office's floorboards. They were eerily similar to the runes on the wall of the mine. Yeah, he'd been doing this for a while.

Now, we were just standing here like jackasses.

"I need my assistant, Carl." He waggled a finger at me without looking up from his book. "No wonder you're such a terrible witch. No patience at all, Officer Nick."

I thought about marching over there and beating his face in for the hell of it, but I heard the door click behind me, and Carl, the boy I'd seen when I was in this office the first time, rushed in. He was dressed in a wrinkled T-shirt and sweatpants, his hair awry. He looked half-asleep.

"I came as soon as I could," he announced, looking around the room.

"Thank you, Carl. As you can imagine, I need your assistance."

When Carl's eyes fell on the runes on the floor, he never blinked, but he did frown with annoyance when he spotted me. "What's *he* doing here?"

"Officer Nick would like us to call the Simulacrum, Carl."

I reached out and grabbed Carl's arm. "You know about the Simulacrum?"

He pulled it free. "Yeah, duh. I help Dr. Lamb."

"Of your own free will?"

Carl looked insulted. "Not that it's any business of yours, daemon."

Their whole arrangement confused me, but Lamb tutted. "Carl, please. Officer Nick is our guest."

Carl frowned as he moved into the circle carved into the floor. "The Simulacrum might not come with him here," he warned Lamb.

I was losing my patience. At least an hour had passed since the Thin Man had taken Antonia, and, honestly, I didn't give a shit what arrangement they had. "Call the fucking thing now!" I shouted, startling them both.

Carl, looking annoyed, pulled his T-shirt up over his head. He had the young, slim, hairless body of young men everywhere. But, unlike them, countless scars covered his chest and trunk, some old and almost white with age, others practically brand new. It knocked the rage right out of me to see.

I took a step toward Lamb. "Did you do this to him?"

Lamb pressed his lips together. "No. Carl does it to himself. Of his own free will."

I looked at the boy who was glaring at me hatefully. "Is that true, boy?"

"I'm not a *boy*," he seethed with insult as he pulled out a long, thin, wavy knife I immediately sensed was an athame. A surly smile spread across his face and one of his eyes glowed gold. "I'm a *kobalos*, you foolish, unlearned daemon."

"A goblin?" I said with surprise. I'd never met a goblin before or any of the Fae.

"Carl is my familiar, and the Fae are my animal to call," Lamb explained as he put his hand on Carl's naked shoulder. He was reading my thoughts in that arcane way he had. Then he smiled. "Did you think *I* alone could call the Simulacrum?"

The goblin gave me a dark smirk. "You daemons are too weak. Too watered down."

Lamb nodded at his familiar. "Proceed, Carl."

Giving me one last nasty look, Carl knelt upon the runes on the floor. He took a few deep breaths as she centered himself in preparation for the summoning. The process was similar to what I had done in the mines, except that he did it faster and with more expertise. As soon as he started cutting a line done the front of his body, the runes began to glow, and the moment his blood touched the floor—it was gold and glimmered on the shiny walnut wood—those runes glowed brighter than ever, almost blindingly so. Despite all the power I had pulled from my familiars and the coven of Satanists, my runes hadn't glowed even half this bright.

Dr. Lamb began to speak. It was not in Angel-speak or any human or Divine-based language I had ever heard. The language was clunky and unmusical like Russian spoken backward.

The runes glowed brighter still, filling the whole room with searing white light. Meanwhile, Carl knelt there, the athame resting at his belly, his gold blood all over the floor, breathing roughly through his magic. Dropping the athame, he reached out with both arms and began to speak that bizarre language, producing a chorus of course alien words whose meaning I couldn't begin to guess at.

The room grew hot and dry like someone had thrown open an oven door. The blast seared my face and the force of it knocked me back a step. It blew books off shelves and sent the papers on Lamb's desk flying. I heard a sound like a rumble and turned my watering eyes up to the ceiling where there seemed to be an indoor tornado developing. I'd seen some shit, but the black, swirling void opening up several feet above my head was enough to steal even my breath away.

Lamb and his familiar began to chant faster, the words running together.

Through the swirl of murky darkness, I saw two long arms emerge. Serrated and cruel. Sand puffed out, residue from that hellhole in some other universe. And the weird chattering began.

I grabbed a chair from the corner and set it down in front of me like a step stool. As the void widened and began to birth that shiny black abomination into our world, I put the toe of my boot on the seat of the chair and, with a quick breath, used it to launch myself upward.

The Simulacrum bellowed as I grabbed hold of its spiky long arms, digging my fingers in for purchase. It tried to shake me loose, but I swung my legs up, wrapping them around its hot, pulsing, repulsive body. It immediately began to withdraw, which is exactly what I wanted. I felt the sucking heat of the void as the creature retreated to its home world, dragging me along for the ride.

| 34 |

Free Falling

WE WERE IN free fall, the creature and I. We'd danced this dance before, sure, but at that time, I was at a disadvantage. I didn't know what I was dealing with. Now, though...

The burning hot, almost airless atmosphere closed around us like the wettest, heaviest fur blanket. It was hard to breathe as we fell through the fiery red sky, our velocity only a little less than it would have been on Earth. I remembered something from science class in high school—hot air rises because it's lighter. The air here was incredibly light, almost like anti-gravity. We fell for a remarkably long time.

The pain of the Thin Man's spiny arms tangled like barbed wire around my forearms hurt like hell, but I mentally shoved all discomforts aside. There was just this driving, maniacal need in me to hang on for the ride and to keep the creature beneath me. I didn't want it to get away.

It screamed. First in its own language and then in Angel-speak. First, it threatened me, and then it promised me anything—everything—if I would just let it go.

"Give me back the children!" I screamed in its face.

After that, its language devolved into a primal wail. And it was still screaming as we both fell to earth.

* * *

The impact drove the creature a few inches into the arid, dusty ground. This time, I landed atop it as I'd planned to, the Thin Man wedged between my thighs. He wasn't going anywhere. I was still tangled in his many barbed arms. I knew this was going to hurt. A lot. Not that I hadn't built up a certain tolerance to pain in the last few days.

Rearing back, I slammed my closed fists into his face. For all his huff and puff, he was remarkably fragile, and when my fist collided with his face, one of his eyes split like a ripe red pumpkin, splattering me with blackish gore. He chattered curses, the sound ringing in my head like a migraine, but I didn't give him a chance to retaliate this time and reared back once more—much of the skin on my forearm tearing away on the rigid hooks of his arms—and smashed my fists down again, pulverizing his other eye. Not that he didn't have others, but he wouldn't be using these anymore.

More screaming. His fangs clacked together like knives. Music to my fucking ears...

I was spewing words the whole time, calling him everything under the sun. Spreading my wings for better balance, I reared back and struck again, driving my fist all the way through his damned head...but he had one last trick up his sleeve. He bucked under me and I felt something like a curved blade sink into the small of my back.

I roared while looking down into the ruined black mirrors of his eyes. He seemed to be smiling up at me. Smiling...and laughing. He had managed to curl his entire abdomen up and send what looked like a long, needle-thin stinger into my lower back. It hurt way more than it should have. In retrospect, it was probably poisonous.

The searing pain made me writhe and arch my back compulsively as my wings beat at the air. The Thin Man used the distraction to backhand me off his body with one claw. The blow packed incredible power and knocked me back ten feet and into the sand. I struggled to push myself upright and saw the creature writhing around in the sand like a turtle trying to right itself.

"Bad angel," it warbled as its many legs clawed at the red earth. It was making a kind of hellish sand angel.

"You have no fucking idea," I gasped.

I couldn't let it get away. Even though moving hurt like hell, I managed to get to my hands and knees in the dust. By then, the creature had managed to flip itself over, but there was a large chunk of its abdomen missing and some of its wet black entrails were dragging along the ground. That stinger had cost it greatly. Reaching around to the small of my back, I grabbed the stinger firmly in my hand. It felt wet and slimy and moving it hurt even more. With a shout, I slid it loose. It wasn't embedded deep, thankfully.

The pain lessened considerably. I looked at what I had in my blood-slicked hands. The Simulacrum's stinger was the size of a knife, a knot of bone attached to a slightly curved and wickedly sharp onyx blade. In a way, it made a very good athame—which gave me a great idea. The wounded creature was trying to crawl away between the sand dunes, black blood gushing from its abdomen. It seemed to be wounded badly.

Getting shakily to my feet, I took a deep breath and leaped at the creature, driving the stinger into the spot just behind the Simulacrum's monstrous head. The thing screamed and a prick of light appeared around the tip the way it had when I'd stabbed its mate with the Morning Star, but when I tried to drag the stinger down the shiny black carapace, it didn't do anything but scratch it slightly. Fuck! This wasn't going to work.

I would need to manifest the Morning Star. But before I was even able to call upon the energy I needed, the Simulacrum whipped around and reared up, gangly and monstrous. With a hiss, it lashed out at me with its serrated scythe-like claws. I turned, narrowly avoiding colliding with a claw as it slammed into the sand, sending a puff of dust up.

I can use a knife in a tight spot. I learned in the Police Academy. But, more importantly, I learned out on the streets. I've used—and misused—any number of athames in my time. As it lashed out again, I moved to one side and, gripping the handle of the stinger underhand style, swung my arm out, lashing at its underbelly as it reared up. I was rewarded with a streak of white light and a scream that rattled my bones. I had hurt it, at last. Really hurt it.

Maddened and in pain, it continued to lunge at me and lash out with its claws and I continued to sidestep it, each time slashing or jabbing at its underbelly. It was big and clumsy…and wounded. I landed far more blows than it did.

"Evil angel," it said and threw its whole weight at me. I could tell I had angered it beyond all rational thought—which I had wanted to do all along. Know your enemy. And then make him make a stupid move. All that Zen stuff. This time, I didn't shift away. Instead, I dropped to my knees and used both hands to angle my weapon upward so the creature more or less impaled itself on its own stinger as it fell on top of me.

It screamed piteously. It sounded almost like a child, and I felt a vague twinge of sympathy even as, with a grunt of effort, I drove the stinger deeper into its soft and vulnerable underbelly. I knew this kind of pain. The kind that rips you apart and puts you back together in a completely different manner. The kind of pain that makes a different person of you. It was hurting like that. It was dying like that.

Its weight was suffocating me, but I gritted my teeth and used all my strength to drag my new athame through its soft underbelly. Black blood gushed out, shiny like motor oil, flecking my face and upper chest. That was followed by one of the brightest bursts of light I have ever witnessed. It blinded me for a moment, and when my vision finally cleared, I saw the creature writhing and melting on top of me, just the way its mate had.

"Have...pity..." it said as it died.

"Pity is for the weak," I told it. I held the stinger in place until the Simulacrum dissolved into black oily slime that was quickly and efficiently eaten up by the parched earth. I didn't know if it was a trick of the wind or not, and I would probably never know the answer, but the Simulacrum's death rattle seemed to echo over the desert for a long, long time after it was gone.

* * *

I walked the surface of that angry Red Planet for what felt like days. I mean, I don't know. It might have been mere hours or weeks. Since there were no sunsets or sunrises—or any other atmospheric changes—it was impossible to know how long a day lasted on this blasted rock.

I walked about a hundred feet, crunching down into ankle-deep sand until I was forced to stop due to sheer exhaustion and take a few moments to catch my breath in the thin, poisonous atmosphere. Then I would continue, head down, eyes on my boots as they marched on in this loose red sand. Rinse. Repeat. Where the hell was I? Everything was red sand and wind that burned my eyes to look into it. I walked hunched over, but it was hot and close, and the sand raking over me seemed to have claws that were trying to rip the skin off my face. Despite the oppressive heat, I wished I had my long coat with me.

Eventually, a true storm sprang up, sandblasting me at maybe a hundred miles an hour, and I had to pull the collar of Sada's borrowed shirt up around my mouth. I struggled to hike on, trying to gauge the horizon, trying to find something that looked alive or like a landmark, without taking any sand in my eyes or mouth.

Antonia. How was I ever going to find her here? It felt almost hopeless.

I jerked to a sudden halt. Only a few feet away, something like a mountain was moving across my path. I hadn't even noticed it through the sandstorm. And that's saying something about the storm because it was as big as a cruise liner and as ugly as an inside-out hippopotamus. It walked on twelve stalk-like legs bent at extreme angles and seemed to have individual organisms growing right out of its enormous bulk—whether human or something else, I couldn't be certain. But they were all screaming in unison as the creature drifted into the horizon, their voices only slightly muffled by the high winds.

And I thought Hell was disturbing.

I felt an intense wave of relief as the enormous thing disappeared into the distance. I glanced around to make certain it had no mates or little ones, and as I did so, I spotted a blot of darkness at the top of the next dune. It looked...familiar, somehow.

I started hurrying in that direction, hoping I wasn't hallucinating due to pain or dehydration. But by the time I had climbed to the top of the dune, the being—assuming it had even been there at all and wasn't a figment of my overwrought imagination—was gone. I stood at the top of that vantage point, tried to shield my eyes, and surveyed the surrounding territory.

Nothing as far as the eye could see. Red sand rippling up and down an endless chain of dunes. Feeling dispirited, I scuttled down the side of the dune, but as I reached the bottom, I caught movement out of the corner of my eye. Turning in the direction of the dark blot, I once again noticed the manlike figure standing at the top of a dune a few hundred feet to my left.

What the hell was going on?

Every time I got to the top of a dune, I saw nothing, but as I climbed down the other side, the figure appeared on the horizon somewhere, sometimes directly ahead of me, sometimes off to the side. I spent what felt like hours or days chasing after my desert phantom, hoping to hell that I wasn't imagining all this.

Time passed. I grew tired and depressed. Eventually, I found myself struggling up the side of a dune, almost ready to collapse and give up. That's when I noticed the man in the distance. He wasn't standing atop a dune this time but in a valley between two rises. I couldn't see any details clearly, but he was wearing something metallic that was winking with light on the upper left area of his breast.

I thought it might be a badge. I started to hurry, but at this speed, the sand was blasting me in the eyes, making it hard to see, and once I'd reached the spot where he was standing, I saw he was gone once more.

"Peter," I said, slowly turning to take in my surroundings. I was finally on the verge of breaking down into frustrated tears.

That's when something grabbed my ankle. I nearly jumped straight out of my skin. But when I finally got my jackhammering heart under control and glanced down, I saw thin, brown fingers scratching at the toe of my boot.

With a cry, I dropped to my knees and started digging frantically at the earth like a dog. Sand blew in every direction, some of it falling back into the hole I was making, but eventually, I got enough out to see the rough outline of Antonia's face. There were vine-like growths up her nose and down her throat, making it impossible for her to speak. Her eyes were wide and frank and stunned. The whites of her eyes had already begun to turn a reddish color similar to this godforsaken place.

I spoke to her quietly while I wiped the sand off her face and worked the vines out of her nose and throat. She gagged as they came out. And as she sat up, she began to cry.

"I found you, baby. I found you," I told her as I clutched her against the shelter of my body and willed us through a new portal into Hell. A place that I at least understood.

| 35 |

Hellraiser

ANTONIA AND I spent a week in Hell. It wasn't as bad as you might think. There is no passage of time in Hell, you see, so we didn't lose any time on Earth. Everything that had happened the night the Thin Man took Antonia was still going on and would continue to do so until we returned.

In that week, we worked on healing ourselves physically and emotionally. And we talked. A lot. The healing part came down to sitting on a comfy wrap sofa in the throne room in our Snuggies, eating pizza, and watching Netflix—which had an odd assortment of programming because the wi-fi couldn't decide where, exactly, we were. It did manage to pick up a lot of British programming, which we thought was pretty interesting.

In the beginning, I was afraid Antonia would freak out about the Watchtower and the rooms that seemed to grow and shrink and change location daily, turning the place into an endless maze. At the very least, I figured she'd be spooked by Baphomet. But Antonia was a real trooper. After her initial shock, she managed to settle into a rhythm surprisingly well.

She had questions, of course. And I saw no point in making up elaborate lies. She'd either accept the truth or go irretrievably insane. But she surprised me. Perhaps her time on the Angry Red Planet had conditioned her for anything, or maybe she had a predisposition to understanding the fundamentals of the craft, but it wasn't long before she settled in.

"What's that?" she said, standing there one morning in her Snuggie, pointing at the oversized curio cabinet.

I opened it with the hook and showed her the vial with the glowy little starfish inside. "I didn't steal it," I told her, afraid she'd think the worst of me. "It was given to me."

She didn't ask to whom it had belonged. "Can I hold it?"

Turned out, it glowed brighter in her hands. "It's warm," she announced.

"It likes you," I said, feeling it was true.

Antonia bit her lips and looked up into my eyes. "So it's all true. You're really...him."

I pulled my Snuggie closer around me like a shield. "It's...more of a job description."

"But you can do it?" She looked troubled before she was able to put words to her thoughts. "I mean, you could take it from me if I gave it to you."

I took the vial back and set it inside the curio cabinet. "But why would I?"

She stared down at her feet a moment. "I've heard it makes you a powerful witch...to do that. Is that true?"

"Do you want to be a powerful witch?" I used the hook to close the cabinet.

"Maybe."

I turned to face her. She still had the fear in her eyes. I knew she would never really get over this experience. It had changed her. It had changed me. But if the craft helped her to grow beyond the trauma of this—well, we would need to discuss working on that together.

* * *

Antonia was nervous the day we went back to Earth. I'd coached her as best I could. She was not to talk about her experience with anyone—except possibly Juliette Alexander, if she needed a therapist. She would need to do her best to slide as seamlessly as she could back into that night—that *moment*, if possible.

She nodded as I took her hand...and then she blushed. "I enjoyed our time together, Nick. I'm going to miss it."

"Me, too," I said, genuinely meaning it. But then I started to worry she might have read too much into that.

Too late, a voice whispered in my mind as I looked into her large, lovestruck eyes and we made the final jump to Earth.

* * *

I was sweeping the floor of the shop, a busy little Snow White, when Morgana came down the stairs. She was dressed in one of her flowy silk gowns, and she had her special date earrings dangling from her ears. I'd given them to her for Yule the year before—small silver crows dangling from red rubies. They'd quickly become her favorite while we were together, and she'd once confessed to me that they reminded her of me. She looked truly happy as she crossed the floor of the shop and set her purse down on the glass display case. "I didn't expect you'd be here so late, Nick," she said. Her voice was, as always, low and soothing, and utterly professional. But there was no familiarity or exasperation in it any longer. Not like when we were together.

"It was a busy day," I said, not looking up. "I didn't get a chance to clean up until now."

"Busy is good," she said, silently watching me broom some debris into a dustpan.

It was late fall, getting cold fast. Halloween season. That always brings the locals in. And when the tourists start coming down from Jersey and New York, apple picking and souvenir hunting, they always seem to find their way to our shop. Today, business jumped nonstop for the full ten hours I'd worked the shop.

She moved toward me while I was picking up the dustpan. She looked worried and even raised a hand the way she usually did to touch me—but stopped herself. "Are you all right, Nick?"

"Yeah." I even smiled. "I'm great."

"You've been quiet. Something bothering you?"

"All clear on the western front. Not a demon or monster to be had." And I meant that. The Thin Man was gone (all of them) and the Lucky No. 8 Mine had been successfully collapsed for all time. No one except the Satanists would ever know I'd been involved in that, but I was okay with that.

I pointed a thumb behind me. "I did catch one shoplifter, though. Little bugger thought I couldn't see what he was doing in the candle aisle."

"Good." She smiled, too.

So we stood there like that, smiling at each other, talking about safe, happy business things. But neither of us was really here. She'd said she wanted a clean break. No friends with benefits. No flatmates. Just business partners. We were work colleagues now, and we both lived separate lives. We saw each other in the mornings and the evenings as we swapped shifts. Sometimes, we discussed inventory or talked about a special event in town. I knew Morgana was always keen on learning if there was trouble of the supernatural variety around, but I no longer discussed that aspect of my life with her.

"Take a look at these," I said as I went behind the counter and brought up a heavy cardboard box full of bubble wrap. Inside lay a half dozen quartz spheres of different colors.

"Obuculums," she said, holding one up to the store lights to examine.

"Locally manufactured, so I got a deep discount." I indicated the glass counter. "I want to put them in with the Harry Potter merchandise. I know it's not related, but—"

"Yes," she interrupted. "I agree. I think they'll be popular with the out-of-towners this Halloween. Put them in."

I nodded and took the crystal ball from her, placing it back inside the bubble wrap in the box. As I was closing the flaps of the box, she grabbed her purse.

"Have fun," I said as she turned to cross the room to the door.

She threw me a little smile as she pushed through the door, the familiar little bell tinkling. After she was gone, one of the flaps on the box popped up. I reached inside the box, took one of the obuculums in my hand, and crushed it to pieces in the box.

* * *

It was a nice night to walk home. I had the old Schwinn with me, its wheels clicking as we went along, but I didn't feel like riding it tonight. I simply walked it along the back roads as I made my steady way toward the Victorian on Lake Ariel—a good five-mile hike, but I was up for it.

It was getting cooler—and less buggy—and I liked it. It gave me time to think about things. All the things that were right in my life. And all of the things that were wrong.

The good things: Sada had been all right. A bad concussion, but she'd recovered all right and gone back to Philadelphia with her mother to look after their coven. For a short time, I thought they were gone from my life. But a few weeks later, Juliette sent a small segment of the coven up my way to settle permanently in the Victorian summer home. They didn't say as much, but I pretty much guessed they were my entourage and worshipers—there if I need them. I wasn't complaining, though, because they were fun, sexy, and smart. They liked board games and pizza. What's not to like?

Lamb? Well, he was another story. An unfinished bit of business, if you will. He knew I was going to come for him one day. I just hadn't picked the right time to strike yet. I also wasn't sure exactly *how*. He and his little goblin Carl couldn't be linked to the school shooting in any way. He wasn't technically responsible for it, so he couldn't be arrested or tried. But that didn't mean I wasn't going to find a way to punish him. I just needed to be creative.

As for the Arcana…well, they were still out there. Somewhere. Probably be back. And I'd probably need to take care of them again. Supernatural Whack-A-Mole, you know? But I wasn't going to let what happened with Agent Kippy Skippy be repeated. I wasn't going through that hell ever again, and if that meant re-learning the craft Satan-style under Juliette, so be it.

Antonia kept her word. And her secret. She'd been to the shop a few times, looking for me in not-so-subtle ways. I knew she wanted to learn the craft. But, so far, I'd been avoiding her, hoping she'd outgrow the need. Maybe. But then again, maybe not.

Josh and Tiger left for L.A. on the night everything went down with the Thin Man. I don't know if it had something with him being repulsed by the vibes in the covens' house or if it was plain old wanderlust, but there you go. I hadn't heard much since about the poor guy, and I worried about him now more than ever. Would

Tiger protect him from the cutthroats of Lost Angeles? I remained hopeful.

And before you ask, no, I didn't go back to The Loop to see Vivian, even after her boyfriend was mysteriously murdered and the remains of Agent Kip's body were discovered. It was being chalked up to some kind of death cult, and I had no desire to discuss the matter with her. I loathed the idea of even stepping into the club and seeing her—knowing what would happen. What always happened. She was right the first time she told me that one of us had to leave town. We were simply no good for each other.

Not that that didn't hurt. Because it did. But sometimes the truth hurts. You get over it.

I sensed a car riding up behind me before I saw the headlights splashed across the asphalt ahead of me. I slowed down as it cruised up beside me, slowly crunching over the gravel. When I turned my head, I had to do a double-take. I was certain it was the Monaco until I noticed the interior was grey, not baby blue, like my old heap. I felt instantly homesick at the sight.

The driver's side window had to be manually rolled down. And then I saw a head full of beautiful afro hair appear. "Hey, Nick!"

"Antonia," I said. I couldn't help but smile. "Did you resurrect my car?"

She laughed. "Nope. But I found this one on Carfinder.com." She tapped the horn for me. "Daddy said when I graduated, he'd help me get any car I wanted, so..."

"So you chose a 1970s Monaco?" I said, raising an eyebrow at that. "No A/C. No electric windows. No GPS. No nothing..."

She shrugged. "I've always liked your car." She pulled to the weedy shoulder and leaned over to open the passenger side. The old door creaked, music to my ears.

"Get in," she said with a blush to her cheeks. "Let me rescue you for a change."

***

I woke up in the middle of the night.

There was no transitional period from sound asleep to wide awake. No cranky fuzziness like I usually experienced. One minute I was asleep, dreaming some ridiculous dream about having high tea with Vivian and Theo Lamb (of all people), and the next I was fully awake, lying on my side, my face in the hair of the woman beside me. Not Sada, but one of her kind.

There was another body on my other side, his arm around my waist. It took me a moment to remember. Amber and Henry. They were fraternal twins. They sometimes warmed my bed. The Satanists often took turns being my bed partners. It was like having a vast, always willing, harem of magical lovers.

Not lovers, I reminded myself. *Brides.*

I sat up suddenly. I had this feeling I had forgotten something important. Something that had to be done. *Now.*

Extraditing myself from the bed, I moved across the room to dress in the dark. Since moving into the Victorian, I'd been using the dresser to store my meager wardrobe of jeans, cargo pants, and pullovers. But instead of going there, as usual, I went to the wardrobe on the other side of the room. I don't know why I felt compelled to, but I wanted to touch the suits and neatly pressed shirts that hung there. The coven said they were mine—if I wanted them. Expensive threads, all with Italian labels.

Somehow, I found myself outside the Victorian, standing on the front porch, dressed in one of my father's ridiculously expensive three-piece Italian suits. Blue silk, it felt like sensual hands caressing me. Pressed shirt, vest, slacks, polished shoes. No tie, thank god. I was not a tie person.

I started walking down the road away from the Victorian. Maybe this was a dream? I mean, it could be. Maybe I really was back in bed, Amber and Henry's sexy bodies pressed against me, and I was only dreaming about walking down a Pennsylvania country road, dressed like a gigolo?

I laughed at that, then stopped. There was a car heading my way. Luxury wheels I didn't recognize. And Baphomet was driving. This *had* to be a dream.

He parked right in the center of the road and got out. "Oh, good. I was afraid I'd missed you, my lord."

"You didn't miss me," I said as he took my hand and kissed my ring. This was the first time I noticed I was wearing one. A large red stone set in black iron coiled like a snake around my middle finger. After he escorted me into the backseat of the car, he went around to the driver's seat and we were off.

The drive was short, maybe ten or twelve miles, but I was not in a hurry. I thought the moonlight shining on the river and between the trees was very beautiful tonight. A gravid, blood-red moon. An omen of things to come.

Baphomet slowed the car when we arrived at the sign for Serenity Falls, the retirement home. We parked right outside the building and I waited for him to come around and open the car door for me. "Better hurry, my lord."

I laughed at that. "He's on my time."

"Yes, of course, sir."

We went inside. That surprised me. I would have thought the doors and windows would be locked. But despite that assumption, I found myself walking the halls, Baphomet shadowing me as I did so.

"I hope you don't mind my coming, sir. This is our first time."

"I don't mind," I said because I didn't.

There was much moaning and crying behind the many doors. Dead dreams, broken sanities, forgotten loves, the pain of abandonment. I could feel each of the occupants' pain as I passed but make no mistake. They were not innocent, any of them. They were, quite literally, lying in the bed of their own making.

I would see them soon.

"Here we are," Baphomet announced as we approached the door at the end. Like before, the moment I thought about it—about wanting to be inside that room—I was suddenly there, standing at the foot of his bed. There was an oxygen mask over his face and a machine monitoring his heart. But no nurse, which was good. I wanted this intimate and personal and just between the two of us.

He was wide awake and looking up at me.

He even smiled with his brown teeth. "Goddamn you," Everett McCarty said. Or, I should say, the thing from that hellish plain of existence that had become Everett McCarty. I suppose, over the years, it had learned and become increasingly human. And then it had done those things to Vivian. I wondered if that was always in the original, not that it mattered. The original Everett McCarty had long since been absorbed into the Angry Red Planet.

I manifested the Morning Star in one hand, lifted it high, and let him see it as I plunged the tines deep into his heart. He writhed and screamed—albeit silently. I held the bident in place and let him suffer, let him burn. Let him see the place he was going. And he despaired.

"My lord!" Baphomet exclaimed beside me. He did not seem entirely displeased.

I made it last for as long as I could until the soul of the beast was completely consumed by my fire. Until the heart monitor wailed and finally shorted out. Until the blackish blood dripped like alien tears from the corners of the creature's eyes and blackened the sheet.

Until that spider-thing crawled from his mouth and dissolved into dust. Until it was all over.

Baphomet laughed and clapped his hands in response. "Sir, you're the best Satan I've ever seen!"

Nick Englebrecht will return in
Guardian Devils
&
Vivian Summers will return in
To the Devil a Daughter

ABOUT THE AUTHOR

K.H. Koehler is the bestselling author of various novels and novellas in the genres of horror, SF, dark fantasy, steampunk, and young and new adult. She is the owner of KH Koehler Books and KH Koehler Design, which specializes in graphic design and professional copyediting. Her books are widely available at all major online distributors and her covers have appeared on numerous books in many different genres. Her short work has appeared in various anthologies, and her novel series include *The Kaiju Hunter, A Clockwork Vampire, Planet of Dinosaurs, The Nick Englebrecht Mysteries,* and *The Archaeologists.* She is the author of multiple Amazon bestsellers and was one of the founders and chief editors of KHP Publishers, which published genre fiction from 2001 to 2015. She has over fifteen years of experience in the publishing industry as a writer, ghostwriter, copyeditor, commercial book cover designer, formatter, and marketer. Visit her website at https://khkoehler.net.

www.ingramcontent.com/pod-product-compliance
Lightning Source LLC
LaVergne TN
LVHW031610060526
838201LV00065B/4794